PENGUIN METRO READS

HALF-TORN HEARTS

Novoneel Chakraborty is the bestselling author of eleven romantic thriller novels, one short story collection, *Cheaters*, and a digital exclusive novella, *Red Suits You*. Four of his novels will soon be adapted into web series. The Forever series was listed among *Times of India*'s most stunning books of 2017; it was also featured among Amazon's memorable books the same year. The two books remained on the bestseller list for ten weeks straight and *Forever Is a Lie* was one of the highest selling books of 2017 on Flipkart. While the third instalment in the Stranger trilogy, *Forget Me Not, Stranger*, debuted as the No. 1 bestseller across India, the second, *All Yours, Stranger*, ranked among the top five thrillers on Amazon India. *Black Suits You* also remained among the top five thrillers on Amazon for fifteen weeks. The Stranger trilogy has been translated into six languages, while *Cheaters* will soon be available in Hindi.

Known for his twists, dark plots and strong female protagonists, Novoneel Chakraborty is also called the Sidney Sheldon of India by his readers. Apart from novels, Novoneel has written and developed several TV shows, such as *Savdhaan India* and *Yeh Hai Aashiqui*. He lives and works in Mumbai.

BY THE SAME AUTHOR

A Thing beyond Forever
That Kiss in the Rain
How about a Sin Tonight?
Ex
Black Suits You
Cheaters
The Best Couple Ever

Stranger Trilogy

Marry Me, Stranger
All Yours, Stranger
Forget Me Not, Stranger

Forever Series

Forever Is a Lie
Forever Is True

half torn hearts

Have you destroyed yourself for someone?

NOVONEEL CHAKRABORTY

Penguin
metro reads

An imprint of Penguin Random House

PENGUIN METRO READS

USA | Canada | UK | Ireland | Australia
New Zealand | India | South Africa | China

Penguin Metro Reads is part of the Penguin Random House group of companies
whose addresses can be found at global.penguinrandomhouse.com

Published by Penguin Random House India Pvt. Ltd
7th Floor, Infinity Tower C, DLF Cyber City,
Gurgaon 122 002, Haryana, India

First published in Penguin Metro Reads by Penguin Random House India 2019

ISBN 9780143442691

Typeset in Adobe Caslon Pro by Manipal Digital Systems, Manipal
Printed at Thomson Press India Ltd, New Delhi

www.penguin.co.in

To,

The Mountain. The Ocean. The Desert.

Forever indebted,

N.

IN A NURSING HOME IN CUTTACK

2018

The nursing home was a small one. The patient's disease was a serious one. She had acquired a rare skin disorder when she had gone to help cyclone victims in one of the coastal villages of eastern Odisha. It was a village that couldn't be located on any map of India. The patient had no family. Not any more. Except for the girl sitting beside her.

The girl sat stock-still at the same place from the time she admitted the patient to the nursing home, which was forty-eight hours ago. She murmured a prayer whenever she felt something calamitous was about to happen. Looking at the patient, the girl wondered why one failed to fathom the bond with someone until that person began slipping away. Did death sever the inner attachment to the near and dear as well? People who meant the world to us at one time, seemed like a distant memory at another. Our own reality changed its face, and a huge part of our life went into accepting that change.

The girl didn't realize when tears began rolling down her cheeks. She brushed them away impatiently. *Why couldn't things just remain the way they were?* she wondered. She swallowed a lump realizing the futility of the question. Not every relationship is about flowing together forever. Sometimes, one just takes a little bit of the other person, surrenders a little bit of oneself to the other person and then continues flowing independently, sensing those acquired bits within oneself and cherishing them always.

Soft, helpless moans broke into her musing and the girl quickly went over to the bed. She caressed her friend's forehead. The moans grew a little louder.

'Sister?' the girl hollered. Nobody came. She walked out of the room and espied a nurse at the far end of the corridor. By the time they returned to the room, the whimpering had stopped. The nurse checked the pulse and then the heartbeat. And then shut the gawking eyes with her palm. The girl plonked down on the chair, knowing fully well what this meant. The nurse rushed out, saying, 'Call the doctor. The patient in room number 9—Raisa Barua—is dead.'

The girl in the room looked at the body. She felt strangely light but broken.

VOICE NOTE 1

Do banjaro ko jab pyaar hota hai,
Unke dil mein thehrao nahi,
Uffan hota hai.

Woh manzilein nahi,
Ek dusre mein safar dhundte hain.
Jiska modh khud ko chubhe,
Aisi raah chunte hain.

Dard ko ek adatan nasha batate hain.
Kareeb aa jaaye,
Toh dabe paer nikal jaate hain,
Faasle badh jaayen,
Toh toofan ki tarah wapas aate hain.

Dusre ke diye zakhm ko,
Apni khuraak banake jeete hai.
Yaadon se kuch lena dena nahi inka.
Yeh lamhon mein khilte hain,
Lamhon mein murjhate hain.

Kabhi saath mein, kabhi bichadhke,
Nai sarhadon ki talaash mein,
Woh na poore idhar ke, na udhar ke hote hain.

Do banjaro ko jab pyaar hota hai,
Unke kismet mein rehna nahi,
Sehna hota hai.

दो बंजारों को जब प्यार होता है,
उनके दिलों में ठहराव नहीं,
उफान होता है।

वो मंज़िलें नहीं,
एक-दूसरे में सफर ढूंढते हैं।
जिसका मोड़ खुद को चुभे,
ऐसी राह चुनते हैं।

दर्द को एक आदतन नशा बताते हैं,
करीब आ जाए,
तो दबे पैर निकल जाते हैं,
फासले बढ़ जाएँ,
तो तूफान की तरह वापस आते हैं।

दूसरे के दिए ज़ख्म को,
अपनी खुराक बनाके जीते हैं।
यादों से कुछ लेना-देना नहीं इनका।
ये लम्हों में खिलते हैं,
लम्हों में मुरझाते हैं।

कभी साथ में, कभी बिछड़के,
नई सरहदों की तलाश में,
वे न पूरे इधर के, न उधर के होते हैं।

दो बंजारों को जब प्यार होता है,
उनकी किस्मत में रहना नहीं,
सहना होता है।

Once done writing, she signed it: *Tushara*. She took a picture of it with her mobile phone and sent it to her fiancé.

He immediately called her up.

'It's wonderful!' Shanay said.

She knew he wouldn't have understood anything. He wasn't the kind who understood the nuances of words. What amused her was that every time she sent him her poems, couplets or lines, he always responded earnestly, with those two words 'it's wonderful!'

'Thanks. Did you check the link I WhatsApp-ed you?' she asked, sounding, as usual, detached even though she had sent him a link to something intimate.

Sitting on the swing in the balcony of her thirteenth floor flat in South City, Kolkata, she had her wireless earpiece plugged into her ears. Far away, in the cloudy twilight sky, she could see the blinking lights of two aeroplanes at opposite ends of the horizon. Although it seemed to her that they were on a certain collision course, they passed each other uneventfully. A faint ironical smile touched her face. She closed her diary as she heard him say, 'I did. It's sexy.' Shanay put his car back on gear as the traffic signal on MG Road in Bengaluru turned green.

'I'm going to wear it for you when we meet next,' she said.

Shanay instantly visualized her in the black lingerie featured in her WhatsApp-ed link. The firm thighs, the natural curves . . . *would she look sexier than the lingerie model in the website*? he wondered.

'I hope you're not kidding?' he said.

'Why would I? I'm okay with your plan.'

'Sure. By the way, I just learnt from a source that I may get nominated this year for the *Business Right Now* awards.'

'Congratulations! Reach home safely now. I'll wait for you on FaceTime,' she said as she hung up. No mushy muahs or cheesy baby-I-love-yous. *Like always*, he thought.

Shanay Bansal belonged to a fifth-generation business family based in Kolkata with roots in Bikaner, Rajasthan. After getting an MBA from Stanford University nobody in his family was surprised when he announced that he wanted to add an online business venture to their portfolio: *click2buy.com*. Life was all about work and more work, in his bachelor pad in Bengaluru, until his parents introduced him to the girl they had chosen as their prospective daughter-in-law. A small *roka* ceremony took place. The wedding was scheduled to be held seven months later.

Although he had met her a few times and telephoned her on a daily basis, if someone asked him to describe her, he would fumble for the right words. He often sensed a strange coldness about her—a coldness that effectively held him at bay. At first he thought she was shy, then assumed she was an introvert. But later, he could tell she was neither of those. Her icy aloofness fascinated him so much so that over time he became secretly obsessed with her. It was as if she was detached to every attachment. It was only recently that Shanay felt bold enough to go beyond discussing the obvious and shared a naughty plan with her on a FaceTime session one night.

'Shouldn't we get to know each other better?' he had asked hesitantly, putting his plan into action. Till then, Shanay had only had one girlfriend. In Class VIII, he had befriended Nisha Jalan. His incorrigible shyness made Nisha dump him after they passed the tenth boards. He couldn't bear the pain of his break up.

'How do you mean?' she asked.

'What if you come over to Bengaluru one weekend? We don't have to tell anyone anything.'

Silence. 'I'm not sure if that's a good idea,' she said.

Shanay was disappointed but he didn't push her again. Her sudden confirmation to the plan this evening, therefore, came as a surprise.

Shanay closed the door of his flat and flopped down on one of his beanbags in the living room, clutching his iPad. He immediately started checking all the Kolkata–Bengaluru flights for the specific day on a travel website. As the page loaded, his phone buzzed with a WhatsApp message. He tapped on the notification. It opened to a voice note from a number not saved in his contact list. Frowning slightly, he tapped on the voice note. A girl's voice spoke:

Hi Shanay,

I know who you are. I know where you work. I know where you live. I know who you are going to marry. In short, I know everything about you.

There's a reason why I'm reaching out to you. But please don't be scared. I'm harmless and not even important so you don't really have to know who I am. Not for the time being. If names matter to you a lot, you can call me Lavisha.

What I'm going to tell you is a story, all right? But it's not my story. Someone close to me narrated it to me with a promise that I wouldn't share it with anyone ever. But with this voice note I'm going to break the promise because if I don't break this promise then several other important promises will never be fulfilled.

Every story has a beginning somewhere—perhaps even a prequel. The great thing about old stories is that they almost always provide a startling new insight with staggering implications that cast an entirely different light on one's perception of the sequel.

Why am I narrating someone else's story to you, out of the blue, and that too anonymously? That's because if you listen to this story carefully and play your part well, you could perhaps change its ending. Right now you're wondering why you should bother to listen or pay heed to this voice note and the rest of the voice notes that will follow until my story is complete. My answer to that would be one simple word: HOPE. You are someone's only hope to steer this story towards an end that may not be a happy one, may not be a justified one, may not even be a right one, but it will be an end that will pave the way for new beginnings. Please bear with me and grant me your patience for now; patience to listen to the voice notes until I'm done narrating them.

I know you're a busy person. But this voice note and the subsequent ones are really more important to you than to me.

The more you know about the story, the more will you be compelled to decide the ending of that story. Please do listen to all the voice notes. Pay heed to whatever I say and try to understand whatever I couldn't articulate because sometimes I won't find the correct words to express matters of the heart.

Before I end tonight's instalment of voice notes, let me ask you a question: do you truly believe the one who lives with you is the only one who was made for you? What if— just, what if—within one's inner world there is another reality in which one lives with someone else? Don't we all have such parallel universes within ourselves? So, to whom does the person truly belong—the one with whom one lives in this physical world or the person with whom one shares the inner realm?

As Shanay finished listening to the voice note, not knowing what to make of it, another one popped up from the same number. He texted back: *who is this?* He called the number. But there was no response. He checked on TruCaller. The name read: *Lavi*.

Shanay stared at the new notification as it blinked on his phone. Out of sheer curiosity, he tapped on it.

Little did he know that a story was waiting to unfold, in which he would unwittingly play an important character.

BOOK ONE

VOICE NOTE 2

Raisa and Nirmaan,
Guwahati, 1996.

There was a mango tree behind the boundary wall of the Reserve Bank of India (RBI) officers' quarters in the Christian Basti area.

The tree was a great attraction for the eight-year-old boys in the vicinity. That summer, there appeared a mango on a branch that was tantalizingly beyond their reach. No amount of stone-hurling or stick-beating could bring it down. One day, Yash, the naughtiest of the lot, scaled the boundary wall and stretched as far as he could to reach that coveted mango. When it was mere inches away from his fingers, he suddenly howled in pain and hurriedly jumped off the wall, and seemed to be itching all over. When they took Yash to his mother, they realized that the boundary wall was infested with caterpillars. From the very next day, the boys started playing elsewhere, on a stretch of land in the campus where sand and bricks were stacked for an under-construction project.

An eight-year-old girl usually sat near the row of bricks that held the sand pile in place, amusing herself by scribbling on the sand. Her boyish haircut made her face appear bigger than it actually was. Her sparkling eyes indicated a sharp mind. She was dusky and wore shorts with half-sleeved shirts. She would arrive sharp at four o'clock in the afternoon and leave at 6.30 p.m. She would always dampen the sand with water from a bottle that she carried and then draw impressions on it with a stick. When the boys shifted base, they thought she was one of them—a boy.

'Wanna play frisbee with us?' asked one of the boys.

Before she could respond, his brother ran up to him and said, 'He won't. Don't you remember what mummy told us? He's a stupid child.' He trampled on her sand arabesque and ran away with his brother.

She saw them whisper something to the other boys. They immediately pulled faces at her. But there was one boy who didn't grimace.

From the next day onwards, the little girl brought with her not just a bottle of water but also a desire to watch that boy playing with the rest. He did glance at her once or twice but she couldn't understand why he wouldn't hold her gaze as she did his. Another thing that the little girl noticed about the boy was that after the others called it a day—at six in the evening—he would linger to throw a stone at the mango tree before leaving.

One evening, after his playtime was over, the boy returned to the apartment where he lived with his parents. He was taken aback to see a mango on his doorstep, the very same one that he had been eyeing for quite some time now. He heard someone speak from behind, 'This is for you. Thank you for not making a face at me.'

Startled by her sudden appearance, Nirmaan hastily rang the doorbell. He couldn't quite understand what the girl meant by 'making a face' and it made him all the more nervous. When his mother opened the door, he quickly picked up the mango and gave it to her.

'Where did you get this?' Mrs Bose asked.

'She gave it to me,' Nirmaan said, pointing to the girl.

Mrs Bose eyed the girl, 'Is she your new friend?'

With a quick, sideways glance at the girl, Nirmaan nodded at his mother. She smiled at her, 'What's your name?'

'Raisa Barua,' the girl answered diffidently.

'Such a lovely name,' Mrs Bose said and raised an eyebrow at Nirmaan, 'Won't you invite your friend in?'

With a nervous smile, Nirmaan reached for Raisa's hand and led her into his home.

Mrs Bose cut the mango in half and gave each child one half. It had a mouthwatering fragrance and tasted delicious.

'How did you know that I'm a girl?' she asked as she sucked on the mango pulp.

Nirmaan paused eating momentarily, pondering the query, 'How did you know that I'm a boy?'

'I knew it because you played with the other boys.'

'I knew it because . . . because . . . ' Nirmaan tried to hazard a guess, but failed.

'I just knew it,' he said and finished his half of the mango. Some of the pulp was stuck in the corners of his mouth and cheeks and although Raisa found the sight funny, she didn't laugh.

That night Raisa peeped out of her bedroom window and noticed Nirmaan on his balcony. They lived nearby and their apartments faced each other. Raisa was about to wave to him when there was a power cut. She scurried indoors, grabbed the flashlight from her mother's cupboard and ran out into the balcony. Directing the flashlight's beam at Nirmaan's balcony, she located him almost immediately. He covered his eyes with his hands, blinded. It made Raisa giggle to herself. She moved the beam from his face to his arms and back to his face again. Suddenly he ran into his apartment. Disheartened, Raisa switched off the flashlight. *Did she scare him off?*

She was about to go back into her room, when a beacon of light shone on her balcony wall. She realized that the light was coming from Nirmaan's balcony and its glare was on her face now. She covered her eyes and somehow managed to switch on her flashlight to see Nirmaan gleefully aiming his flashlight at her balcony. Raisa ducked down and playfully crouched behind the cemented portion of the balcony with an amused face and a heart that was beating fast. She could see the beam of light hover above her head on the windows of the adjoining drawing room, looking for her. Then the light was switched off. Fearing that Nirmaan would leave, Raisa stood up and saw that Nirmaan's mother had joined him. Together they waved at her. She waved back eagerly.

His mother went back in, but Raisa's mother came out just then, boxed her ears and took her inside. She hit the bed after getting slapped twice by her mother for not having been asleep already. She closed her eyes feeling excited for no apparent reason.

VOICE NOTE 3

The following two seasons painted Raisa and Nirmaan's friendship in deeper hues. During a fancy-dress competition in school, their mothers decided to dress them as Krishna and Radha. They looked incredibly cute together and won the first prize. They spent most of the day with each other. Apart from his parents, Raisa was the only one whose company Nirmaan looked forward to, both in the colony as well as at school. He had once asked his mother, 'Why can't Raisa and I stay together with you and Baba?'

Mrs Bose had laughed at that and had kindly explained the difference between family and friends. *Friend*. Although Nirmaan had other friends, calling Raisa a friend sounded inexplicably strange to him.

That spring, when Nirmaan brought out a bicycle that had two smaller wheels on either side of the rear tyre, Raisa couldn't help laughing.

'Nobody has those on their bikes,' she teased.

Glancing at her and then at the other kids who were racing by on their bikes, Nirmaan's heart sank. Abandoning his bicycle, he retreated into one of the surrounding buildings. He looked the picture of misery sitting on the bottom stair, hugging his knees to his chest. Raisa parked her bicycle outside and came over.

'What's the matter, Nirmaan?' she asked.

With long, shuddering breaths and head sunk into his knees, Nirmaan mumbled, 'I can't balance myself like the others so Baba got those supporters for me. Without them I can't cycle. But with them, people make fun of me.'

Raisa caressed his hair and said, 'Look at me.'

Nirmaan didn't.

'Look at me, Nirmaan. Now!'

He looked up. Raisa wiped the tears from his face and said, 'I'll teach you how to balance while riding a cycle. Come with me.'

'You will?' Nirmaan said, looking at her in disbelief.

Raisa smiled and nodded, 'I will. Get up now and follow me.' He stood up, dusting his pants and joined her.

Nirmaan mounted his bicycle.

'Not this one. Sit on mine.'

Nirmaan parked his bicycle and mounted Raisa's. Raisa positioned herself behind him.

'I'm holding you from behind to make sure you don't fall sideways, but you must keep pedalling, okay?'

'I'll fall!' Nirmaan was genuinely scared.

Raisa came in front of the bicycle and extended her hand to him.

'Hold it.'

Nirmaan held her hand.

'Tightly.'

Nirmaan tightened his grasp.

'Last Sunday I watched a movie. In it, the hero said that if you hold someone's hand and wish the person luck with all your heart, then nothing will ever go wrong. I wish you luck, Nirmaan, with all my heart.'

Looking into her eyes, he felt reassured. She let go of his hand and went behind the bicycle again.

'Now look in front and pedal. I'm right behind you.'

Nirmaan moistened his dry lips and started pedalling slowly, looking at his feet. Raisa urged him to look up and straight ahead. The bicycle kept wobbling until Nirmaan mastered the art of looking straight ahead. With Raisa pepping him up, Nirmaan discovered a new thrill. With each passing second, he gained more confidence and better control over the bicycle. He had overcome his own fear. Half a minute later and he still hadn't fallen over. *Of course Raisa is holding me from behind and* . . . a quick turn of the head told him she was a long way behind him now. The unprecedented thrill made him pedal harder. The wind buffeted him fiercely and sang in his ears. He had never believed a fear so terrifying could ever be truly conquered. But now the wind was real, the thrill was true, the fact was he was cycling without any support . . .

'See, I told you, Nirmaan,' Raisa's voice reached him.

Nirmaan turned his head and shouted, 'Thank you, Raisa!'

Before he could slow down or steer the bicycle away, Nirmaan, who had been speeding a little, crashed into a low wall beside the bend in the track.

Raisa came running to him. The front of the bike had been damaged. They exchanged sheepish glances. She noticed his palm was grazed.

'I'm sorry, Nirmaan,' she said.

'Why are you sorry? I didn't fall because of you.'

'I'm sorry because I lied to you. I saw no movie where anything was said about bringing good luck by holding hands.'

As Raisa's absurd lie seeped in, Nirmaan understood that she had only said it to help him defeat his fear.

The next day at school, when a surprise test was conducted, Nirmaan couldn't complete half the assignment because of his injured palm. When the teacher distributed the papers, she reprimanded Nirmaan severely for scoring the lowest marks. After she was done humiliating him to her heart's content, she turned around to write something on the black board when something hit her squarely on the back of her head.

'Ouch!' she roared and spun around. A brick-shaped eraser lay on the floor at her feet. 'Who threw that eraser?' she yelled.

Nobody answered as she panned her gaze on the students from left to right and back again.

'Who threw the eraser at me?' her voice rose ominously. Still nobody answered. Nirmaan noticed that the student sitting by his side was about to raise his hand to point at the culprit: Raisa. He quickly stood up.

'It was me, Teacher,' Nirmaan said.

Raisa, sitting a couple of rows ahead of him, turned around to look at him in sheer disbelief and then stood up herself.

'You shouldn't have hit him, Teacher,' she said. Everyone gaped at her audacity.

The teacher summoned their parents. Although
Nirmaan told Raisa that they should confess to their
respective parents, she couldn't find the right moment to
tell her mother about the school summons all through
the evening. That night, she had a quiet dinner as always,
sitting alone in a corner of her room. It was either that
or the kitchen because her father didn't appreciate a girl
child sharing his dining space. His prejudice paved the way
for a neurotic father–daughter relationship. Sometimes he
ignored her completely and at other times, when he came
home sloshed, he clasped her tight against his chest and
wept. The stench of cheap country liquor revolted Raisa,
but at the same time, his display of affection made her feel
loved, something she didn't feel too often. Raisa didn't
know whether she loved or hated him. Worse, she didn't
know whether he loved or hated her. On the other hand,
her mother was a loving and caring woman who rarely
spoke in her husband's presence. Although Raisa liked her
mother, she could never understand why she periodically
developed black eyes or bruises around her eyes or neck or
cuts on her lips.

That night, when Raisa finally worked up the courage
to tell her parents about the school summons, she went to
her parents' bedroom and found it locked from the inside.
This was nothing new. Once or twice a week, they locked
themselves in their bedroom after dinner. Her mother
had told her that when grown-ups prayed in their room,
children were not allowed inside. Raisa never disturbed
them, but that night was different. She was about to knock
when she heard a strange noise from within that disturbed

her so much that she scurried back to her room, jumped into her bed and burrowed under the blanket.

The next day at school, Nirmaan appeared in the teacher's room along with his parents, but Raisa came alone. Nirmaan's father kindly covered for both children and they were soon allowed to go.

As soon as Mrs and Mr Bose left, Nirmaan turned to Raisa as they mounted the stairs to their classroom on the first floor.

'Why didn't your parents come?' Nirmaan asked.

'I didn't tell them,' she replied.

'Why?'

'Do your parents make weird noises while praying?' she asked.

Nirmaan shook his head, not understanding a word she said.

'Mine do. They aren't like your parents, Nirmaan.'

VOICE NOTE 4

A few months went by and it was time for the annual sports day in the RBI quarters. Although both girls and boys had the same athletic events, they competed separately. Nirmaan stood second in most of the boys' events, losing the first place to Yash. Raisa came third in one of the events and lost in the rest. Huffing and puffing after his last event, Nirmaan ran up to the stone bench where Raisa was also sitting, catching her breath.

'I didn't win a single event,' she said sadly.

'Neither did I,' Nirmaan shrugged.

'Now we'll have the mixed events.'

'Be my partner?' he proposed.

'Sure!' she replied enthusiastically.

It was then that they heard the announcement of the names of the couples in the mixed events. Raisa was paired with Yash while Nirmaan was with a girl called Vini.

'Now we won't win at all,' Nirmaan mourned and plonked down beside Raisa, his expression both angry and disappointed. Raisa stood up.

'If both of us want to win, one of us will have to lose,' she said enigmatically.

Nirmaan frowned and watched Raisa amble over to Yash.

The first event was the marble-and-spoon race. The partnered pair stood at opposite ends of their track. First, the girl would set off with the handle of a spoon clenched between her teeth, a marble wobbling in its bowl. She would need to reach her partner balancing the marble on the spoon and relay it to the boy. He would then put the spoon in his mouth and return to the girl's starting point. The first pair to successfully complete this exercise without dropping the marble would be the winner.

When the whistle was blown, the girls started walking towards their respective partners. Raisa, with Yash waiting for her at the other end, kept glancing sideways. Two girls were alongside her and then overtook her. One was Smita and the other Vini. She let Vini go past her, but gradually caught up with Smita. As they drew abreast, Raisa flung out her arm, striking Smita's shoulder. Raisa's marble dropped. And so did Smita's.

'Sorry, I noticed a bug on my hand,' Raisa apologized.

Smita burst into tears when it was announced that both she and Raisa had been disqualified. Vini, meanwhile, reached Nirmaan, who went on to complete the event and win the race.

If both of us have to win, one of us will have to lose. Looking at her, Nirmaan now understood what she had meant. His success had the fragrance of her victory as well.

VOICE NOTE 5

That evening Raisa waited for her father. She wanted to show him the only silver cup she had won. She felt that if her father would embrace her for once without the stink, it would be rewarding enough for her. Although her mother kept telling her not to wait up since her father always came home late on Sundays, she preferred to wait on the sofa with the silver cup on her lap. At around ten in the night, when her father came home, she opened the door. One look at him and her cup clattered to the floor. Mr Barua, his eyes bloodshot, pushed the door open with great force and staggered in. Raisa noticed that he was swaying the way he always did whenever his breath stank. He collapsed on the floor beside the sofa. Raisa was about to try and help him up, when her mother stepped in and told her to go to her room. Raisa obeyed.

She rarely cried as a child, but that night the tears just wouldn't stop. She didn't know exactly when she dozed off. It was a cry that woke her up with a start. As the haze of sleep lifted from her mind, Raisa heard more cries that seemed to be coming from her parents' bedroom. She jumped out of bed and ran to their room. It wasn't locked. To Raisa it meant that they weren't praying. Pushing the door slightly open, she peered in with her heart thumping hard. She got the shock of her young life. On the big bed was her mother and on top of her was her father, naked, beating her while thrusting his pelvis up and down violently. Raisa began to shake with fear, watching her mother begging her husband to let her go. But he was slobbering on her mouth, slapping her cheeks and continuing those seemingly demonic hip movements.

Raisa wanted to help her mother but her limbs went numb and stiff as if she were paralysed. Her mind went blank. Only her eyes stayed wide open and whatever they were witnessing was getting imprinted into her core. Her squirming mother kept sliding up and down and fighting her father, but she was unable to free herself. Raisa wanted to slither down the floor by the door and weep at her mother's helplessness, but she couldn't even do that. And then her mother caught sight of her. That moment sucked the life out of Mrs Barua. She abruptly stopped fighting her husband. No more whimpers or whines emanated from her. Her husband clutched her for a few seconds before collapsing beside her with a groan. Mrs Barua slowly sat up, adjusting her clothes, covering her inebriated and naked husband, still looking arrow straight at Raisa. The latter was wide-eyed and open-mouthed. Her mother got out of bed and stood up looking dishevelled and weak. She limped towards her daughter as if it hurt to move. As she drew nearer, Raisa noticed her tousled hair, smudged vermilion and a streak of blood from her lips to her chin.

Mrs Barua looked deep into her daughter's eyes and knew that whatever she had just witnessed would remain seared into her little girl's brain no matter how much she tried to justify it at this juncture. Mrs Barua simply held her daughter against her bosom. Soon mother and daughter started conversing in the language of pain whose words were tears.

VOICE NOTE 6

Knowing that her husband would invariably repeat himself and fearing that Raisa may witness it again, Mrs Barua asked Mrs Bose if Raisa could spend the weekend at their place, citing some lame excuse. She knew perfectly well that it wasn't a solution at all.

'Sure,' Mrs Bose was happy to have Raisa.

On the first night, when Raisa sat down with Nirmaan and his parents to dine, she couldn't help but cherish every moment, crazily wishing that she had the same routine at home. It wasn't the food, it was the heart-warming togetherness. It wasn't the routine, it was the fact that his parents were there for Nirmaan. That feeling was alien to Raisa. Hence, appealing. And heart-crushing.

It started to rain late in the night, the pitter-patter of the raindrops woke Raisa. She went to Nirmaan's room to wake him up.

'Nirmaan, get up. Let's go for a picnic,' she shook his arm.

'Picnic? Where?' Sitting up in bed, disoriented, for an instant, Nirmaan thought he was dreaming.

'On the terrace.'

'Ma will scold us.'

'She won't if you do as I say.'

Nirmaan rubbed the sleep out of his eyes.

'We'll need two umbrellas and something to eat.'

Nirmaan went to his parents' room and fetched a large, black umbrella from the cupboard without waking them up. Meanwhile, Raisa opened the refrigerator and found several canisters of Frooti and a box full of sweets. She tucked the box under her arm and picked up a Frooti in each hand before softly elbowing the refrigerator door shut.

When Nirmaan joined her in the drawing room, he said, 'I don't know where the other umbrella is. Will one do?'

Raisa pondered for a moment before saying, 'We'll just have to make do.'

She stealthily unlocked the main door.

'What are you doing?' Nirmaan was more scared than curious. But the thrill of the forbidden was immensely attractive.

'Told you,' Raisa chided gently, 'we need to go up to the terrace.'

Like an obedient child, Nirmaan followed Raisa as she drew back the bolts and wedged the door ajar, and together they climbed the stairs to the terrace above the fourth floor.

They sloshed to the middle of the terrace under the umbrella, with Nirmaan clutching Raisa's dress as it poured heavily around them. She lowered the umbrella and they made themselves comfortable under its vast black canopy, as if it were their den. Raisa handed a Frooti to Nirmaan and said, 'You're lucky, Nirmaan.'

'Meaning?'

'Meaning you have good luck with you.'

'What's luck?'

'I don't know. I've often heard Ma use this phrase to describe other people. Both you and Aunty,' Raisa replied.

Nirmaan looked at her as she stared at the weeping night sky, taking care not to get wet.

'Can't best friends share their good luck?'

'Best friends can only share Frooti, not luck,' she shook her head.

'Are you sad about anything?' Nirmaan probed.

Raisa nodded.

'Here,' he said leaning towards her. 'Ma says that when someone is sad we should give them our shoulder to lean on. It helps them feel better.'

Raisa put her head on his shoulder. *Aunty is right. It does feel good*, she thought.

VOICE NOTE 7

Mrs and Mr Bose were frantic when they found neither of the kids in their beds in the morning. They frenziedly looked for them all over the housing campus. Mrs Barua joined the search party as well. It was only when they asked the security guard to check all the terraces that he found the children, fast asleep. Mrs Bose who rushed up, paused for a moment to look at the two kids lying side by side, hands clasped, an open umbrella by their side, the morning sunshine warm on their faces. They resembled two innocuous petals of a freshly flowered bud. When Mrs Barua joined Mrs Bose, they couldn't help but smile.

'Now, one by one, bathe and get ready. We'll go to the Kamakhya Temple today,' said Mrs Bose as soon as she brought the truants home.

'But I don't have a change of clothes,' Raisa protested.

'That's okay, dear. Wear Nirmaan's clothes today. As soon as we get back, I'll take you home. In fact, Raisa, you bathe first.'

Nirmaan saw Raisa go into the bathroom but come out immediately.

'Listen, lock the bedroom from outside,' she instructed him, 'I'll knock when I'm dressed, and you can let me out.'

'Okay,' Nirmaan agreed.

'But where are my clothes?' she asked.

'I'll ask Ma.'

'Put them on the bed.' Raisa stepped into the en-suite bathroom and locked herself in.

When Nirmaan asked his mother about fresh clothes for Raisa, she told him to take his pick from his closet because all of them were clean and pressed. Nirmaan carefully extracted a T-shirt and a pair of shorts without disturbing the tidy pile of clothes in the cupboard. He placed it on the bed and was about to walk out, when he paused by the door, a naughty smile on his face. *I'll surprise Raisa*, he thought.

Nirmaan shut the door and quickly hid himself under the bed. Minutes later, Raisa came out. He could see her feet. He could tell that she was wearing his shorts. It was when she was going towards the door that Nirmaan emerged from under the bed and bounded upon her, yelling a monstrous 'hu-hu-ha-ha!' In pure reflex, she snatched up a jar of talcum powder from the dressing table and hit him on the head. Everything happened in a flash. Holding his head, Nirmaan collapsed on the floor. A second later blood oozed out of his head and tears out of her eyes.

Although it wasn't a major injury, the doctor asked Nirmaan to rest for a couple of days. He missed his school. Raisa visited him with her mother, but a furious Nirmaan refused to see her. When Raisa narrated the whole incident to her mother, she understood why her daughter had reacted like that: abhorred a man's touch . . .

On the one hand, Raisa was filled with remorse for the hurt she had caused, and on the other, she felt that Nirmaan ought not to have scared her that way in the first place; and that he too ought to be as repentant as she was. The two mothers did their best to patch things up between their children, but the cold war continued.

One day, a couple of months later, Mrs Bose visited Mrs Barua.

'I've come to tell you that Nirmaan's father has been given a promotion. We're moving to Calcutta,' she said. 'Everything happened so quickly that I couldn't tell you before.'

'Oh! Why don't you all come home for dinner before you leave?' Mrs Barua asked.

'Thank you very much, but there's so much packing still to be done. And we're leaving the day after tomorrow.'

When Mrs Barua broke the news to Raisa, she skipped dinner claiming she had a stomach ache. The next day, she watched as all of Nirmaan's household items were loaded into a huge truck. The following day, a car arrived to take Nirmaan and his parents to the airport. As she leaned out of her balcony, Nirmaan got into the car. That was when Raisa realized that it didn't really matter who apologized first or who was at fault. Nothing mattered except the fact that she would miss her best friend if he left her.

Raisa ran to the main door of her flat, opened it and jumped down the stairs in her bare feet. By the time she came out of her building, the car was at the main gate, waiting for the security guard to open it. She ran towards the vehicle, shouting Nirmaan's name but stumbled and fell. She stood up again, ignoring her injury and ran as fast as she could to catch up. The car sped through the gate and on to the road. Reaching the main gate, panting, Raisa could only hope that Nirmaan had glanced back at least once and that he knew she had been there. With moist eyes, she put her hand into her pocket and withdrew a photograph in which they were dressed as Radha and Krishna.

VOICE NOTE 8

Hi Shanay,

I'm sure you're wondering who Raisa and Nirmaan are and how this matters to you. I could have jumped directly to the point without telling you anything about Raisa and Nirmaan's backstory but that would not have served the purpose. I've told you about their beginnings because if you don't understand that, you will not be equipped to make a valid choice by the end of this story.

The good thing for Raisa and Nirmaan at the time when the latter left Guwahati was that they were both young and neither carried the burden of a heavy past. All they carried with them was their friendship; their feelings for each other were instinctive, impulsive and visceral. It is important for you to know that whatever they shared at that time, therefore, was pure and beyond anyone's manipulation.

Let me continue the story from the next note onwards.

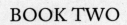

BOOK TWO

BOOK TWO

VOICE NOTE 9

Raisa and Afsana,
Kolkata, 2002.

It was the first day of school after summer vacation. Nirmaan excused himself from class after the first period and was heading for the boys' toilet when a paper ball hit him between the shoulder blades. He spun around to see who had thrown it but couldn't figure out the culprit from among the students in the corridor on their way to their classes. He casually picked up the paper ball and, unfolding it, found a single word inscribed in bold black letters with a sketch pen: *MORON*. He was sure it was one of the boys from his own class playing a silly prank.

When the physics teacher asked him to bring all the students' files from the laboratory, Nirmaan got pelted again; this time, just as he had stepped on to the landing of the floor where his class was. He turned around in a flash and glimpsed someone in a skirt scurrying out of sight in the stairwell. However, the pile of files in his arms obscured his line of vision; he couldn't get a proper look. He placed the files on the floor and picked up the paper ball. This time it had the word: *DOGGY*.

When the bell rang, signifying the end of the recess, he trooped into his class with everyone else. He saw a word chalked in bold letters on his bag: *LOSER*. It infuriated him. He asked around to find out if anyone had seen who had done it. Nobody had.

After school, he boarded the school bus with his friends and was soon having a good time chatting in the last seat, when another paper ball hit him. This time the word was *PIGGY*.

Nirmaan spotted a girl in the front seat turning away. She was so quick that he couldn't register her face. He decided to confront her. As he drew nearer, he saw that the girl's face was hidden behind a Nancy Drew novel.

Nirmaan cleared his throat and said: 'Excuse me?'

The girl lowered her novel. He gaped at her.

'Remember me, or do I need to tell you my name, numbnuts?' Raisa asked. They were seeing each other after six years.

VOICE NOTE 10

Nirmaan and Raisa were standing in the aisle of the school bus.

'When did you take admission to St Peter's High?' Nirmaan was still shocked. Was it the same Raisa who had panicked so badly when he had played a childish prank on her; with whom he had sat on a terrace on a rainy night; the girl who had given him the most succulent mango he had ever had by way of introduction; the girl who had taught him to ride a bicycle? He looked at her as she talked. Her long hair was tied with a red hairband into a ponytail; she had pearl studs in her ears; and her skin seemed unusually soft. There was a tiny mole on her chin, which hadn't been there before. It made her look even sweeter.

'Two months ago, Deuta got transferred here,' she said, grabbing the strap overhead when the bus jerked as it set off. 'But we got our flat in the RBI quarters only yesterday. We were staying in a hotel when I took the admission test for this school.'

'Did you know that I was studying here?' Nirmaan asked.

'No, dumbo. But Deuta said that most of the kids from our RBI quarters study here, so I hoped to find you here. If not, I'd have found you in the quarters.'

For a little more than a moment, they silently gazed into each other's eyes. Raisa shrugged.

'God, I still can't believe it!' Nirmaan exclaimed.

Raisa raised her free hand and pinched his cheek hard. 'Now, do you?'

Nirmaan cupped his cheek, shocked and embarrassed, and quickly looked around to see if his friends had noticed.

The long-lost friends disembarked from the bus by the Ultadanga footbridge. They weaved through the crowds at the bus stop and headed towards the RBI officers' quarters adjacent to the Bidhan Nagar railway station. Forced to walk in a single file due to the milling crowd, they found it difficult to make conversation. At times Raisa would be ahead of Nirmaan and sometimes, he.

'You forgot me, didn't you, Nirmaan?' she accused.

'No way!'

'Yeah,' she scoffed nastily, 'that's why there were no letters.'

'You didn't write either!' Nirmaan retorted, literally running to keep up with her.

'Idiot! Did you give me your address? You simply went away in that stupid car. I chased after it, but you didn't turn around even once or even say goodbye.'

'Did you follow the car?'

'Yes, duffer!'

'I'm sorry, Raisa, for whatever it is that I need to be sorry about.'

Through the crowd, Raisa shot him a smile. Nirmaan caught up with her a moment later.

'But you don't know how happy I am to see you again,' he realized that Raisa was again ahead of him. He called out to her, 'Raisa!'

She stopped, turned around, and walked back towards Nirmaan.

'Screw you!' she scowled.

'What?'

'Hug me, stupid.'

Nirmaan immediately enfolded her in his arms.

'*Ki hochche eta* [What's going on here]?' an old geezer sneered in Bengali, seeing two youngsters embrace in public.

Raisa broke the hug, looked at the sanctimonious old-timer, flicked him off rudely and said, 'Dadu, this is for you.' Grabbing Nirmaan's hand, she ran laughing into their housing campus.

The first thing that Nirmaan told his mother when he went home was that Raisa was in town. After quickly freshening up, he accompanied his mother to Raisa's apartment.

'It's wonderful to see you after so many years,' Mrs Barua beamed at Mrs Bose and Nirmaan. 'How have you been? And how big our little Nirmaan has become,' she added, ruffling his hair.

'We're all good. How have you been? You're looking well,' Mrs Bose replied, genuinely happy to see a fresh-looking Mrs Barua.

Raisa emerged from an inner room and joined her mother. She greeted Mrs Bose, gave a high-five to Nirmaan and took him inside.

As they entered her room, Nirmaan looked around slowly and scowled in exasperation, his arms akimbo.

There were four wooden crates firmly nailed shut; several planks of wood that, he could tell, were actually components of Raisa's bed waiting to be reassembled; a tall, rectangular box covered with gunny sacking that had to be an almirah; an iron chest, also wrapped in jute gunny; and suitcases of various sizes piled higgledy-piggledy. An old photograph had been glued to the door panel of one of the built-in wardrobes. He went closer to peer at it and realized it was their fancy-dress picture.

'How stupid we look!' he exclaimed.

'You definitely look stupid. Not me!' she rebutted.

'I need to have a copy of this.'

'You will, but now help me out,' she said, gesturing at the cartons.

'What's all this?' he asked.

'I didn't have time to unpack,' she shrugged. 'You have to help me set up my room.'

'Oh!' Nirmaan's eyes widened. 'But I have maths tuition in half an hour.'

'You were my best friend, Nirmaan. Act like you still are.'

It took them exactly four hours to unpack everything and set up the room precisely the way Raisa desired.

The next day, they boarded the school bus together. As soon as they stowed their bags away in their respective classrooms in school—Nirmaan in section B, Raisa in section D—they met in the badminton court behind the main school building. Although Nirmaan asked Raisa to stay with the girls of her section, she stuck to him like glue. She found it difficult to talk to someone new.

'Unless you talk to them, how will you get to know anybody?' Nirmaan argued.

'I don't know. Just stay with me until I get a friend here, okay?'

Nirmaan's batch mates were seeing him with a girl during school hours for the first time, which he knew would raise unnecessary comment. Ever since they had graduated to Class IX, Nirmaan had noticed that whenever a girl and a boy were seen hanging out together, everybody immediately assumed that they were dating.

During recess, Raisa took her lunchbox and went to Nirmaan's classroom and gestured him to come out.

'Now what?' he asked.

'What "now what"? Aren't you going to share your lunch with me?'

'I'm discussing an important assignment with my friends. I won't have lunch today.'

'But I'm starving. I promise I won't take long. I can't eat alone, especially knowing that you're around.'

'Oh, all right!' Nirmaan gave in, terminating whatever desire he had to counter her. He could sense the tittering and sniggering among his group in the background.

The duo quickly made their way to the edge of the sports field and sat down on a small patch of grass in the shade of a tree.

'Time for some good food,' Raisa said as she opened her lunchbox. A dead cockroach and the tail of a lizard lay inside.

VOICE NOTE 11

Upon Nirmaan's suggestion, Raisa promptly complained to her class teacher, who told the students to stop harassing the new student and threatened them with dire consequences if any further bullying was reported. That day, the last period was music class. When Raisa excused herself to the washroom, three other girls excused themselves one after the other and followed her out.

Raisa washed her hands in the washbasin when she emerged from the toilet cubicle and as she approached the restroom door, she noticed a tall, stout girl standing beside it. She recognized her as one of the girls in her section.

'Hello, teacher's pet,' the girl said nastily.

Raisa heard sniggering behind her and turned to see two more of her classmates.

'What happened?' Raisa asked, feeling her throat go dry. The tall girl shot a glance at the ones behind Raisa. They pounced on her and in a flash, had her pinned down on the filthy, damp floor; one pinioned her arms while the other clamped her hand over Raisa's mouth. Raisa struggled in vain. The tall girl crouched down to lean close to her and smiled at the naked fear in Raisa's eyes.

'Don't you mess with us by being a teacher's pet, okay?' she grated. 'The next time we see you complaining about a cockroach in your lunchbox, we'll make you eat a live one. Got it?'

Raisa could only glare at the bully. She stopped squirming when she saw the tall girl fish out something from the pocket of her skirt.

'Got it?' she growled, pressing hard with the sharp end of a compass into Raisa's forearm until it drew blood. Raisa nodded in terror and agony. The bully smirked and removed the compass. A knock on the washroom door interrupted the proceedings. The tall girl slipped the compass back into her pocket and gestured the others, who immediately let go of their victim and got to their feet. Raisa was left on the floor. One of the bully's henchwomen unbolted the washroom door and the three girls trooped out. The girl who had knocked, yet another fellow student in Raisa's section, entered the washroom. She barely threw Raisa a cursory glance before vanishing into a cubicle. Raisa knew her skirt would have a wet patch.

She washed the gash that was bleeding. She wrapped her handkerchief around the wound and was about to leave the loo when she heard the other girl speak aloud from inside the toilet:

'The first-aid room is to the left of the staffroom.'

Although Raisa didn't know her classmate's name yet, she was grateful for the stranger's help.

'Thanks,' Raisa said aloud and limped out of the washroom.

After Raisa got her forearm bandaged by the school nurse, she ran into the girl who had directed her there.

'It's good that I got you here. Here, let me dry your skirt,' the girl said.

She took out a small, battery-operated hair-dryer and knelt down to dry Raisa's skirt.

'You brought your dryer to school?' Raisa asked.

'I bring a lot of things to school. But this I brought for a different reason.'

Raisa stood patiently till the dark patch on her skirt lightened considerably.

'I'm Raisa Barua. Can we be friends?' Raisa asked. It would be good to have someone in class to have her back.

'Can you meet me tomorrow morning outside the washroom adjacent to the chemistry lab?'

'Isn't that locked?' Raisa clearly remembered seeing a large, rusty padlock on the door when she had exited the lab the previous day.

'It is. But we'll break in tomorrow. Game?'

A twinkle appeared in Raisa's eyes as she grinned mischievously.

'Game!'

'I'm Afsana Agarwal. Friends,' the girl agreed raising her hand for a high-five.

'By the way, you didn't say why you brought a dryer to school?'

Afsana smiled mysteriously, 'I'll tell you tomorrow. Just wait for me by the chemistry lab.'

VOICE NOTE 12

In the evening, Raisa called out to Nirmaan while he was out playing cricket with the boys in the colony.

'I've made a friend in school,' Raisa said. She was sitting with Nirmaan by the stairs of the community hall during a break in his game.

'Thank god! Now I'll get a breather, phew!' Nirmaan said, pretending to wipe sweat off his brow.

Raisa pinched his arm hard. He yelped.

'You've got no idea about the ribbing I have to put up with in school when they see us together. I have an image to maintain in school.'

'Image?'

'I'm this studious, master-of-all, popular boy who doesn't talk to girls much,' Nirmaan said.

'A gay image,' she nodded sagely.

'Shut up, Raisa!'

'Ever since we've met again, I have this feeling that you're ashamed to be seen with me. What is it with this what-will-they-think attitude all the time?' Raisa stood up, truculent, arms akimbo.

Nirmaan looked up at her and then, with a rueful grin, pulled her down beside him.

'I'm sorry. But you've got to understand, it's no longer the way it used to be.'

'What? Don't you want to be my best friend any more?'

'It's not that. I don't know how to explain this to you. From the time I got here, I've encountered immense competition. I understood that not everyone is a well-wisher. Not everyone wants you to be happy. One has to be on guard always. My parents, especially Baba, expect a lot from me. He has high hopes from me. You won't believe it, but last year, when I ranked second in the half-yearly exams, he didn't let me eat for two days.'

'Are you serious?'

'Yeah. Ma was distraught, but he assured her that the fasting would never let me stand second ever again.'

'Mothers are all like that. They can't stand up to our dads,' Raisa said, thinking of her mother.

'Baba can't bear to see me come second in anything. Especially academics. It's his dream that I top Class X, then XII, and then get into an IIT. That's why I always feel this pressure of being someone who I'm probably not on the inside. But to retain that other persona, I often do things that I don't really want to. Like I don't really want to stay away from you, but this person that I am in the eyes of my batch mates wants to avoid you. Are you getting what I'm saying?'

Raisa looked pensive. She gazed into the stairwell and said quietly, 'We're growing up, Nirmaan.'

He could have hugged her at that moment. She had succinctly summed up his rambling roundaboutation. Yes, they were growing up. They had grown up since their Guwahati days. On the face of it, it was less than a decade, but the change that the few years had wrought within, Nirmaan knew, was of such magnitude that it was beyond estimation.

'I really want to talk to you, but you see, a few minutes from now, I'll have to go to my social studies tuition class. And then after dinner, I have to study for the maths class test tomorrow. Do you know what I've realized?'

Raisa looked at him expectantly.

'The most frustrating thing in this goddamn world is to live up to someone else's expectation of you. Especially if that someone is your own father.'

Neither spoke for a while. Then Raisa stood up.

'Hmm, I too have expectations from you, Nirmaan *beta*,' she said in a deep voice. And giggled.

'Shut up, *kameeni*!' retorted Nirmaan.

'Wow! That's the first time you called me a name.'

'I'm sorry. It was a slip.'

'I loved it.'

'What?'

'I think you calling me a kameeni is cute. May I call you *kutta*? Kutta–kameeni. Best friends for life.'

Nirmaan was in splits. 'You're absolutely mad!'

'Anyway,' he grew serious again, 'who is this new friend of yours? Is it a boy?'

'No. Boys don't talk to me. Her name is Afsana. She is so much like me. And tomorrow we're going to do something.'

'What?'

'I don't know what exactly. That's what is so exciting, isn't it?'

Nirmaan gaped at her for a few moments and then said, 'Yeah, sure.'

The next morning as Afsana stepped on to the landing of the school's third storey, which, being the laboratory floor for the senior students, remained deserted during the morning session, she noticed Raisa was already there, leaning against the wall. Afsana walked up to her briskly.

'How are we going to deal with this?' Raisa asked, indicating the rusty padlock on the lab door with a jerk of her thumb.

She watched in awed admiration as Afsana quickly and efficiently jimmied the lock with her hairpin, pushed open the door and slipped in. Before Raisa even knew it, Afsana was already out of the room, a small vial in her hand.

'What are you doing?'

'It's game over for those bitches!'

Afsana extracted two ski masks from her satchel and handed one to Raisa.

'Those bitches always spend some time in the ground floor washroom as soon as they come to school. That's our point of ambush. Hurry up now,' Afsana said.

Both scurried down the stairs to their classroom. After a few minutes, the three girls came into the room together. They dropped their school bags on their seats and walked out. Afsana and Raisa followed them.

As the trio entered the washroom, the duo stood guard outside. After half a minute, Raisa and Afsana slipped in and locked the door stealthily. Two of their adversaries were in front of the large mirror by the washbasins while their leader, the tall, hefty one, was missing. Raisa and Afsana wore their ski-masks. The latter soaked both their handkerchiefs with drops from the chloroform vial. They snuck up behind the two girls and pressed the handkerchiefs on their mouths. The swiftness of the attack took their victims by surprise and muted their shouts. Before they knew it, the chloroform had rendered them unconscious. Satisfied with a job well done, the masked duo stood up just as one of the toilets was flushed. They silently flanked the cubicle door. The moment the tall girl emerged, Afsana and Raisa pounced on her. She struggled for a moment, but by the time the assembly bell rang, she too was unconscious. Afsana and Raisa stood still, listening for a few minutes as the sound of the students stampeding to the assembly hall receded. Afsana delved into her bag and extracted a make-up kit. In the washroom, the two girls quietly and quickly applied foundation, lipstick, eyeliner, mascara and whatnot on the faces of the three sleeping girls. As soon as they were done, they took off their masks, unlocked the washroom door and peered out to make sure the coast was clear. They dragged out the three girls one by one and left them propped upright on the bench by the washroom door. The two girls then slipped into the assembly hall. Before the assembly came to a close, they returned to their classroom feigning illness and sat well away from each other so nobody could tell that they were together.

There wasn't a single student in the school who didn't laugh at the sight of the three sleeping beauties with their kitschy make-up, dark-red lipstick on garish-white faces, hair poofed-up with hairspray and red ribbons tied into bowknots around their necks. The news spread like wildfire until a teacher arranged for one of the school staff to take the girls away to the sick bay and summoned their parents. All three regained consciousness a good two hours later. Their parents demanded that strict disciplinary action be taken against the ones who had perpetrated this mischief. However, the identities of the miscreants remained a mystery because the two girls had been wearing masks. The principal ordered the teachers to search every student's bag. Nothing was found.

Afsana and Raisa stayed behind in the campus after school. A worried Nirmaan asked Raisa how she planned to get home if she missed the school bus. Raisa asked him to tell her mother that there was an extra class and that her friend would drop her home. Nirmaan didn't want to lie, but with a little wheedling from Raisa, he agreed to collude in their little charade. He glowered at Afsana who, he now knew, was his best friend's new friend.

As soon as he left, Afsana took Raisa to the decommissioned washroom beside the chemistry lab. Raisa was amazed to see that Afsana had the keys to the lock.

'How did you manage that?' she asked.

'I broke the original lock a long time ago and replaced it with one that I brought from home. Nobody knows because nobody opens it,' Afsana grinned.

When they entered the old washroom and locked the door from inside, the overpowering smell of jasmine startled Raisa. But that was not the only surprising thing there. It was a small, unkempt and clearly neglected place, predominantly dirty, but in a corner she saw a canister of a room-freshener, some fashion magazines, a book of Hindi poetry, a discoloured Walkman, a lighter and couple of cigarette packets.

'What's all this?'

'Welcome to my time-pass zone. I read magazines here, smoke and listen to songs, mostly after school. Now you are allowed here as well.'

An astonished Raisa picked up the cigarette packet.

'I've dreamt of smoking ever since I saw my father smoke,' she confessed.

Afsana took the packet, extracted two cigarettes, lit both and retaining one, she gave the other to Raisa.

'Suck gently,' she suggested.

Raisa did as told. A sense of forbidden pleasure invaded her as she exhaled the smoke. The girls smiled at each other and puffed again.

'Thanks for avenging my insult,' Raisa said blowing smoke into the air.

'Not only yours. They have been harassing a lot of girls of late. I wanted to get back at them earlier, but I needed the right partner,' Afsana said, leaning against the washroom window.

'Now you've got one,' Raisa chuckled and winked at her. As they exhaled together, the smoke coalesced in the air and became one.

VOICE NOTE 13

Nirmaan had a natural flair for event management: budgeting for an event and spearheading a team to execute the plan. He was unanimously chosen, therefore, as the head of the student committee to arrange the upcoming Teacher's Day celebration across all classes in the school.

After planning everything in minute detail with the monitors of all the sections, Nirmaan was strolling with Raisa towards their school bus, which was parked outside the school campus, when a car came to a halt beside them. The rear passenger window was rolled down and someone screamed out gleefully, 'Rice!'

Nirmaan looked at the girl quizzically and said, 'What?'

'Affu!' Raisa exclaimed and added, 'Nirmaan, don't tell me you have forgotten my friend!'

Nirmaan had not. But he didn't want to remember Afsana either. He didn't like her for some reason that he couldn't quite pinpoint. She was rash, impulsive and a brat: everything Nirmaan hated. She gave off a vibe that signalled that if given a responsibility, she would deliberately screw it up. Moreover, he was fairly sure that she was the main reason for Raisa's poor academic performance. He was also confident that all Raisa's lately learnt Hindi and Bengali profanities that instantaneously afflicted him with hiccups, came from Afsana. He had even recommended that she stay away from this girl, but all he got in return was an earful of even filthier swear words from Raisa.

'Coming?' Afsana asked, looking pointedly at Raisa.

The latter threw a pleading glance at Nirmaan. He understood what he had to do.

'Okay, I'll tell aunty you have an extra class. But this is not right!'

'Right and wrong are subjective notions,' Afsana quipped, opening the car door for Raisa. Nirmaan glared at her. Raisa gave him a quick hug.

'Thanks!' she said and climbed into the car. It soon sped away.

Inside the car, Afsana seemed excited about something. Having been her only friend for the last three months, Raisa knew very well that whenever Afsana felt excited, someone somewhere paid a price big time.

On Teacher's Day, as the teachers wandered around visiting various classrooms, they were pleasantly surprised by the gala preparations. This day had never seemed this grand before. A student presented them with a red rose as they entered the classroom. After this was done, they were led to a corner where a solitary candle burned, above which hung multicoloured balloons. The teacher held the flame below the balloons till one of them burst. A fortune cookie would fall out, containing a line or two praising the teacher, written by the students themselves. After this, the teachers were given small gifts and a helping of roshogollas from one of the five big bowls. After all the teachers had visited the classrooms, the last two bowls were taken to the staff room to be distributed amongst the remaining teachers and staff. It was towards the end of the day that some of the teachers started having strange headaches, others felt dizzy while some felt an uncontrollable bubble of mirth rising up from within them. Some sat still on their chairs, too afraid to stand up and others chuckled insanely. The principal, Mrs Dasgupta, on the other hand was weeping copiously, alone in her room. Only the vice principal, Mrs Gujral, who had been late to school that day, seemed normal.

It was eventually discovered that the only common food item that everyone had had was the roshogolla. A quick test of the remaining few roshogollas revealed that the syrup had been laced with a large amount of cannabis (bhang).

'Where did the roshogollas come from?' Mrs Gujral howled at the teachers the next day.

After a shocked silence, one of the teachers replied, 'Class IX, ma'am.'

'Who is the batch head in Class IX?' asked Mrs Gujral.

'Nirmaan Bose.'

VOICE NOTE 14

The next day in school, just before the recess, Nirmaan was standing by the water purifier, lost in a reverie. His plastic tumbler was overflowing, when someone reached past him and turned off the faucet. He turned to see Raisa.

'What happened?' she asked, her eyes flicking to his chest a few inches right of his tie where his 'Batch-Head' badge was always pinned to his shirt. That space was empty.

'Where's your badge?' she frowned.

He ignored Raisa and walked away.

'Hey, Nirmaan, what happened? Did someone beat you? Tell me, I'll squash his balls.'

Nirmaan stopped. He turned to face Raisa.

'I've been suspended for a week. Someone injected cannabis into the roshogollas on Teacher's Day,' he said shortly. He looked so miserable that Raisa's heart sank. Next came the guilt punch on her conscience.

'Who?' Raisa choked. She cleared her throat and repeated, 'Who injected cannabis into those roshogollas?'

'Don't know and don't care. How the hell am I going to get the suspension letter signed by my parents? Baba is going to kill me.'

'I—' Raisa was just about to confess when the recess bell rang and students poured out into the corridor from all directions. Watching Nirmaan walk morosely back to his classroom, Raisa hated herself like never before.

'We shouldn't have done that, Affu,' Raisa said. Both girls were playing table tennis in the sports room after playing hooky from their maths class, citing severe headaches.

'Hmm. But we didn't know that this would be the outcome when we did it, right? I mean we didn't deliberately do it to get your friend suspended, did we?' Afsana justified their mischief.

'That's true but—'

'But we can't undo the damage. We can be sorry, but we can't undo it.'

Raisa knew Afsana was right and that made her feel worse. She hit a fast forehand. Afsana missed it.

'Did you apologize?' she asked, picking up the ping-pong ball.

Raisa threw her TT bat on the table and went to sit on one of the plastic chairs in the room.

'Should I?'

Afsana dragged another chair over to Raisa and straddled it to look straight into Raisa's eyes.

'You once told me that he is your best friend. In that case, you should answer the question yourself,' Afsana said.

'Affu, what if he starts to hate me? I don't want Nirmaan to hate me ever. I mean I wouldn't shed a single tear if the rest of the world loathed me, but Nirmaan . . .' Raisa stretched her legs and looked up at the ceiling, weighing her options. Afsana bounced the ping-pong ball on her TT bat.

'Although both of us are responsible for it, you're right: I, being his best friend, should be the one to apologize,' Raisa reasoned. 'But before that, I have to make sure he doesn't suffer for this screw-up.'

That day, Raisa was in time to catch the school bus along with Nirmaan. He sat in the front of the bus, on the first seat, far away from his friends and was quiet for the entire journey. It was only when they entered the RBI housing colony that Raisa broke the silence and asked Nirmaan when he would show the suspension letter to his parents.

'I have maths tuition now. I'll show them the letter after dinner,' he said and walked towards his building. Raisa ran to hers and got busy preparing an official looking table on a sheet of paper. When this was done to her satisfaction, she took an empty milk-powder tin can, hammered out a tidy slot into its lid and then sat by her window to keep an eye on the entrance of Nirmaan's building. Fifteen minutes later, she saw Nirmaan leaving for his coaching class. She immediately went to his apartment.

'Hello, Aunty!' Raisa greeted Mrs Bose.

'Hello, Raisa! How are you?'

'I'm good. Hello, Uncle,' Raisa noticed Mr Bose dressed in formal clothes, sitting on the sofa, sipping tea. He nodded at her.

'Nirmaan just left for his tuitions,' Mrs Bose opened the door wide to usher Raisa inside.

'I know, Aunty. Actually, I have come to meet you two. We've been given an assignment by our teacher. We need to collect funds for an old age home named Umeed. I would be very grateful if you could make a contribution. Please?'

Mrs Bose included her husband in her pleasant smile and said, 'That's wonderful. How much do we need to donate?'

'That's up to you, really,' Raisa flashed her most appealing smile.

Mrs Bose went inside one of the rooms and returned with a fifty-rupee note.

'Will this do?'

'Certainly,' Raisa said, extending the slotted can. Mrs Bose slipped the note through the slot.

'Aunty, you need to sign here,' she offered a paper on which, Mrs Bose noticed, there were three columns: name, amount and signature. Mrs Bose signed it and returned the sheet to Raisa.

'Uncle as well,' Raisa pleaded.

'Do we both need to sign?' Mrs Bose frowned.

'That's okay. Bring it here, Raisa,' said Mr Bose, putting his teacup down. His wife took the pen and paper to him and he signed it without a fuss.

'Thank you once again.' A happy Raisa left.

Sitting in her room, she practised forging Nirmaan's parents' signatures almost five hundred times before she mastered them. Feeling confident, she went down the stairs and sat on the narrow bench beside the main gate.

Half an hour later, as Nirmaan returned from his tuition and was wheeling his bicycle through the gate, she waylaid him.

'Go and fetch me your suspension letter.'

'What? Why?'

'Just do as I say. And don't show it to Uncle or Aunty.'

Nirmaan took a few seconds before he said, 'Okay.'

It took a minute for him to go home and return with the letter.

'Don't tell me you wanted to see what a suspension letter looks like?' he muttered as he gave the letter to Raisa.

She knelt down on the ground with the letter on the bench. Nirmaan watched in disbelief as she signed the letter on behalf of his parents and most importantly, just like his parents. This accomplished, she stood up and handed back the letter to him.

'You don't have to show this to your parents now.'

Nirmaan glanced alternately at the letter and at Raisa. A moment later, he hugged her tight.

'Thanks a million-trillion-zillion times, Raisa.'

'Are you happy?' she asked.

After giving her an obviously-I'm-happy look, he beamed at her and said, 'You bet I am.'

'All right, now I have a confession to make.'

'What?' Nirmaan was still staring incredulously at his parents' signatures, unable to believe his eyes.

'Affu and I spiked the roshogollas with cannabis.'

Nirmaan's smile disappeared. He slowly raised his head to look at his friend, who looked apologetic.

'No, you didn't,' he breathed.

'Yes, we did. But, believe me, we didn't know that you would be suspended for it.'

'I knew that idiot Afsana would ruin you. Why don't you stay the hell away from her?' Nirmaan demanded, finally speaking his mind.

'Calm down. I told you we were both involved.'

'But I'm sure it was her plan, wasn't it?'

'In a way.'

'What "in a way"?' Nirmaan mimicked her cruelly and sat down heavily on the bench.

'She wanted to inject vodka, but cannabis was my idea. We got it from one of her cousins.'

'I've been suspended, Raisa. Do you even know what that means?'

Raisa sat beside him and said, 'I know. But at least now you won't have to involve your parents. Moreover, you have one hundred per cent attendance. One week off won't make a difference.'

'But what will I do for an entire week at home? What will I tell Ma and Baba?'

'Who said that you will sit at home? You will go to school on time and return from school on time, but you won't enter school, that's all. And I'll be there to keep you company.'

Nirmaan glared at her.

'You can study if you want to, at a bus stop or wherever, we won't disturb you.'

'We?'

'Affu will be there too. If you're my best friend, she is my soul-sister. I can't do anything without her involvement.'

'It has only been a few months and she has already become your soul-sister?'

'Time has nothing to do with people coming close or drifting apart, Nirmaan. It happens like that,' she snapped her fingers.

Nirmaan sighed.

'Moreover,' she went on, fishing out the fifty-rupee note from the can, 'we have money as well,' Raisa beamed.

Nirmaan couldn't help smiling at his best friend and bumped his head to hers lovingly. She headbutted him right back, but with greater force.

'Ouch! What's wrong with you?' Nirmaan rubbed his head.

'Sorry. Ma says that if we bump our heads once, both of us will sprout horns, unless we bump our heads twice.'

VOICE NOTE 15

'Wow! Is this where you live, Affu?' Raisa was awestruck at the sheer magnificence of the bungalow in the CF block of Salt Lake. They had graduated to Class X with Raisa just about scraping through and Afsana with mediocre scores in all the subjects. This was the first time Raisa had accompanied Afsana to her place.

'I stay here. I live when I'm out of it,' Afsana replied cryptically, walking into the house.

Raisa felt like she was walking into a film set where everything looked close to perfection, boasting of class and opulence.

As the two girls entered the vast hall room, a servant came over to take their school bags. Raisa readily handed over her bag to him and then noticed that Afsana was clutching hers even as she removed her shoes.

'Sorry, Affu. It's not every day that someone offers to take my bag,' Raisa placed her shoes by Afsana's.

Afsana laughed and said, 'And it happens to me every day so I don't care.'

She ordered the servant to bring two cold drinks to her room. The girls went upstairs.

'How many bedrooms are there in this house?' Raisa asked.

'Six,' replied Afsana, impassively.

'This only gets better. And how many people?'

'Twenty.'

'Twenty? That's like impossible. How can you live with twenty people even if the house is this big?'

'You have no idea how.' Afsana entered a room. Raisa followed and paused by the door, stupefied.

'Gosh! Don't tell me this is your room.'

'It is.'

There were two life-sized posters—one of Michael Jackson in his 'Bad' avatar and another of Tom Cruise from his *Top Gun* days—above a small, cozy-looking bed.

'The first thing I do when I wake up every morning is kiss Tom. I want to marry him,' Afsana said.

'Shut up! We can't both marry the same guy,' Raisa went ahead and planted a kiss on Tom Cruise's lips.

'Sorry, sweetheart, I can kill for Tom,' Afsana said, grinning.

'Okay, let's do one thing. You keep him during the day and I'll keep him during the night.'

'How convenient!'

They laughed and shared a high-five as they collapsed on the soft bed together.

'No Tom needs to come between us,' Afsana said.

'Exactly. I, anyway, won't ever marry,' Raisa quipped.

'Why so?'

There was a momentary silence as Raisa stared at the designer lights suspended from the ceiling.

'Marriage is garbage,' she replied.

'The world is garbage,' Afsana sighed and shut her eyes. The servant tiptoed in and placed two bottles of Coke on the bedside table.

'How many times do I have to tell you that I don't need straws?' Afsana yelled at the hapless servant, who meekly took the straws away.

Raisa sat up. She took one of the bottles and gave the other to Afsana.

'It's so nice to command people like that, isn't it? I wish I could do that.'

'We all like what we don't have, Rice. I would like to have a place where only my parents and I stay, like you do.'

'And I could kill for a place like this, Affu. I wouldn't mind even if I had to live with fifty people!'

'My point exactly.'

Afsana sat with her back against the wall, her head tilted up and her eyes closed as she gulped her Coke.

'Is there any problem, Affu?' Raisa asked, realizing for the first time that her soul-sister was not sounding like her normal self.

'The Afsana who lives here and the one you see in school are two different people,' Afsana said heavily.

'What do you mean?' Raisa scooched up close to her curiously.

Afsana opened her eyes, glanced at Raisa for a moment and then squeezed them shut again. Seconds later, tears rolled down her cheeks.

'Affu!' Raisa cupped her friend's face in alarm.

'Do you know why I'm such a brat?' Afsana asked. 'It's because that's my best chance to get noticed.'

Afsana's tears disturbed Raisa in ways she hadn't felt before.

'I told you there are twenty people staying here,' Afsana continued, with shuddering breaths. 'That sounds good when you say it, but the ugly part is nobody has time for anybody. Look at my parents. They don't even know which class I'm in.'

'Really?'

'The first time I got their attention was when I broke a costly vase. Both of them scolded me. I liked it. And I kept doing something out of the ordinary whenever I wanted their attention. And now they think I'm a brat. They give me everything I want but they don't know what I really need.'

Raisa hugged her and Afsana broke down, her face burrowed into Raisa's shoulder.

'Promise me you won't ever leave me, Rice. I know we've known each other for only a year, but I've never had anyone so close to me before.'

Afsana tightened her embrace. Raisa marvelled at the way people lived a grammatically incorrect life, just waiting for the elusive emotional punctuation to happen. Nirmaan's every action and very existence was dictated by the pressure of his father's aspirations for his son. There was a time when Raisa wanted to redeem herself before her father without even knowing what her mistake was. Affu too seemed to be labouring under a sense of neglect, even though her father wasn't even an alcoholic like hers. *Wait a minute*, Raisa thought, and said aloud, 'Affu, is your father an alcoholic?'

'Not really.' Afsana rubbed her eyes and excused herself to the en-suite bathroom. Raisa got off the bed and went over to the study table laden with academic books untidily strewn all over it. She slid open a drawer in the desk and casually picked up the thick encyclopaedia that lay within. She caught sight of an old issue of the salacious *Debonair* magazine beneath it. Raisa picked it up with a shy giggle. A half-naked man and a skimpily clad woman adorned the cover. She heard a sound and spun around, holding the magazine aloft, 'Affu, they're naked!'

But it wasn't Afsana. It was a boy in a leather jacket and jeans, with a bandana around his brow to keep his long hair from falling into his eyes. He stared at her in frank admiration.

'Wow! Who are you?' the boy asked.

'Raisa. You?'

He walked up to her, his hand extended, 'Rick.' They shook hands. Raisa was suddenly alert. She could feel her hackles rise. Except for Nirmaan, she was always uncomfortable around boys—something about the way they looked at her made her jittery.

'Did anyone ever tell you that you're damn beautiful?' Rick asked.

Raisa's throat dried up. She gave him a tight smile and said, 'Thanks.'

Afsana came out of the bathroom and paused. Raisa's eyes darted to her. Rick followed her gaze.

'Is she your friend?' Rick asked Afsana, cocking his head.

'Get lost!' Afsana snarled. The abrupt rudeness hit Raisa.

Rick narrowed his eyes at Afsana, suddenly looking mean. To Raisa he said, 'We'll meet again.'

'No, you won't,' Afsana quipped.

Raisa looked alternately at the two of them during this exchange. Rick left. Afsana followed him to the door and slammed it shut.

'That's why I prefer to keep my room locked,' she said.

'Isn't he someone from your family?' Raisa asked.

'He is. My uncle's eldest son.'

'Then why were you so rude to him? He *is* family.'

'I hate him. He is a rascal and a player.' Afsana clambered on to the bed.

'Who's a player?' Raisa joined her.

'Players are men who can't be anything else but *men* all their lives, if you know what I mean. Forget him.'

Raisa couldn't.

VOICE NOTE 16

'Who told you that you're beautiful?' Nirmaan asked.

Raisa, who had come to his flat on the pretext of trying to learn algebra from him, told him about Rick. They were seated on chairs flanking his study desk in the glow of the table lamp between them. The confession made Nirmaan look at Raisa sceptically.

'Why do you sound so surprised?' Raisa frowned, 'Am I not beautiful?'

For a moment, Nirmaan was at a loss for words. He had always liked her but he had never asked himself before if he considered her beautiful. What is being beautiful? Is it about having a flawless skin (which she did), about possessing a healthy figure (which she did), nice features (which she did as well)? The fact that he liked her told him she must be beautiful. The fact that she helped him win all those races in Guwahati as a kid made him believe she was beautiful. The fact that she helped him get away with the suspension letter convinced him that she was beautiful.

'Who's Rick?' he asked.

'Affu's cousin.'

'Where did you meet him?'

'At Affu's place.'

'He said you're beautiful the very first time he met you?'

'Yeaaaaah,' Raisa drawled and shrugged in a what's-wrong-in-that manner.

'That sounds weird.'

'Come on. I'm thrilled and you are focusing on the boy instead.'

'So what should I do if someone finds you beautiful? There are so many girls who find me cute. I don't take them seriously.'

Nirmaan feigned to focus on the algebra problem while Raisa seemed momentarily lost.

'You mean that I too shouldn't take Rick seriously?'

'No. You shouldn't,' Nirmaan said and noticed her frowning. He chose to explain, 'Look, Raisa, this boy doesn't know you and so he finds you beautiful. It doesn't mean that you're not. What I mean is, I've been your friend for so many years. Have I ever told you that you're beautiful? Do you know why? It's because I know you're beautiful. Friends don't point out the obvious. Imposters do.'

Raisa sighed as if Nirmaan had just burst her little bubble of joy.

'See you tomorrow in school,' she said dejectedly and stood up.

'What about algebra?'

'Do I look like I'm interested in algebra?' She left.

* * *

Afsana was absent the following day in school. Nirmaan was busy with his friends preparing for an upcoming inter-house debate competition. Without her partner-in-crime, Raisa felt like a toothless hag. She slept through the classes.

After school, she noticed someone waiting by a motorbike outside the school gate. One look and she recognized Rick. His hair was loose.

'Hi!' he said when Raisa approached him.

'Hi!' For some strange reason, she felt happy for the first time that day.

'Going home?' he asked.

'Yes.'

'Want to go for a ride?'

'But—'

'I'm not a kidnapper,' he smirked. The way he said it made her heart beat faster.

'Okay.'

The thrill in her brushed aside her apprehensions. She straddled the pillion seat and the bike roared away.

Instead of taking Raisa straight home, Rick took her to an amusement park in Salt Lake.

'Have you been here before?' he asked.

'I've only heard about it from my friends.'

They rode almost all the rides in the park, ate, talked and within a span of two hours, Raisa felt he wasn't a stranger any more. Rick seemed to imbue her with a weird sense of self-confidence that she had never felt before.

As the two rode the toy train, it passed through some shrubbery within the park campus. Suddenly Raisa giggled pointing at something. Rick followed her finger and saw two couples, one pair behind the other, smooching. Rick grinned and looked at Raisa.

'Why, what's wrong?' he asked.

'Didn't you see what they were doing?'

'What?' Rick egged her on deliberately.

'I don't know,' Raisa turned her face away.

'Have you ever kissed a boy?' he asked.

Raisa could feel all her muscles clench and goosebumps appear on her arm as Rick held her hand. Suddenly the pleasure in her heart was substituted with a hunch that something disturbing was about to happen. She tried to break free of Rick's warm clasp, but couldn't. She looked at him. He was leaning towards her, drawing closer with every passing second. When he reached dangerously close to her mouth, Raisa stood up and jerked her hand free furiously. Rick let go of her hand and watched as Raisa hopped off the slow-moving toy train before it came to a halt. He followed her.

'I like you, I love you,' Rick said aloud, catching up with her. She stopped, so did he. She turned to look at him. Rick felt emboldened and came to stand directly in front of her. He gripped her shoulders and gently clipped her lips. She bit hard on his lips. Too hard. Rick pushed her away, wiping the blood off his lips.

'You bitch!'

'You swine!' Raisa said.

Rick punched her savagely and she toppled to the ground. Her nose was bleeding. He stared down at her for a moment, moistening his lips and then offered her his hand.

'Now get up and don't fight me when I smooch you.'

Raisa took his hand, stood up and threw the fistful of earth she had scooped into her other hand into his open eyes. Rick howled in pain as she ran away holding her injured nose.

Later that evening, when Nirmaan's mother told him that she had met an injured Raisa with another girl in the RBI campus, he abandoned his dinner midway and rushed to her flat.

'With whom did you fight?' was his first question upon entering her room. It was only when he switched on the light that he noticed Afsana sitting on the bed with her back against the wall. Raisa had run straight to her and Afsana had taken her to a doctor first before bringing her home.

Raisa was on a chair by the window.

'Switch off the light, Nirmaan,' she said.

He complied, repeating his query.

'Affu's cousin,' Raisa replied.

'That guy who said you're beautiful?'

Raisa muttered a soft yes.

'Why?' he asked.

'He was trying to be smart.'

'Is he in our school?'

'He is in Bhawanipore college,' Afsana chose to reply.

Nirmaan ignored her, staying focused on Raisa and said, 'Then where did you meet him?'

'Outside school. He said he would drop her home on his bike but took her to Nicco Park where he tried to smooch her,' Afsana replied.

Nirmaan stood quiet, seething with anger.

'Why the hell did you get on his bike? Are you mad?' he hissed.

'I thought—' Raisa started, but didn't say anything more. Realizing that she didn't want to talk, Nirmaan threw an accusing glance at Afsana and stormed out.

Silence crept back in.

'You know, Affu,' Raisa said in a soft, confessional tone, 'my father has raped my mother. And beaten her up as well. I have seen it with my own eyes. She always surrendered like a slave. I don't want to be a slave. I had promised myself long ago that if any man ever touched me, I would beat him to a pulp. This touching thing—' she trailed off and tried again, '. . . until Rick tried to smooch me, I felt good being with him but the moment—'

Afsana was quiet, absorbing every word.

'I don't think I'll ever be able to have sex with anyone. The thought of physical intimacy stifles me, threatens me, breaks me and in a way alienates me from myself. When Rick held me by my shoulder, I thought he would rape me. I thought he would make me his slave and . . . Affu, is sex really important?'

'I don't know. I think love is important and sex is necessary. But we often confuse ourselves by thinking what is important is necessary and what is necessary is important.'

'That's deep, Affu,' Raisa went over to Afsana and put her arms around her.

'Why? Don't you like deep stuff?' Afsana caressed Raisa's forehead.

'I do. I think deep too when I'm sad.'

'I think deep when I have nothing else to think about.'

'So, do you mean no boy will ever be mine if I don't have sex with him?' Raisa asked.

'At some point you'll have to. Everyone does.'

'Aren't you afraid of sex, Affu? Isn't it such an "ugh thing"? Just imagine a boy sticking something inside you. Yuck! Why can't we stick something inside them instead?'

'From what I've seen in my family, I'm more scared of love.'

The two girls sat in silence in the darkness of the room. Then Afsana suddenly said, 'Stay away from Rick. He's a B-hole.'

'I will. Such an A-hole he is. Wait a second, B-hole?'

'Bum hole.'

'Oh! It's the same as A-hole.'

'Yeah. A-hole is his good name and B-hole is his nick name.'

'I think he should also have a third name: C-hole!'

Afsana looked at her enquiringly. Raisa's amused face answered her. She gave a hard peck on her soul-sister's cheek.

VOICE NOTE 17

The half-yearly exams for Class X were over. Raisa, yet again, managed to barely scrape through in all the subjects. Afsana had slightly more than average marks while Nirmaan successfully topped the entire batch.

Raisa went to his flat one evening to copy Nirmaan's history notes. She saw him talking to someone on the landline phone in his room. He raised two fingers, implying that he would need two more minutes. Raisa didn't mind. She extracted his history notebook from his school bag and began copying the notes. The two minutes stretched to half an hour and then to a full hour. Raisa wouldn't have noticed the time had she not heard Nirmaan giggling and trying to crack lame jokes on the phone, which sounded very unlike him. As soon as he was done, the hangover of the phone conversation was evident in the form of a faint smile on his face.

'What's up with you? Why are you smiling to yourself?' Raisa asked.

'Am I? Shit, sorry,' Nirmaan said and sat beside her.

'Who was it?' she asked.

'A newcomer. I was updating her about the stuff that she has missed in class till now.'

Her? You were updating her about what she missed in class by telling her stupid jokes, Raisa completed it in her mind.

The next day Raisa went to Nirmaan's class during recess to share her lunch—pani pitha, which was his favourite too—but she didn't find him there.

'Where's Nirmaan?' she asked one of his classmates.

'I saw him go out with Sakshi.'

'Sakshi who?'

'The newcomer.'

Afsana approached her from behind.

'Hey, waiting for Nirmaan?' she asked.

'He's not here.'

'Absent?' Afsana casually helped herself to the pani pitha in Raisa's lunchbox.

'No. He's out with Sakshi.'

Afsana stopped chewing and looked at Raisa. Before she could say anything, Raisa was gone. She followed her out. In the distance, they could see Nirmaan and Sakshi walking together in the parking area, chatting and smiling.

'What?' Afsana joined a dejected-looking Raisa.

'I don't know,' she replied, but Afsana knew what was wrong.

'Listen, Rice,' she said, 'Nirmaan isn't your property. He's a friend, not your boyfriend. Let him roam around with whomever he likes and let us enjoy these pithas.'

'I know he is not my property, but . . . '

Raisa reluctantly averted her eyes and walked away in the opposite direction with Afsana.

The following weekend when Raisa met Nirmaan while he was playing cricket with the others, she couldn't help but laugh. For the first time he had shaved off his thin line of moustache and the peach fuzz on his chin.

'You look like a girl!' she exclaimed.

'Shut up!' Nirmaan bristled.

'But why did you have to shave?'

'Sakshi thought I would look better if I shaved.'

Raisa checked her laughter.

'Moreover, everyone but you think I look better now,' he retorted.

'You look like a fool,' Raisa snapped and marched off leaving a bewildered Nirmaan behind.

Sakshi started riding in the same school bus as Nirmaan and Raisa. Although Raisa could effortlessly excuse herself and barge in between them, she didn't want to.

A few evenings later, Raisa went to Nirmaan seeking his help to complete her science project. He was again busy on the phone. His tuition time came and went, but he stayed glued to the phone, smiling all the while. The I-am-not-myself-any-more tinge in his smile told Raisa it had to be Sakshi at the other end.

It wasn't jealousy or any kind of insecurity that gripped her. She sensed a new indifference in Nirmaan's attitude towards her with his increasing proximity to Sakshi. What hurt her was that when Nirmaan was the first person to whom she had confided about Rick, why couldn't he have told her about Sakshi without her having to nudge him to it? Raisa eventually discussed it with Afsana.

'She wastes his time all the time and he doesn't seem to mind it at all.'

They were sitting together on the last bench in their Hindi language class, chatting softly while one of the students was reading out a passage from the book aloud.

'If he doesn't mind it, why the hell do you care?' Afsana retorted.

'Can best friends be substituted, Affu?'

'No,' Afsana replied.

'Can there be more than one best friend?'

'No.'

'Then, wasn't I ever his best friend? Was it all fake?'

'No.'

'Stop being monosyllabic, Affu!' Raisa hissed in her ears.

'*Aap dono,*' the Hindi teacher said, '*bahar.*'

Afsana and Raisa happily obliged and went to stand outside the class.

'What do you want me to tell you?' Afsana asked, irritated by Raisa's obsession with Nirmaan's behavioural changes.

'I'm okay if he's with Sakshi, but his indifference is killing me. You know, for the last two months he has talked to me only when I approached him. This is simply not done!'

'Rice, people transform, their preferences alter and priorities change. Get used to it. Not every friend remains with us forever. Forever is only a bestselling concept in books and movies. Apply it to life and it will flounder.'

The words affected Raisa deeply. If Affu was right, then what would she do without Nirmaan? Is that all life was about? Things change just like that and we are all left to suffer?

'Affu, will you too forget me one day?'

Afsana looked at her and with a serious face, said, 'I only talked about friends. Not about soul-sisters.'

Raisa managed a smile and they shared a high-five.

Without Nirmaan, I won't be able to live; but without Affu, I won't exist, Raisa thought.

Raisa took Afsana's words seriously and decided that instead of feeling frustrated because someone's preferences had changed, it would be better for her to change her priorities as well. And she did leave Nirmaan alone.

A few months later, on her way home from the vegetable market with her mother, she saw Nirmaan sitting alone on one of the benches in the RBI quarters.

'Ma, you go ahead, I'll be home a little later,' Raisa told her mother and headed towards Nirmaan.

He noticed her but didn't react when she sat down beside him. They looked at each other and she could tell that he had been crying.

'Will you tell me what happened or are you waiting for a film director to say "action"?'

'My marks dropped in the unit tests. I came second.'

'Oh no! Are the results out? I thought that would be next week.'

'The results aren't out officially, but our class teacher told me that this time I've stood second. This is the first time after so many years that I have come second.'

'God, Uncle is going to be harsh, won't he?'

'"Harsh" is a mild word. He's away on an official trip and will call tonight after dinner. I'm fairly sure he'll disown me and tell me to get out of the house.'

'Chill. You still have a week more to face him. Tell him about it when the results are officially out. And don't forget to have a fever or stomach ache or headache or whatever you can conjure up two days prior to that. It would be best if you tell him you have brain cancer. I have seen in the movies that people turn real sympathetic towards brain cancer patients. In any case, if Uncle tells you to get lost, come over to my place. I'll call Affu as well.'

Nirmaan looked at Raisa and a smile spread on his face.

'I missed you, Raisa,' he said.

'Hmm,' Raisa said doubtfully. Then she asked, 'By the way who came first?'

Nirmaan didn't reply.

'Do I need to use a loudspeaker?'

'Sakshi,' Nirmaan blurted out.

For a split second, Raisa felt immense joy surging through her, as if Sakshi were her own daughter and she, Raisa, was proud of her.

'What are you saying?' she exclaimed.

'She would complete her lessons and then call me to waste my time.'

'But I thought she was your best friend,' Raisa's words held a whiff of sarcasm, which Nirmaan couldn't sniff.

'Best friend?' Nirmaan gave her an incredulous look.

'Yes, best friend. In fact, I thought you two were an item as well. Best friend turned lovers, you know,' she sneered.

'I'm sorry, Raisa,' Nirmaan finally smelled the sarcasm.

'Affu said your indifference towards me was normal. And I thought our friendship was over. That it was time for me as well to change my best friend. You and Affu are my heart and soul, if you don't know this already.'

Nirmaan knelt down before her and said, 'I don't know what happened to me in the last few months. It was as if I were under a spell. I'm really sorry, Raisa. I know you must be hurt.'

'Hurt? You have no idea, Nirmaan!' she turned her face away.

'Tell you what, the next time you see me doing anything like this, or any other stupid stuff, just slap me hard, okay? It'll drive some sense into me.'

Raisa turned and instantly slapped him hard. He cupped his cheek in sheer disbelief.

'Just checking. Do you want it this hard, or harder?'

VOICE NOTE 18

'What's this?' Raisa freaked out at the sight of the slashes on Afsana's wrist.

They were meeting after a good one month post their Durga Puja vacation during which Afsana's family had compelled the recalcitrant girl to accompany them on a pilgrimage to all the holy places in north India.

Raisa was perched on the teacher's desk and Afsana was sitting on the teacher's chair. It was a free period.

'I tried killing myself last night,' Afsana said matter-of-factly.

'Killing? Please tell me this is a joke?' Raisa pleaded, tentatively stroking the livid marks on Afsana's wrist.

'It's not a joke. A boy and his family had come to see me yesterday.'

'What do you mean "see you"?'

'My parents have fixed my marriage.'

'Marriage?' Raisa hopped off the desk and gaped at Afsana in amazement. 'What rubbish are you saying?'

'I was a little surprised when Mom asked me to wear conventional Indian clothes and bring tea for the guests.

Then the boy's folks started asking me weird questions. Actually, you know the boy is a man. He is twenty-seven.'

'Twenty-seven? And you are only sixteen!'

'I know. It's my dad's colleague's son. They want us to get engaged now and marry as soon as I turn eighteen.'

'You can't get married like that, Affu.'

'Exactly. Hence, just as I was about to kill myself, I wondered why the hell should I waste my life only because my parents want to get me married. I've decided that I won't go home again after school today. I've brought a few clothes and some other essentials with me.'

'But where will you go if not home?'

'I don't know. Any suggestions?'

The girls brainstormed the whole day until school was over. In the end, Raisa said, 'Do you remember you once opened the old rusty padlock of the chemistry lab?'

'Yes, with a hairpin.'

'Can you still jimmy a lock?'

'Anytime,' Afsana quipped.

The sparkle in Raisa's eyes clearly indicated that she had hit upon the very solution.

An hour later the two were on the mezzanine floor between the top floor and the terrace of Raisa's block in the RBI quarters. The low-ceiling floor had two locked rooms on either side of the stairs, with thick pipes from the terrace going into one of them.

'What's in there?' Afsana indicated to the second locked room.

'I don't know. I don't think I've ever seen it open in the three years that I've lived here.'

It took Afsana little more than two minutes to unlock the thick metal lock to reveal a dusty, cobwebbed little room. The tiny window was broken and had an empty bird's nest on the outer ledge.

In the next hour, Raisa managed to smuggle out some candles, a box of matches, a broom, a bedsheet and a pillow from her apartment without arousing her mother's suspicions. Raisa swept the attic room clean, after which they set up the room together.

'Damn! I wish I could live here with you,' Raisa said, wiping the sweat off her brow.

'I can't thank you enough, Rice,' Afsana hugged her.

'The next time your parents try to get you married, just give me a little more time.'

They burst out laughing.

That night, Raisa finished her dinner hurriedly and when her mother went into the kitchen, she stealthily packed two chapattis and a little sabzi in a piece of newspaper. She told her mother that she was off to Nirmaan's place for some schoolwork and went directly to Afsana. She knocked thrice—their code—and Afsana opened the door. The room gleamed delightfully in the candlelight.

'This is so adventurous. Why didn't your parents fix your marriage before?' Raisa moaned, sitting down beside Afsana as the latter wolfed down the food.

The next day, Raisa skipped school feigning a stomach ache and spent the entire day with Afsana in the small room, playing ludo, snakes-and-ladders, chatting and smoking.

'Do you know, Rice, I want to study science,' Afsana confided.

'Science? Not arts or commerce?'

'With arts or commerce, I won't be allowed to leave the city. If I study science, I can do engineering in some other city and never return.'

'Never?' Raisa sounded disturbed.

'Naturally we'll go together, stupid,' Afsana said.

A smile lit up Raisa's face.

'In that case, I too will opt for science,' she replied, knowing perfectly well that she had never scored even average marks in science subjects or for that matter in any other subject.

'But all that will be possible only if my parents report to the police that I'm missing.'

'They should, right? Otherwise I could adopt you.'

The girls giggled.

'I'm counting on it,' Afsana grinned. 'As soon as they file a police report, I'll emerge from my hiding and threaten to elope if they don't allow me to study science.'

'What if they still insist that you get engaged to that elderly guy first?'

'They will. I know. And I'll get engaged. Actually, I kind of feel sorry for him. His first would-be-wife will never be his wife!'

After another paroxysm of mirth, Afsana continued desultorily, 'But I can't be married off against my wishes. I'm a minor now. By the time I finish my graduation, I'll be grown up enough to manage my own life without the need of a stupid husband or even my parents. Therefore, there's no question of ever coming back to them.'

'All this is so exciting!' Raisa exclaimed.

The following evening, Nirmaan ran to Raisa's place after school. On the verge of ascending the stairs to her floor, he noticed her in the stairwell, going further up. Curious, he followed her and realized she had a guest.

'What are you two doing here?' Nirmaan exclaimed. He was shocked to see Afsana. Then he noticed the cigarettes.

'You girls smoke?!'

'Nirmaan, shut up and listen: first thing first. This has to be a secret!' Raisa shushed him.

'Secret? I just saw her photograph in the "missing persons" section of the local newspaper. I came to tell you about it and now I see this.'

The missing persons' report made Afsana and Raisa share an enthusiastic high-five. It confused Nirmaan even further.

'Are you girls on drugs?'

'We were waiting for Afsana's parents to file a police report. Now you'll have to help us a bit, Nirmaan,' Raisa beseeched, her palms pressed together.

'What is it?'

'We need to inform Affu's parents that she'll come home only if they give it in writing that they'll allow her to study science in plus two.'

'Study science? Is this what this is all about? She absconded because she wanted to study science?'

'Oh, you'll never get it. Are you going to help or not?'

Nirmaan nodded, knowing fully well that he didn't have any other option.

'Please help, otherwise we'll have to toss you out of the window,' Raisa said.

That night, Raisa telephoned Nirmaan and asked him to smuggle some food out for Afsana because there were guests at her home and her mother wasn't letting her out of her sight. Nirmaan somehow managed to steal some food from his home, excused himself citing a post-dinner walk and reached Afsana. As he watched her eat, Nirmaan could see that she was famished.

'Can I tell you something?' he asked.

'Sure,' Afsana said.

'I think you should just go back home without making any demands at all. They're your parents, after all. They'll understand whatever it is that you want them to do.'

Afsana paused to glance at him and then resumed her meal. This was the first time they were meeting without Raisa. When Afsana was done, Nirmaan stood up to leave.

'Can I ask you something?' Afsana asked.

'Yeah.'

'You could have just given me the food and left. You didn't, why?'

The response came a few seconds later, 'I don't know. Perhaps it's just courtesy to be there when someone is eating.'

Afsana felt he wasn't telling the truth. She took out a cigarette from its box. She flicked the lighter a couple of times but couldn't light it as the window was open. Nirmaan cupped his palms around the lighter's flame and helped her. Although he didn't say anything, he noticed the brand that she was smoking.

'Bye,' Nirmaan said and was at the door when her voice stopped him.

'I'm sorry,' she said.

'For what?'

'Rice apologized for that cannabis-in-the-roshogolla thing. I didn't get a chance to.'

'That's all water under the bridge now.'

'Then this is a long-overdue apology,' Afsana replied. They smiled at each other and then Nirmaan was gone.

The next morning, Raisa told Nirmaan not to go to Afsana's hideout.

'Why, what happened?' he asked.

'She said she'll go home on her own.'

Nirmaan couldn't help but smile.

It was evening when Afsana returned home. Although her parents agreed that both her engagement and wedding would only take place after her graduation, they insisted on the alliance that they had chosen.

Afsana joined science tuitions. Although Raisa followed suit, she slept through most of it, and everything that the teacher taught went over her head. In no time, the board exams arrived. Raisa spent most of the time cooped up with Afsana, studying. The exams took place and two months later, the Class X board results were announced. Nirmaan topped not only their school, but also the other schools in eastern India. Afsana scored enough to secure a seat in the science stream for her senior secondary. Raisa failed in four subjects. She had to repeat Class X with neither her best friend nor her soul-sister.

VOICE NOTE 19

Hi Shanay,

Raisa loved both Afsana and Nirmaan. It was as if the creator had sliced her soul into three sections: the one part within her yearned for the other two. If Nirmaan completed her, then Afsana embellished that completion. The failure in studies didn't hurt Raisa. She had never had big academic aspirations anyway. However, it was hard to believe that two people who were not related to each other by blood or class, could form the most essential and most basic part of one's existence. It was as if the other two had been there in the creator's subconscious when one was being created and the connection was felt the instant they met. Have you ever wondered that the most important experiences of one's life aren't caused by events but by a few specific people? And when you see them moving ahead in life, there are bound to be emotional repercussions. The fact that Raisa had to repeat a year while Afsana and Nirmaan went on ahead in life tore her from within. Landmines of queries filled her, which exploded as fear. Raisa was sure that both Afsana and Nirmaan would miss her as

*well, which they did, but there was something else that she wasn't
ready for. It was something that changed her life forever.*

*You'll know what I'm talking about from my next voice
note onwards.*

Shanay was supposed to be in an important meeting
with one of his product's distributors in Hyderabad. That's
what he had told his fiancée two days ago, but the truth
was that he was on leave—his first since he had started the
online operations. He also told his fiancée that he wouldn't
be taking any calls for these two days. The first reason for
this lie was that he needed some time alone, away from
everything and everyone.

He had stayed put in his Bengaluru flat for the last forty
hours. The chaos he was feeling within after the last voice
note made him skip dinner. This turmoil was the second
reason that he had lied. The voice notes gave him a hint, or
so he thought, about how exactly he might be related to the
story being narrated to him. The more he thought about
it, the more he felt that the initial voice note could well
be true: that his very life, perhaps, would actually change
when the story ended. *But what was the end?* The question
only exacerbated his ferment.

His phone vibrated. It was his fiancée calling. He
had told her he would return that night from Hyderabad.
Shanay kept staring at his fiancée's name flashing on the
phone's screen. It stopped ringing. For the first time since
they had met, he hadn't picked up Afsana's call.

BOOK THREE

VOICE NOTE 20

Afsana and Nirmaan,
Kolkata, 2003–05.

It was a hot and humid April day. The more she perspired, sitting by the rocks surrounding a big banyan tree a few metres outside her new school campus, the more she felt her wound stinging.

Afsana, like all the other freshers in Class XI, was asked to draw cat-whiskers on her face with a sketch pen and introduce herself to the seniors. The five other newcomers, in the science stream, happily obliged their seniors without missing a beat, except Afsana. She stood her ground even after being warned that she would pay dearly for it. And she did. Right after school, she was ambushed in the classroom by four seniors. But they had underestimated Afsana. She pulled out a knife from her bag, but not before one the seniors, enraged by her rebellion, stabbed her in the leg with a broken ruler. However, when Afsana brandished the knife, they reluctantly let her go.

Her sweat trickling into the gash exacerbated the pain in her injured leg.

As she sat wondering what to do next, she heard a bicycle bell. She turned her head to see Nirmaan.

'Afsana?' he said, astride his ranger bike.

'Are you in this school as well?' she exclaimed in surprise.

'I did get into a few others, but chose this one because it's the closest to my place. Saves time for my tuitions.'

'Ah, I see.'

'Waiting for someone?' he asked.

Afsana raised her injured leg with some effort to show him the reason for her sitting alone beneath the big tree.

Nirmaan immediately parked his bicycle and came over to her.

'How did this happen?'

'The ragging went out of control. Why, weren't you ragged?' she asked.

'I was. We were asked to slap ourselves twenty times saying aloud *mera baap chor hai*,' Nirmaan replied sheepishly.

'I don't like people telling me what to do.' Afsana presumed that Nirmaan must have complied with his seniors' demands.

'That's why you get hurt,' Nirmaan said wryly.

'Whatever!'

'By the way, I didn't either. They slapped me fifty times.'

'Oh!' Afsana was taken aback.

'I, too, hate being told what to do,' Nirmaan shrugged.

Afsana thought this was a different Nirmaan whom she was meeting in the new school.

'Is someone coming to take you home?' Nirmaan asked, glancing at her wound.

Afsana shook her head. 'No. I've already told my dad that I don't need his car any more.'

Nirmaan shot a what's-wrong-with-you look at her and then asked, 'Do you want me to call a rickshaw for you?'

Why is he suddenly so caring? Afsana wondered and said, 'My house is too far away for a rickshaw ride.'

'In that case . . . ' Nirmaan pondered and then looked at his bicycle. Afsana followed his gaze.

'Only if you don't mind,' he said.

She couldn't fathom why he had offered to take her home on his bicycle. Also, she couldn't understand why she had said yes. It was awkward to perch on the top bar of the bicycle without bending the knee of her injured leg.

'You're such a weakling!' she grumbled as Nirmaan panted, pedalling with the extra weight on his bicycle.

'Nothing of the sort,' Nirmaan gasped, understandably annoyed. 'It's just that I'm not used to carrying someone on my bicycle. You are the first one to sit on it.'

'Not even Rice?'

'No. She thinks I can't cycle well and that she may fall off.'

Afsana sensed he was smiling as he said this.

'Why?' she asked.

'Did you know that a long time ago, back in Guwahati, it was Raisa who taught me how to ride a bicycle for the first time?'

'It's a good thing she did, otherwise it would have been difficult for me to get home today,' Afsana said.

'Do you mean she taught me to ride so that one day I could drop you home on it?' Nirmaan asked in a thoughtful tone.

'No, I didn't mean anything like that. Moreover how would she have known that I would meet you someday when, back then, she herself was yet to meet me?'

'Hmm,' he grunted.

Afsana knew Nirmaan was a topper but, talking to him, she found him a little slow on the uptake.

'Don't you miss Raisa?' Nirmaan asked.

'Not until today. We were together most of the time during the holidays until she went off on a vacation. But today, being the first day in this stupid school, no senior would have dared to rag me if Rice had been there with me. I think I'll miss her even more in the coming days.'

'I know. I missed her too in school. I so wish our last school had plus two in it,' Nirmaan said.

'Tell me about it. By the way, why do you miss her? You guys live in the same colony, no?'

'We do, but when Raisa failed, my dad asked me to stay away from her.'

'How mean! Had he not been your father I would have punched him for this.'

'My father is like that. He only likes successful people. He believes losers should perish.'

'Rice isn't a loser.'

'I didn't mean that. Nor am I staying away from her just because Baba wants me to.'

'Still you guys don't meet often,' Afsana said.

That's true, Nirmaan thought.

After fifteen more minutes of casual chit-chat, they arrived at her house.

'Stop here,' she said.

'Is that your house?'

'Yes. I'm the daughter of a rich man. Why? Is that a crime?'

'Huh?' Nirmaan didn't get her.

'Thanks for the ride. Bye,' she said abruptly.

'Bye. Get well soon,' he responded and cycled away.

Nirmaan shared the incident with Raisa that evening when he chanced upon her during a post-dinner stroll. Raisa immediately went home and called Afsana.

'I'll kill those bitches,' she said. 'How dare they hurt you!'

'Calm down, Rice. I'm good enough for them.'

'How is your leg? Nirmaan told me about it.'

'It's better now.'

'I'm happy that at least you two are in the same school. When I saw him go to a different school today, in a different uniform, I realized just what it was to be alone.'

'I can understand. Thanks to Nirmaan though, I reached home on time today.'

'See, I always told you he's a sweetheart.'

'Hmm. You know, I deliberately made him cycle extra today,' Afsana chuckled.

'Gosh, why on earth did you do that?'

'He was huffing and puffing, doubling with me on his bicycle. I wanted to see if he would complain.'

'Poor guy!'

'He didn't complain though.'

'I think it's high time that you two become friends,' Raisa declared.

'Naw!' Afsana said. But in her mind she agreed with Raisa.

VOICE NOTE 21

The injury kept Afsana away from school for the entire week. Raisa started frequenting her place every day after school for an hour. With Rick gone for higher studies in the UK, Raisa felt comfortable there. That Friday, Raisa looked a little disturbed when she visited Afsana.

'Do students stare at you in your school and giggle?' she asked, looking at her bust in a full-length mirror in Afsana's room.

'No, I'm not a clown,' Afsana said, her entire attention focused on her butterscotch ice cream.

'Then, is something wrong with me?'

'Wrong? . . . As in?' Afsana looked at her.

'I don't know,' Raisa was confused. 'Just look at me properly and tell me,' she turned around to face Afsana.

'Nothing,' Afsana said, carefully scrutinizing Raisa from head to toe.

'Then why is it that the boys always stare at me weirdly and then snigger. That never used to happen before.'

'Boys?' Afsana said with a slight frown and then burst out laughing.

'What?' Raisa sat down beside her mirthful friend.

'Dumbo, we're growing up now.'

'That I already know even though I hate biology. But so what, Affu, if we are growing up?'

'So my dearest and cutest Rice baby, you have breasts now.'

'As if I didn't know that I had breasts. Why would any boy want to stare and giggle at them? Nirmaan never does.'

Afsana could have kissed her for her innocence. She got out of the bed, fished out a brassiere from one of the drawers in her wardrobe and threw it at Raisa.

'Try it,' Afsana said.

'Mom wears these,' Raisa said.

'Just shut up and try it.'

Raisa turned her back to Afsana, doffing her school shirt and then the white shimmy that she wore beneath.

'Nirmaan would never see you the way other boys do,' Afsana continued, gazing appreciatively at the flawless and supple skin on Raisa's back.

'How do you know all this, Affu?'

'You may have bigger breasts than me, Rice, but I'm way more mature than you.'

'Hmm, true,' Raisa agreed fidgeting to fasten the hook of the brassiere. Afsana stepped up and helped her with it.

'Thanks,' Raisa said, turning to her.

'Now wear your shirt,' Afsana recommended with a gracious smile.

When Raisa had slipped her shirt back on, Afsana steered her to the mirror. Raisa was delighted to see her breasts in considerable control.

'Wow! This is good.'

'Our cup size is different, so ask aunty to buy you some.'

Raisa hugged her tight and said, 'I miss you so much, Affu. Nobody suggested a bra to me, not even Ma. She didn't even tell me anything about sanitary pads.' After a pause she added, 'What a fool I made of myself.'

Afsana knew her voice was choked.

'It's okay, Rice. Now no one will mock you.'

'Thanks for being there for me.'

'Don't mention it because I miss you too, my sis-doll.'

'I miss you more,' Raisa broke the hug to look into Afsana's eyes. 'You don't know this, but I no longer have any friends in school. My current batch mates were once my juniors. I don't jell with them. I wear a plastered smile on my face because their jokes suck. They suck. In fact repeating this year without Nirmaan and you sucks!'

'Don't be upset, sweetheart. You have to work hard this year because I want you to be in my school next year, okay?' Afsana said, breaking the hug.

'I know I'm stupid. Nirmaan and you are the intelligent ones.'

'Says who?'

'Deuta did. When I showed him my report card he beat me with a belt. See.'

Raisa hitched up her skirt. A long reddish welt was faintly visible on her outer thigh. Afsana deduced that the mark wouldn't have been quite so faint a month ago. As she gently caressed the scar, she could tell Raisa was sobbing.

'I lied about going on a holiday last month. I was at home the whole time. I actually didn't want you to see my bruises.'

Afsana remembered now that soon after the board results were out, Raisa had told her that she would be going away to visit relatives in Guwahati.

'Why did you lie, Rice?'

'I don't know, Affu. You were so busy with the admission tests and all. I didn't want to upset you with all this, so . . . '

'Listen, Rice, if you ever lie to me again, I swear I'll never speak to you. I mean it!'

'I'm sorry, Affu.'

'You should be. You shouldn't hide anything from your soul-sister.'

'I'll never lie to you again, god promise,' Raisa's eyes moistened further as she pinched the skin on her throat as she swore. Afsana wiped the tears from Raisa's face and said, 'It's okay. And don't forget to buy some brassieres.'

Raisa smiled through her tears.

'I'll leave now. Relax, don't come downstairs, I can show myself out,' she said, picking up her bag from Afsana's study table.

Afsana walked with a slight limp to her study table. As she sat down and opened her physics textbook, Raisa barged back into the room huffing.

'What's happened now?' Afsana asked with a frown.

'You said Nirmaan doesn't ogle at my breasts because he's my best friend.'

'Yeah, so?' Afsana shrugged.

'But you aren't his best friend so has he ogled at your breasts? Be honest with me, Affu. I'll kill him if he has.'

Afsana paused to think before she replied.

'No, he hasn't,' she said and wondered why she had hesitated.

'Good for him. Okay, bye Affu,' Raisa was about to leave when Afsana stopped her.

'Rice, do you have Nirmaan's phone number?'

VOICE NOTE 22

Afsana dialled Nirmaan's landline number fifteen times that night. Each time Nirmaan picked up the receiver, she just breathed heavily into the telephone, smirking goofily.

'I know you're there. Why don't you say something? What's the point of calling if you don't want to talk?' he snapped.

Afsana herself had no idea why she was calling him. Every time she promised herself that this was the last time, the weird thrill it gave her compelled her to dial the number again. It was only when Nirmaan's father bawled down the line, threatening to file a police report about the crank calls, that Afsana decided it was indeed enough and desisted. However, sleep eluded her that night, and she tossed and turned wondering why she had been so silly in the first place. Then she thought why she had paused before responding when Raisa had asked if Nirmaan had stared at her breasts? She'd have slapped any boy who would've dared to do something like that. But Nirmaan? Would she like him to see her . . .? Afsana covered her head with her blanket. She knew she was blushing but it was so involuntary that she could do nothing about it; nor could she stop the unprecedented sensations in her body, in her heart. It wasn't as if she had met Nirmaan only recently. She had always known him as Raisa's best friend. But, during the bicycle ride, she seemed to have rediscovered Nirmaan, and her own self, in a new way. It was disturbing to her, but comforting as well. She tried to assess the feeling and all she could conclude was that it was like she had found something that she had previously lost. She hadn't actually had a feeling of loss until this moment when she felt that she had regained that something. What was that thing? She sat up on her bed and bringing the phone on to her lap, dialled Nirmaan's number yet again. After three rings, Nirmaan answered.

'Hello,' he said.

'Hello,' Afsana echoed in a deep voice.

'Who is this?'

'What is my problem?' Afsana asked.

'Your problem? What is your problem?' Nirmaan repeated.

'That's what I want to know as well. What is my problem?' Afsana maintained the pitch.

'How do I know what your problem is?'

'If not you, who else would know?'

Afsana heard Nirmaan shout, 'Nobody, Ma,' and he cut the line.

Afsana started laughing to herself.

When she got a chance the next day at school, Afsana sneaked out to the parking space. There were three ranger bikes of the same model in the lot, but it took her only a few seconds to recognize Nirmaan's. There was a Batman sticker on its mudguard and a Superman sticker on the handlebar that she had noticed on her ride back home the previous week. With a quick glance around to make sure she wasn't being watched, she dropped down on one knee and pricked the rear tyre of Nirmaan's bicycle with her compass.

The moment the final period of the day was done, she quickly positioned herself in a doorway to keep an eye on the entrance of Nirmaan's classroom. He soon emerged and she tailed him from a distance. When he disappeared into the parking area, she hung around outside. A distressed-looking Nirmaan came into view, this time wheeling his bike alongside. She called out to him.

'Nirmaan!'

He looked up and noticed her. He waved to her and then paused seeing her approach him.

'How is your leg?' he asked.

'Absolutely fine. No pain now.'

'That's good.'

Afsana eyed his bicycle.

'Hey, is that a flat?' she asked casually.

'Probably one of the seniors did this,' Nirmaan lamented.

'Honestly, this school is full of jerks. Someone injured me first and now some idiot punctured your tyre,' Afsana said.

'I don't think there's a bicycle repair shop nearby.'

'There is,' Afsana lied.

'Where?'

'It's not very close, but within walking distance.'

'All right. Could you please take me there?'

A happy Afsana took his side and as they were about to exit the school compound, she spotted someone outside the school. She instantly turned around. Nirmaan found it odd.

'What happened, who's that?'

'Do you see that boy in a white shirt and black jeans?' she asked, keeping her face averted.

'The one with the red rose in his hand?'

'Yes. He's a *chipkoo* [clingy]. He stays in my locality. I've noticed him follow me before as well.'

'If you like I can ask him to back off or even complain about it to the school authorities,' Nirmaan offered looking at the boy.

'No need. Please let's go out today through the rear entrance,' she said.

'Okay,' he agreed and wheeled his bike around.

In the twenty minutes of meandering through winding lanes in search of a non-existent bicycle-repair shop, chatting about this and that, Afsana enjoyed herself like never before. Nirmaan was becoming more and more appealing with every passing second. As he talked, she felt as if she were finally moving towards something, when so far she had just been wandering with no destination in mind. Even though she too was talking to him, in her mind, she was imagining a world where she had the power to design her life her own way, where there were no parental pressures, no societal stigmas, no rules on how to live one's life and no rituals to define relationships. Where she wouldn't have to suppress any wish, or sacrifice any desire, or adjust to any norm.

When a tired Nirmaan finally asked querulously where this elusive tyre shop was exactly, Afsana deliberately turned a corner into a lane that led towards a small tea shop and stood staring at a niche beside the stall, her mouth agape.

'What's wrong now?' Nirmaan sighed.

'I swear there was a bicycle repair shop here until last week.'

'Oh!' Nirmaan looked at the empty space with despair. 'My rotten luck,' he said.

Afsana couldn't believe just how gullible he was.

'Let's take a taxi back to your place. We can harness the cycle to the roof of the car,' she suggested.

'But your place isn't on the way,' objected Nirmaan.

Gullible is all right, but something has to be done about his stupidity. Can't he understand that I want to be with him for a bit longer? she thought.

'I have to meet Rice also,' Afsana said aloud.

'Oh! Great, let's go then.'

Between other inconsequential talks during the shared cab ride, Nirmaan told her about another chipkoo who kept calling him at night. Afsana laughed in her mind but stopped herself short as the word chipkoo hit her. She wondered what stopped her from telling Nirmaan that the chipkoo with the red rose outside their school was actually the man her parents wanted her to marry. The fantasy world that she had dreamed about a few minutes ago slipped away like sand does no matter how tight one's grasp is.

VOICE NOTE 23

For once in his life, Nirmaan couldn't register a word that his mathematics tuition teacher was saying in class. It was wholly unlike him. His distraction manifested out of nowhere when he realized that he had scribbled the letter 'A' in the top corner of his notebook and was staring at it. Then he wrote 'N' beside it before averting his eyes from it. He soon found himself staring alternately between those two letters.

'What do you think, Nirmaan?' the teacher asked.

There was no response.

'Nirmaan?' the teacher repeated.

The rest of the class gaped at him. Nirmaan looked around, abstractedly. He assumed that the teacher had reprimanded him for not paying attention.

'I'm sorry, sir.'

'What are you sorry for? I asked you what you thought the next step in this problem should be,' the teacher gestured at the blackboard. It took Nirmaan a few seconds to study the problem and figure out the next step.

'Good,' the teacher said in approval. Nirmaan relaxed but he wasn't relieved.

Rohan, the boy sitting next to him, nudged him and wiggled his eyebrows at the letter 'A' in his notebook. Nirmaan shook his head. He couldn't explain it to Rohan because he himself didn't know why he had written the first letter of Afsana's name. He had never been this silly before.

When an injured Afsana had rode home on the top bar of his bicycle a week ago, Nirmaan knew his every breath would brush her ear. It had made him uncomfortable in a curious way. He hadn't been that close to a girl before except Raisa. However, his proximity to Raisa felt platonic unlike Afsana's nearness. Why? If it wasn't relevant, he wouldn't have felt the need to analyse the feeling, therefore perhaps it was important for him to unravel this mystery.

As he had pedalled on that day with Afsana in front, he understood his emotions like a torrential river that was flowing in a particular direction but had suddenly discovered undeclared tributaries of curiosity, awakening and confusion. In fact, the emotional vortex in those tributaries made him look for Afsana in school the next day and the day after. But she was absent. It was on the third day that he asked Raisa about it.

'How is your friend's leg?'

'Can't you call her Affu?'

'I prefer to call her Afsana,' Nirmaan was wary lest Raisa became suspicious about his private emotional turbulence.

'The doctor has asked her to rest. She'll be back next week,' Raisa said.

When one impatiently wants time to fly, it teases you with the illusion that it has slowed down inexplicably. The next week, for Nirmaan, took ages in arriving. He knew that it was not every day that he would be able to give her a ride home. When they had looked for a bicycle repair shop together, he felt he had been uncharacteristically talkative. It wasn't nervousness alone that had made him so—the currents of his feelings in the tributaries also provoked him as they flowed with unmanageable brio in the presence of Afsana.

The tuition was dismissed for the evening. As Nirmaan stood up, he told Rohan he wanted to talk to him.

Rohan had been Nirmaan's friend from the previous school and was in a steady relationship with Shruti, a girl from Loreto Convent. Nirmaan thought it would be best to consult someone with experience.

'What is it?' Rohan asked.

Both of them were cycling through the quiet lanes of Salt Lake.

'How is Shruti?' Nirmaan asked. Rohan and Shruti had been together for two years now.

'She left me,' Rohan said matter-of-factly.

'What?' Nirmaan braked sharply and then, noticing Rohan moving ahead, caught up with him again.

'Why did she leave you?'

'She was two-timing.' He immediately added, 'Forget her. What did you want to talk to me about?'

'I like this girl,' Nirmaan said.

'Who?' Rohan shot a this-is-a-revelation glance at him.

'The name is not important. I like her but I don't know what to do.'

'When did you meet her?'

'Two years ago.'

'Two years? And you're telling me this now!'

'I mean I met her two years ago, but this "liking thing" happened recently and I don't even know why it happened.'

'And now that it has happened, do you like this "liking thing" towards her?'

'Yes.'

'Hmm. Does she like you?'

'I don't know. Perhaps not. She is the best friend of my best friend though.'

'Who? Raisa?' Rohan asked. Everyone in their earlier school knew Raisa was Nirmaan's closest friend.

'Yes. Any idea what I should do?'

'First, find out if she is already with someone or not because it hurts to know later,' Rohan said and added sagely, 'Love may be blind but you need to keep your eyes open otherwise a lot of shit could happen to you.'

'But how do I know if she has someone in her life or not?'

'You just said that she is Raisa's best friend. Ask her!'

VOICE NOTE 24

Nirmaan was nervous about sharing his feelings with Raisa, especially because he had himself asked Raisa once to sever her friendship with Afsana. It was ironical. A couple of years ago, if somebody had told him that he would have sleepless nights because he had certain out-of-the-ordinary feelings for Afsana, he would have slapped that person. It was ludicrously improbable. But that was what life was all about: to encounter something highly unlikely—and then manipulate the journey to harness that incongruity.

In that single moment, when he saw Afsana sitting beneath the banyan tree by his new school and chose to approach her, everything changed. What if that moment hadn't happened? What if Afsana hadn't injured her leg? What if Afsana hadn't applied for admission to the same school as him? What if she hadn't fled her home and later studied hard to secure a seat in the science class? What if she had never been Raisa's friend? What if Raisa had never taught him to ride a bicycle? What if Raisa had never given him that mango? When Nirmaan sat staring stupefied at his dinner plate that night, tracing back his life with a series of questions from the moment when he'd had no other option but to approach a distressed-looking Afsana a few days ago, it all seemed totally inevitable. The ways by which he arrived at that point could have happened in multiple ways but the root event—his first meeting with Raisa in Guwahati—and the result—approaching Afsana by the banyan tree—would always remain the same.

After dinner, he told his parents that he was going out to get some fresh air. He went to talk to Raisa.

'I have an important thing to ask you,' he said the moment Raisa opened the door.

'It's good that you came. I too have something to ask you. Let's go downstairs,' she replied.

They made their way to their usual spot where they often sat post-dinner, a bench in a secluded corner of the housing colony. In the fading light, they were barely visible.

'Somebody proposed to me yesterday and I'm confused,' Raisa said as soon as they sat down after blowing the dust off the bench.

'Who?' Nirmaan held himself in check with immense will power although he was itching to tell her his story.

'Kapil Juneja. He's obviously a junior, but now I'm in his class. He says he has loved me from the day he first saw me in the class.'

'Oh! And what about you? Do you like him too?'

'I don't know.'

'Then how do you want me to help you if you don't know whether you like him or not.'

'How do I know if I like him if I know nothing about him? The "first-sight thing" doesn't always work, does it?' Raisa said.

'Hmm,' Nirmaan was confused. He too hadn't fallen for Afsana at the first sight and he didn't know her well either. So what was it that he was going through? Infatuation? Was it hormonal changes or something that happened to almost everyone his age? Temporary? He didn't want whatever he was feeling for Afsana to be something temporary. And if it really was about hormonal changes, then why Afsana specifically? Why not anyone else? Why not Raisa considering she was his closest female acquaintance?

Nirmaan's thoughtful trance was broken by the sound of the snapping of fingers.

'Hello! You should be the one talking and I should be the one listening here,' Raisa said.

'I think you should give it some time,' Nirmaan said answering his own inner quandary.

'But I like the way Kapil looks at me. What if he stops looking at me after I say "no"?'

'How does he look at you?'

'Umm . . . as if I'm not really a being for him but an idea. His most amazing idea perhaps.' Raisa was carefully choosing her words, 'A kind of startling idea that takes one by surprise when it strikes.'

This is by far the most matured avatar of Raisa ever, Nirmaan thought wonderingly.

'A notion,' Raisa continued, 'that he isn't quite sure why it struck him, but he is happy that it did. One never knows how, where and why one could have an epiphany, can one?'

Silence.

'Okay, I don't know what I just said,' Raisa confessed.

Nirmaan swallowed a lump. He understood Raisa's meaning perfectly because that was exactly how he looked at Afsana as he bore her home on his bicycle the other day. It was all too unreal. The only difference in his case was that he hadn't yet declared himself to her because he wasn't as sure of himself as Kapil. If he had really seen Afsana as an idea then that idea had blossomed into a concept within a week. As he sat listening to Raisa that concept had already turned into a story. And when a person becomes someone's story, it's difficult to sever oneself from it.

'Do you know what, Nirmaan, there's someone inside me who wants to give Kapil a chance, see what it's all about; I'll probably discover that he is interested in me because I'm actually interesting or that he is simply curious because he merely fancies my outer appearance. His proposal affected me, otherwise I wouldn't have discussed it with you. Like whatever you wanted to tell me tonight, I'm sure, has affected you as well,' Raisa concluded. She looked at Nirmaan expectantly. It was his chance to talk.

Nothing happened for some time. Nirmaan sat still, seemingly lost. Raisa shook his arm, 'Oi! What's up?' she asked.

'Nothing,' Nirmaan's throat was dry. 'Nothing,' he repeated, more confident this time.

'What "nothing"? You said you wanted to tell me something, didn't you?'

'Yes. But it's . . . it's nothing.'

Raisa could read an abrupt reticence in his hesitation. She didn't pester him.

As soon as Nirmaan was back in his room, he sat by his study table listlessly. Although there wasn't any test the next day, he needed to revise his physics tuition notes. The pressure of remaining ahead of his class made him sigh. He drew out his physics textbook only to find a scrap of paper staring at him. It read:

You are the cutest thing I've ever seen.

– The girl who punctured your bicycle.

VOICE NOTE 25

It was the first time Afsana was meeting Tarun Somani, the man recommended by her parents, in a restaurant. They were to get married as soon as she graduated. She was pissed off and seethed within; however he seemed gung-ho about making a good impression on her.

When the waiter placed the menu on the table, Tarun slid it across to Afsana. Following several abortive efforts to meet her after school, Tarun had telephoned her father and asked his permission to take his daughter out on a date. Afsana's father had readily agreed, but Afsana had dug her heels in. This date with Tarun was the result of the verbal duel that had ensued, and here she was, perusing the menu.

'What will you have?' Tarun asked. In his mind he had already decided to have a Mysore masala dosa and was anxiously waiting to see if she desired the same.

'Maybe . . . umm . . .' Afsana took her time making up her mind. 'Okay, I'll take a Mysore masala dosa.'

The similarity in their choice made Tarun beam.

'Great!' He quickly gave the order to the waiter before returning his gaze to Afsana.

'I love south Indian food,' Tarun declared in an attempt to break the ice.

'I love non-veg,' she replied.

'Non-veg?' he sounded appalled.

'Butter chicken is my favourite.'

'Oh! I didn't know your family was okay with non-veg. We abstain from non-vegetarian food.'

'My family doesn't know. But do you know that I'm a minor?' Afsana asked, looking arrow-straight at him.

'That's why we're not yet married,' he nodded.

'Don't you think people need to get to know each other before they get married?'

'There's a lot of time left before we get married. We can get better acquainted by then.'

'And what if we fail to bond during this interim period? What then? Are you going to call off the wedding? Will our parents allow us to call it off?'

Afsana's maturity made Tarun swallow a sudden lump in his throat.

'This marriage won't be called off,' he said. 'We either like each other or we don't.'

'I know that!'

'You have to understand, Afsana, we'll eventually have to get married because our parents have to merge their businesses. If we somehow adjust and learn to accept each other we can live happily irrespective of this business thing.'

This was the moment, Afsana felt, when she had to reveal the secret in her heart or he would never understand what she was hinting at. She braced herself.

'I love someone else,' she said baldly.

Tarun gaped at her for an instant before laughing out loud derogatorily.

'I didn't crack a joke.'

'Sorry. You reminded me of something.'

'What?'

The waiter arrived with their order. Tarun quickly ripped off a piece of his dosa, dipped it in the hot sambar and ate it.

'I too loved someone when I was your age.'

Afsana resented his condescending tone.

'And I too thought I would marry her,' he said, 'But I couldn't because she loved someone else. I was hurt, I cried, but now when I think about it, I can't help but laugh. Perhaps it's because I cried then that I'm able to laugh about it now. It was only a phase, but at that age it seemed too real, too genuine and too forever to let go. But . . . ' he scooped out a spoonful of the coconut chutney.

Afsana waited for him to continue as she gobbled a large portion of the dosa herself.

' . . . now I know it was only an infatuation. So, I can totally understand when you say you're in love. Don't worry, it'll pass.'

Afsana didn't appreciate any of Tarun's monologue. Even if it were an infatuation, who the hell was he to tell her that?

'What if you did marry the girl you thought you loved? Would you still say it was an infatuation?' she asked.

Tarun was struck speechless for a moment. He stuffed more dosa into his mouth, giving himself time to think for an apt reply.

'No, but—'

'So anything that blossoms into marriage is love and that which doesn't is infatuation. Only adults can allow themselves such privileges.'

'Only kids allow themselves such ignorance,' Tarun chuckled.

The sneering chuckle as well as the 'kid' label infuriated Afsana. *You don't call a seventeen-year-old a kid*, she thought, and gobbled up her dosa faster than she normally would have done.

'I'm getting late. I have tuition,' she replied curtly.

'I'll drop you off.'

'Thanks, but no thanks.'

Tarun understood that the next time he would have to work twice as hard to win her.

Afsana took a shared auto-rickshaw to the Ultadanga footbridge where she was due to meet Raisa in another half an hour. While she waited for her soul-sister, Afsana thought about Tarun's words. *What if her feelings for Nirmaan were only infatuation?* Her heart felt heavy even considering this possibility. What was a painful thought now, could it feel like a joke, say, ten years later? She prayed not. She took out a one-rupee coin from her pocket. Kissing it on one side she told herself: heads, it's love; tails, it's infatuation. She tossed the coin in the air and the moment it landed on her palm, she closed her fingers over it. *Heads or tails?* Her heart was beating fast. She put her fist into her pocket. It had to be heads. When one was sure, there was no reason to believe in something as nonsensical as a toss of a coin, she told herself. The next minute, she saw Raisa hurrying up the steps of the bridge. She waved to her. Raisa waved back and within seconds was by her side.

'Look what I got today, Affu?' Raisa said, gasping for air, and extended a red rose to Afsana.

Afsana sniffed it appreciatively.

'I can't explain how amazing it feels when someone gives you a red rose with that certain look on his face,' Raisa said.

'What look?' Afsana returned the rose.

'Like I'm the world to him.'

'To whom?'

'Kapil. The boy who proposed to me recently. He loves me.'

Afsana noticed that her soul-sister looked rather flustered.

'Are you sure he loves you or is he only infatuated with you?'

Raisa looked as if Afsana had slammed the emergency brakes on her excitement train.

'What do you mean?'

The two girls walked down the length of the bridge, bought jhaal moori from a roadside hawker near the HUDCO housing society and strolled towards the Kakurgachi crossing on the footpath. Afsana told her about her date with Tarun.

'How does it matter what it is?' Raisa said.

'It does, Rice. Infatuation is like when you take an airplane; it takes you high all right but it brings you down in a jiffy as well and then there's nothing. Love is a long train journey in which you spend hours going through all your basic activities; it's almost a home on the move and, most importantly, the journey stays with you.'

Raisa gave her an exasperated look and exclaimed, 'Oh my god! You too are in love!'

'Like hell I am!' Afsana crushed the paper cone that had contained the jhaal moori. At that point, she suddenly felt that her life was all messed up.

Silence reigned as they ambled on aimlessly.

'Are all three of us screwed the same way, by any chance?'

'Three?'

'See, Kapil loves me, but I'm not sure if I should accept him even though he isn't a bad guy. Nirmaan loves someone, but there's something troubling him and now you're saying you too are in love . . . '

'Wait a minute. Nirmaan is in love? Did he tell you that?'

'He didn't exactly tell me about it but I could guess that he too loves someone. When we were talking a few nights ago he abruptly went quiet as if he knew what he wanted to say but couldn't phrase it properly and feared I would misinterpret it. I didn't nudge him about it because I thought it's always good if these things come out naturally . . . Affu?'

Raisa realized she was walking alone. She paused and looked around to see her soul-sister seated on the kerb, crying.

Raisa, who couldn't conjure up a proper reaction to Afsana's sudden gut-wrenching grief, ended up weeping as well. Raisa had seen Afsana cry only once before. It was when Afsana had told Raisa about her parents' indifference towards her. But these weren't tears of condemnation, this was an open floodgate of devastation.

It was not for want of trying that Raisa failed to inveigle a name out of Afsana. What was the point of furnishing Raisa with a name if Nirmaan really loved someone else? What could Raisa have possibly done, except perhaps sympathize with her? Now she would have to follow Tarun's tack and years later, tell herself and other love-struck teenagers that her feelings for Nirmaan were merely a passing adolescent crush. However, in her heart, she would always know the truth about the strength of her love.

With a mighty effort of will power, Afsana clamped down on the urge to abuse Nirmaan over the telephone for not falling in love with her. She wanted to castigate him for not giving her enough time to express her feelings to him and for selfishly making her fall in love with him when he wasn't really into her. When the tears eventually abated, she realized all of this was just too childish. She tried to sleep out all the quandaries within her heart, but couldn't. After indulging in another pointless exercise of blaming her destiny and life, she wondered who the girl was, anyway, whom Nirmaan loved. Raisa was not sure who she was. She did ask Raisa about the piece of paper she had secreted into Nirmaan's physics textbook.

'What piece of paper?' Raisa had asked.

It was proof enough that Nirmaan hadn't told her anything about it. And it only meant he wasn't even curious about the matter.

The next day, she stalked Nirmaan during school hours. First, it was during the morning assembly. In all, he talked with three girls: a little more with the third girl than the first two. They shared a laugh about something as well. Afsana didn't know any of them because they were in other sections but she made a mental note of them. Especially the third one. During one of the classes, she casually walked past his classroom to see if he was sitting with any of the three. He wasn't. During recess, she was fairly certain that she would see him with one of them, but she didn't. Contrary to her expectations, Nirmaan walked out of the school alone. It only made the itch of curiosity in Afsana even stronger. She followed Nirmaan to his home but stayed outside the RBI quarters, because she didn't want Raisa to catch her hanging around there. It was possible that the mystery girl was either absent from school that day or wasn't from their school at all. She waited outside by the auto-rickshaw stand. In twenty minutes, he emerged again, changed into his civvies and cycled away quickly to his tuitions. She followed in an auto-rickshaw. Fifteen minutes later, Afsana watched him enter his tuition class in Salt Lake. She waited outside. It was after an hour that Nirmaan came out along with the other students, all boys. A normal girl in love should have been happy seeing no girl by his side, but Afsana was no longer normal.

Where is this girlfriend of his? Afsana punched her palm. As Nirmaan disappeared from her sight, she decided to return home. As she turned to leave, she had her heart in her mouth.

Raisa was standing behind her. Caught red-handed, Afsana ran up to her and hugged her soul-sister tight.

'Promise me you won't tell him,' she whispered.

'First pay my auto-wallah. I don't have money,' Raisa said.

VOICE NOTE 26

For the umpteenth time, Afsana reached for the small clock on her study table. It was only an hour before the alarm would go off and she would have to get ready for school. She kept the clock back on the table and flipped over to the other side of the bed. She repeated this exercise after a few minutes. She had been waiting for Raisa's call, as per their deal, but no call had come.

When Raisa discovered that it was Nirmaan for whom Afsana's heart both blossomed and bled, she felt profoundly sorry for her soul-sister. *Profuse bleeding of any blossom had to signify love*, Raisa decided.

'Leave it to me,' Raisa told her when the two shared an auto-rickshaw home.

'You don't have to do anything, Rice, please. Promise me you won't sympathize with me for this,' Afsana said impatiently, wiping the tears from her face.

'Why would I sympathize?'

'Because Nirmaan loves someone else and I love him and we can't be together. That's why. And don't even tell me what people normally say, "forget him, move on" or any such nonsense. I'll be all right on my own in a while.'

As she dropped off Afsana, Raisa promised to talk to Nirmaan. She also promised not to mention Afsana's name unless absolutely necessary and would call her if her name came up. Afsana was waiting for this call. It was much later that morning when Raisa called to say that Nirmaan was down with flu, so she hadn't been able to talk to him the previous evening.

'He is skipping school today and so am I. I'll call you in the evening and let you know if there are any developments.'

'No. Call me the moment you have a talk with him. I'm skipping school too. And waiting,' said Afsana and hung up.

It was after breakfast that Raisa visited Nirmaan. The maid answered the door. She went to Nirmaan's room to see his mother sitting beside him looking intently at the clock as Nirmaan held a thermometer in his mouth. He tried smiling at Raisa. She raised a finger to her lips to shush him. Nirmaan stopped smiling. His mother gestured Raisa to sit down beside her without averting her eyes from the clock. However, Raisa remained standing in the doorway. Nirmaan's mother removed the thermometer and murmured, 'One hundred and two.' She shook the thermometer to restore its mercury level and looked at Raisa, 'No school today, dear?'

'No, Aunty. I had stomach cramps this morning.'

'Sit beside Nirmaan. Let me see what the maid is up to.' Nirmaan's mother left the room. Raisa got into the bed and made herself comfortable.

'It's good that you came,' whispered Nirmaan in a feeble voice.

'Why? Were you waiting for me?'

'Not waiting because I knew you had school. But happy you didn't go. Did you say yes to the boy who proposed you?'

'Forget it. I have something more important to talk to you about.'

'What?'

'Afsana loves someone,' Raisa said watching with interest as facial muscles twitched on Nirmaan's face.

'Don't you have anything to say?' she snapped, irked by his silence.

'That's . . . ' Nirmaan tried to find the right words, 'great!' He just wanted to be left alone after hearing this bombshell, but couldn't say so. He closed his eyes, hoping she would take a hint.

'Not really,' she continued. Nirmaan opened his eyes and frowned.

'The one she loves supposedly loves someone else.'

'She too?'

'What?'

'Nothing.'

'What did you mean, Nirmaan?'

Looking at Raisa he knew the meaning of those narrowed eyes. She would keep at it like a dog with a bone until he clarified his cryptic statement.

'It's nothing, really,' Nirmaan protested in vain, making a last ditch effort to sidestep the topic. In his heart, however, he was already wondering at the irony of the situation: he had feelings for Afsana but wanted to be sure of them before telling her and now he knew that she was suffering the pangs of unrequited love with some undeserving fool who didn't reciprocate her feelings. There wasn't any point in approaching her now, he concluded, even if what he felt for her was genuine.

'Who is the girl you love, Nirmaan?'

Nirmaan shot an incredulous look at Raisa. *How on earth did she know this?*

'What?' He feigned innocence, but failed miserably.

'I know it. You have someone. Now tell me, who is it?'

'Nobody.'

'Nirmaan, I'll tell Aunty about it if you don't tell me.'

'Okay!' Nirmaan tried to sit up and Raisa helped him. 'There isn't anybody. I mean, I don't have a girlfriend per se. I only . . . ' he paused, 'like someone.'

'Name, Nirmaan, name!' Raisa was glaring at him.

'You won't laugh or beat me, promise?'

'Name!'

Nirmaan took a deep breath, closed his eyes and said aloud, 'Okay, it's Afsana.'

For few seconds, nothing happened. Then Nirmaan opened his eyes slowly. He saw Raisa had covered her face with her palms. She didn't know whether to laugh, cry, faint or die. These two silly people in her life, who liked each other, were in troughs of deep depression and making her miserable in the bargain, because both thought the other loved someone else. It was time for her to have some fun now.

'I didn't expect this from you, Nirmaan. She is my soul-sister, how could you—'

'Yeah, but she is not my sister. And I just like her . . . '

'A few years ago you told me to stay away from her and now you are saying you like her? All right, tell me this, do you like her or love her?'

'I don't know. All I know is that she has been on my mind all the time for the last few weeks. That's love, isn't it?'

'Hmm. How do I know? I'm yet to know that myself, but do you even know how she is going to react to this?'

'Oh no. She doesn't need to know. Please, Raisa, I shared this with you hoping you'll keep mum about it. Let it be our secret.'

'I'm sorry, Nirmaan. I'll have to tell her about this. And that too, right away,' Raisa got out of the bed and sauntered to the phone in the corner of the room.

'Raisa, wait!' he was on the verge of getting out of bed himself when Raisa called out to his mother.

'Aunty, Nirmaan is getting out of the bed.'

'Stay in the bed, son. Take rest,' his mother commanded from the kitchen.

Raisa dialled Afsana's number, avoiding Nirmaan's helpless pleas.

Within the next hour, Afsana rang the doorbell of Nirmaan's flat. His mother answered the door. As she inquired about Raisa, the latter came out of Nirmaan's room to receive her.

'Aunty, this is Affu.'

'Affu?' Nirmaan's mother repeated with a frown.

'I'm Afsana Agarwal.'

'She is like my sister and is in the same school as Nirmaan.'

'That's nice,' his mother replied. 'Take her inside.' She shut the door and disappeared into the kitchen as the girls marched into Nirmaan's room.

As they entered, Nirmaan who was waiting with bated breath for Afsana's arrival, shut his eyes and feigned weakness and sleep.

'Get up, Mister Oscar-winner for best actor,' Raisa nudged him hard. Nirmaan opened his eyes and smiled goofily.

'Look who is here,' Raisa said and made herself comfortable again in his bed.

'Come on!' she gestured to Afsana to hop into the bed. Nirmaan made some space for her.

'What's going on?' Afsana asked. After being urgently summoned to Nirmaan's place, she was nervous, anxious, happy, bemused and scared.

The moment Afsana settled in the bed, Raisa stood up with a mysterious smile that confounded both Nirmaan and Afsana.

'Lend me your ears,' Raisa made a bow.

'Why are you being so dramatic?' Afsana asked, her patience running low.

'As you know, Affu, my best buddy likes someone.'

'She knows?' Nirmaan was startled.

'Sshh!' Raisa said, 'Be quiet. This is my show.' Turning to Afsana, she continued, 'Nirmaan likes someone. It's true. He actually doesn't know if it's only liking or love.

He's stupid anyway.' She turned to Nirmaan, 'As you now know, Affu loves someone as well.'

Afsana hung her head in deep embarrassment.

'The girl that Nirmaan "likes" and the boy that Affu "loves" are both present in this room,' so saying, Raisa burst out laughing, clutching her tummy.

'What's that supposed to mean?' Afsana elbowed her while Nirmaan said plaintively, 'Stop kidding about my emotions.'

'You two idiots! Affu, Nirmaan likes you,' she told Afsana and to Nirmaan she said, 'Affu loves you, duffer!'

Both looked at each other as the room filled with Raisa's loud laughter.

'You two are such jokers!' she said. Between bouts of mirth, she relayed to both the comedy-of-errors that had wreaked such havoc in their young lives. Listening to Raisa, the two felt all the more awkward. Eventually, Nirmaan managed to smile sheepishly at Afsana, every hair on his body rising, while Afsana, with goosebumps all over her arms, stole furtive glances at him.

Raisa took their hands and clasped them together.

'I really like you, Afsana,' Nirmaan blurted out clumsily.

Raisa thwacked his head, 'You love her!'

'Sorry, I love you,' he corrected himself.

Afsana could have laughed out loud herself, but controlled herself and said, 'Same here.'

'Now hug her, dumbo, and kiss her,' Raisa commanded.

'What?' Nirmaan looked appalled. Afsana was also taken aback.

'Shut up, Rice!' she said.

'That's what they do in English movies,' Raisa argued.

'But we're Indians,' Nirmaan countered.

'So is this when the couple time-travel to Switzerland and sing a song? Are you two going to do that, seriously?' Raisa scoffed.

There was a short silence before the three of them collapsed in a heap on the bed, roaring with laughter.

VOICE NOTE 27

In the days that followed, Afsana as well as Nirmaan understood what it meant to have someone else as the centre of their universe.

One day after school, she gave him a piece of paper.

'This is for you,' she said. Nirmaan started reading.

Socho ke tum aur main,
Ek kitaab mein qaid,
Do kirdaar hote.

Chand panne humari duniya hoti.
Panno ke mudhne se dikhne wale daag, humare gile-shikve.
Unn panno ke number, humare rishtey ki umra.
Dus pe milte,
Tees mein bichadhte,
Sau mein fir milte.

Chote, bade, mushkil, aasan tarah ke shabd,
Humari zindagi ke unginat armaan.

Shabdon ke beech ka khalipan,
Ek dusre se kaha gaya jhooth.
Shabdon se boone panktiyon ke beech ka sunapan,
Bina bataye samjhne wali sachai.

Jahan alpviram,
Humare nadaani bhari man-mutao ke din.
Jahan ardhviram,
Humari shaq se panpe galatfehmi ki shaam.
Jahan purnviram,
Humare befuzool ke jhagdon ki raat.
Jahan prashnachin,
Humara ek dusre se lambe dino tak roothna.
Jahan ek naya adhyay,
Humari nayi shuruaat.

Agar koi kitaab khula chodhta,
Hum milne ke liye tadapte.
Agar firse padhne lagta,
Hum roke der tak gale milte.
Agar kabhi koi shuru se padhta,
Hum bhi shuruaat se apne anth ko jee lete.
Agar koi adhe mein kahaani chodh deta,
Hum usse apna kismet samjhke, apne mein simat jaate.
Agar koi kitaab ko barson tak na chchuta,
Hum saath budhe hote,
Aagr koi kabhi kabhi kitaab kholta,
Hum jawaani ki aag mein bhasm ho aate.

Socho ki tum aur main,
Ek kitaab mein qaid,
Do kirdaar hote.

सोचो कि तुम और मैं,
एक किताब में कैद,
दो किरदार होते।

चंद पन्ने हमारी दुनिया होती।
पन्नों के मुड़ने से दिखने वाले दाग़, हमारे गिले-शिकवे।
उन पन्नों के नंबर, हमारे रिश्ते की उम्र।
दस में मिलते,
तीस में बिछड़ते,
सौ में फिर मिलते।

छोटे, बड़े, मुश्किल, आसान तरह-तरह के शब्द,
हमारी ज़िन्दगी के अनगिनत अरमान।
शब्दों के बीच का ख़ालीपन,
एक-दूसरे से कहा गया झूठ।
शब्दों से बुनी पंक्तियों के बीच का सूनापन,
बिना बताये समझने वाली सच्चाई।

जहाँ-जहाँ अल्पविराम,
हमारे नादानी भरे मन-मुटाव के दिन।
जहाँ-जहाँ अर्धविराम,
हमारे शक से पनपे ग़लतफहमी की शाम।
जहाँ-जहाँ पूर्णविराम,
हमारे बेफ़िज़ूल झगड़ों की रात।
जहाँ-जहाँ प्रश्नचिह्न,
हमारा एक-दूसरे के साथ लम्बे दिनों तक रूठना।
जहाँ-जहाँ एक नया अध्याय,
हमारी नई शुरुआत।

अगर कोई किताब खुली छोड़ता,
हम मिलने के लिए तड़पते।
अगर फिर से पढ़ने लगता,
हम रो के देर तक गले मिलते।
अगर कभी कोई शुरू से पढ़ता,
हम भी शुरुआत से अपने अंत को जी लेते।

अगर कोई आधे में कहानी छोड़ देता,
हम उसे अपनी किस्मत समझ के, अपने में सिमट जाते।
अगर कोई किताब को बरसों तक न छूता,
हम साथ बूढ़े होते।
अगर कोई कभी-कभी किताब खोलता,
हम जवानी की आग में भस्म हो जाते।

सोचो कि तुम और मैं,
एक किताब में कैद,
दो किरदार होते।

'Do you write poems?' he asked, genuinely surprised.

'Why? Can't brats write poems?'

'This is really good, Affu.'

'Thanks. And I don't write poems. I just scribble down my thoughts, that's all.'

His eyes went to the signatory, Tushara.

'Who's Tushara?' he asked.

'Tushara is my pen name. It means ice. Something that is all solid but, at times, it melts.'

'Has this Tushara melted for anyone yet?' he asked, without taking his eyes off her.

'Only for one, yeah,' she blushed a bit and hugged him.

It wasn't just mushy romance that lit up their lives. Nirmaan loved how she calmed him down whenever his father's views about his future frustrated him. He didn't want to pursue engineering. He wanted to start his own business. He wanted to create something out of nothing. Samuel Walton was his role model. He wanted to be an entrepreneur but couldn't tell his father about his ambitions and aspirations.

'Okay, I did tell Baba once that I wanted to start a business. Make something of my own,' Nirmaan said.

'What did he say?' Afsana asked, curious.

'He said that there's no respect for people in business, only money. For him respect is everything. He told me he didn't want me to even think about it again and to focus on getting into IIT.'

Afsana took her time before replying, 'Why don't you do your engineering, then do an MBA and then start whatever you want to? That way your father will also be pacified and you don't have to compromise on your dreams.'

Nirmaan nodded and said, 'That's exactly what I have planned to do.'

'I'm anyway sticking with you whether you're an engineer, an MBA or an entrepreneur.' He took her hand and kissed it. Nirmaan was pleasantly surprised at how soon she'd become the point where he felt emotionally rejuvenated. Both were slowly becoming each other's spiritual highway where they could drive ahead of their fears and rise beyond where they already were.

Afsana joined Nirmaan's tuition. With every passing day, they could sense a process shaping up within them. It was both exhilarating and scary; exhilarating because it made them long for the other in unexpected and unprecedented ways; scary because in an attempt to live the togetherness to its hilt, they knew they were gradually growing vulnerable to life's sadism. Especially Afsana. She was yet to tell Nirmaan about Tarun. The man to whom her parents were hell-bent on getting her married. She had discussed it with Raisa once, but she had asked her to not tell Nirmaan about it.

'Do you remember your plan, Affu? The one you told me last year, where you would graduate from a college outside Kolkata and not return? Now just add Nirmaan to that plan. Both of you can study elsewhere and get married when y'all get a job. You don't have to return to your parents if they can't accept their daughter's choice,' Raisa said.

Afsana, in agreement with Raisa, chose to keep mum.

During the Durga Puja festival that year, Raisa took it upon herself to give Afsana a makeover. She had picked up all the Bengali nitty-gritty from Nirmaan's mother and helped Afsana wear the traditional red-bordered saree, draped in the archaic Bengali style, with a big red bindi. Although the white and red bangles were essentially the mark of a married Bengali woman, Raisa borrowed them from Mrs Bose and bulldozed Afsana into slipping them on. In the end, Raisa transformed a Marwari girl into a Bengali lady. The inherent sweetness in Afsana's face was subtly highlighted with the transformation. They hopped into her car after Raisa called Nirmaan from Afsana's place and asked him to be ready for a surprise.

It was Maha Ashtami. As Afsana's car entered the RBI quarters, they noticed Nirmaan in a white kurta-pyjama, talking to some other boys. He eyed the car that drew up in front of the yard. Raisa disembarked first before helping Afsana step out of the car. Nirmaan was stunned and then went numb. Afsana in the red-bordered saree, with the red bindi and bangles was the most vibrant image of a woman he had ever seen. She had the aura of a deity. As Afsana stood a few metres away from him, blushing

somewhat, he fell in love with her all over again. Before
he could approach her, Nirmaan's mother came up from
behind him, recognizing Afsana. She held Afsana's chin
and exclaimed in surprise at the transformation.

'*O ma, ki mishti lagche!* [so sweet she's looking!]' she
exclaimed.

'I dressed her up, Aunty,' Raisa chipped in, beaming.

As Nirmaan joined them, his mother turned to him
and said, 'Remember, Nirmaan, I need a daughter-in-law
this pretty.'

Raisa started giggling and Afsana had to elbow her
hard. Nirmaan stood by, both shy and awkward. Together
they made their way to the huge Durga idol that was
inside a large colourful pandal in the centre of the playing
ground, surrounded by the tall apartment buildings.
Nirmaan introduced Afsana to his father for the first time.
She touched his feet reverently. He blessed her and was
surprised when he heard her surname.

'You look like a Bangali *meye*!' he remarked.

The next moment the pushpanjali was announced by
the purohit. The people in the pandal gathered in front of
the Durga idol. Nirmaan, Afsana and Raisa stood together
in the first row. As the purohit proffered a large tray laden
with flowers and leaves and petals, everyone scooped up
as much as they could. Nirmaan took a handful and gave
some to Afsana and Raisa. They clasped the flora in their
joined palms, as a mark of obeisance to the goddess.

'I've never done this before,' Afsana whispered to Nirmaan.

'It will become a habit now,' he said. She grinned,
getting his drift.

As the purohit started chanting a mantra over the amplifier, the group chanted along except Nirmaan, who was intoning his own personal prayer in his heart, eyeing Afsana from the corner of his eyes.

VOICE NOTE 28

Although Nirmaan had been to the Calcutta Book Fair that year with his parents, he made sure he visited it again on a Saturday with Afsana.

The famous Maidan where the Calcutta Book Fair was held, was teeming with local people as well as foreign tourists. Raisa met her friends by the ticket counter. Nirmaan bought three tickets while Afsana bought three vanilla cones from the ice-cream hawker at the entrance. They entered the fair together. Afsana soon noticed that Raisa seemed rather preoccupied.

'What's up with you?' Afsana asked.

'He slashed his wrists for me,' Raisa replied.

'Who?'

'Mihir.'

'Who's Mihir? You never told me about him, Rice? What happened to Kapil by the way?' Afsana turned to face Raisa, holding her by the shoulders.

'Kapil and I were never in a relationship. He liked me but I didn't. Now he is history. But when would I tell you about Mihir? Do you guys even have time for me these days?

You two are a couple and I'm the *kebab mein haddi*!' Jerking out of Afsana's grasp, Raisa walked on ahead in a dudgeon.

Afsana and Nirmaan exchanged guilty glances and caught up with her.

'Hey, are you angry with your soul-sister?' Afsana made a puppy face. Raisa couldn't help but hug her.

'And your best friend,' Nirmaan tried the puppy face as well and failed miserably. Raisa broke her hug and pinched him hard. Nirmaan shrieked.

'I'm not angry with you guys,' Raisa threw over her shoulder as she stepped into one of the bookstalls.

'Then what's the matter?' Afsana and Nirmaan followed her in.

'Mihir is the older brother of one of my classmates. He saw me at her birthday party and has been pursuing me ever since. Yesterday he proposed to me after school and threatened to kill himself if I didn't accept his proposal. Today his sister told me he's in hospital after slashing his wrists.'

Afsana frowned. Raisa seemed engrossed in browsing through some books on a shelf but Afsana knew for certain that she wasn't interested in any of them. She grabbed her arm and said, 'Come with me.' She dragged Raisa out of the stall, commanding Nirmaan, who would have followed them, to stay where he was, so that the girls could share some private sister-time.

They went behind one of the book stalls and sat down on the grassy lawn beside a group of college students who were making the most of the informal atmosphere of the fair, singing songs as one of them strummed a guitar.

'Now tell me, do you like Mihir?' Afsana came straight to the point.

'I don't know,' Raisa said, looking away.

'Rice, even when Kapil expressed his interest in you, you weren't sure whether you liked him or not. And now it's the same. Is there someone else on your mind because of which you aren't giving anyone else a chance?'

Raisa made eye contact with Afsana for an instant, and then looked away to stare into the crowd with a faraway look. Raisa was afraid that Afsana would read the truth in her eyes.

'I think I like him,' she said hesitantly.

'Then what's the problem? Say yes and see how it goes.'

'I'm scared. What if it doesn't work out? What if he misunderstands me or . . . beats me? What if he rapes—'

Afsana grasped her hand and pressed it.

'Not every man is like your father, Rice,' Afsana said.

'I know but—'

'At some point you'll have to just trust life. Look at me. Do you imagine that the fact that I haven't told Nirmaan yet about Tarun doesn't bother me? But I trust life. I'm sure that things will fall into place because my intentions are pure. So, say yes to Mihir if you like him because we can only hope, Rice, and although we imagine that we are, we can't really be in control of our destiny. Some decisions are already made; we only think we made it all happen ourselves.'

Nirmaan approached them.

'Are you guys done with your sister-talk? I can't stand around in the stall alone like a fool.'

Afsana and Raisa stood up.

'Yes,' Raisa told Nirmaan and turning to Afsana, she repeated, 'Yes.'

Afsana acknowledged it with a faint smile and a pat on her back. Minutes later, Afsana and Nirmaan stood at a distance looking on indulgently as Raisa fooled around with a person dressed as a clown.

'There is something Rice is hiding from me,' Afsana told Nirmaan in an undertone.

'I don't get you.'

Afsana sighed and said, 'Nothing.'

'What did she say about Mihir? Is he a good boy?' Nirmaan asked.

Afsana gave him a speaking glance.

'Don't misunderstand me, but I don't think she can judge boys properly.'

'She'll say yes to Mihir.'

'That's nice. I hope it all goes well for her sake.'

Raisa joined them. The loudspeakers in the fairground buzzed with an announcement asking people to disperse and make their way to the gates as it was time to close for the day. As the three strolled towards the exit with paper-packets of jhaal moori in their hands, Raisa grabbed Afsana's arm and pointed at something behind a large tree. Afsana followed her finger and noticed a couple kissing passionately.

'*Eto chumu khaash na*! [Don't kiss so much],' Raisa suddenly screamed at the couple and darted out through the gates. Afsana followed her out, giggling away. Nirmaan couldn't understand what was going on. He saw a red-faced man emerge from behind a tree with a menacing look, searching for someone or something in the crowd. Sensing that neither Raisa nor Afsana was anywhere in sight, Nirmaan turned his back to the man and exited the fairground.

Outside, he found the girls in splits.

'What's with all this silly childish behaviour?' Nirmaan growled.

The girls laughed harder.

'Oh God, you should've seen their faces!' Raisa's stomach hurt with her mirth.

'Come on, it was terribly rude of you. What if it were us over there, smooching? Would you have liked someone to do that to you?'

Raisa stopped laughing. So did Afsana.

'Have you two smooched?' Raisa was wide-eyed. 'That too in my absence?'

'Shut up, Rice!' snapped Afsana and started walking away.

'Have you?' she asked Nirmaan.

'Shut up, Raisa!' an embarrassed Nirmaan followed Afsana.

For a moment, Raisa wondered if she had inadvertently touched a nerve and then shouted, 'Wait!' She hurried after them.

VOICE NOTE 29

A week later, it was Saraswati Puja. Every boy in school wore the traditional kurta with either pyjamas or jeans, while the girls swanned around in gorgeous sarees.

The previous night, Afsana had telephoned Nirmaan to tell him that she was going to wear a black saree with a red border. This kept him up for the best half of the night with his imagination busy. And yet when she alighted from the car in front of the school gate, he couldn't believe his eyes. She waved at him but he was too frozen to wave back. When she came right up to him and asked, 'Do I look all right?'

There was no response.

'Nirmaan?' she shook his arm.

'Huh? Yes, oh yes, you look amazing!' he replied. Only he knew what had induced that temporary frozen state and he found it disturbing. He felt restless and glanced around.

'Are you waiting for someone else?' Afsana asked.

'Me? No.'

'Should we go inside?'

'Sure.'

Nirmaan's steps faltered, so Afsana took the lead. She turned around, 'Are you all right?'

Nirmaan nodded unconvincingly.

Right through the morning assembly, the Saraswati Puja celebration and later, when the classes were dismissed for the day, Afsana couldn't help feeling that Nirmaan was avoiding her. When she sought him out in his class, he seemed busy with his classmates. Such deliberate evasion was completely unlike him. Dejected, she left. It was only then that Nirmaan, looking at the empty space where she had been standing a moment ago, wondered how he could tell her that the first thing he had noticed when she had got out of her car in the morning was her navel. His eyes had been roving over the exposed areas of her body. He hadn't done so a few months ago when he had seen her in a saree for the first time during Durga Puja. Then why now? What was the layer in their relationship that he had peeled off that had made him do so? The stifling sensation that this feeling produced told him that this could be a critical turning point in their love story. He was certain that it wasn't love that made his eyes wander that morning. Love could never be this specific or objective. Or could it? Nirmaan had never been more confused.

When he excused himself from his classmates and made his way to the washroom, he passed by Afsana who was chatting in the corridor with her classmates. They noticed each other but this time his aloofness cut her to the quick. If he was upset with her about something, he ought to come clean and say it to her face, Afsana thought, without playing weird games. If they couldn't be honest and upfront with each other, they had no business being in a romantic relationship.

An hour later, when school was over for the day, Afsana waited for Nirmaan outside his classroom. He was one of the last ones to emerge with a couple of other boys.

'I want to talk,' she said bluntly. Her eyes told him she meant it. He bade his friends goodbye and seemed nervous as he turned to her.

'Let's go inside,' she marched into his classroom and Nirmaan followed her. She shut the door.

'What is it?' he said.

'That's what I want to know. What is it with you today? You were fine last night on the phone,' Afsana said aggressively.

'I don't know what you're talking about,' Nirmaan said without making eye contact.

'Why have you been avoiding me today?' Emboldened by his silence she stepped towards him. 'Do I need to rephrase my question?'

Nirmaan gazed at her uneasily for a few moments and then said, 'I must apologize to you.'

'For what?'

'I had bad thoughts about you.'

Afsana frowned trying to understand his meaning.

'I always thought my feelings for you were pure, but this morning, when I laid eyes on you, bad thoughts came to me. I even imagined you naked. I'm deeply sorry. I don't want to see you that way. I mean I want to, but not by objectifying you . . . ' he trailed off and hung his head in shame. Afsana drew close to him and placed his arms around her waist and then put her arms around his neck. This was the first time his skin was touching hers in a kind of intimate way. His hand, almost involuntarily, moved to her navel and his thumb began to gently circle her belly button. She could feel goosebumps forming all over.

'Why were you ashamed of imagining me naked?' she asked softly.

'I don't know,' he whispered, continuing to caress her navel.

She rose on her toes and rubbed the tip of her nose on his. Warming up the rhythm, he tilted his face so their lips brushed against the other's.

'I don't mind if you imagine me naked,' she breathed, 'because I know that your imagination could only enhance my beauty.'

Nirmaan's grip on her waist tightened and he moved in closer, her nubile breasts just about pressing into his chest. He slowly raised his lips and kissed her forehead and said, 'I hope this won't destroy our relationship.'

Afsana, with her eyes closed, murmured a no at first, and then feeling his lips gliding on to her cheeks, whispered, 'After this, no distance can ever kill our closeness.'

His hand travelled to the fine hairs on her nape. The tips of his fingers feathered her skin, tickling her senses. Her body that was gently caged in his arms, squirmed slightly in his embrace.

'Don't you dare leave me, ever,' he muttered.

'Don't you dare think that I will,' she retorted.

He sucked on her luscious lower lip as she enclosed his upper lip. They felt that the rapture of their intimacy was potent enough to gift a poet somewhere with the final stanza of his long awaited poem; or inspire an infant to pronounce his first word; or convert an atheist into a believer; or make the old lament the loss of their youth.

The kiss broke and they gazed at each other with a sense of relief and an ache to indulge further.

'Now we know love in its totality,' she said with a twinkle in her eyes.

VOICE NOTE 30

The shuffle between coaching classes for the engineering college entrance examination and schoolwork lowered Nirmaan's rank in the Class XI final exams and he stood third in his class, missing the second rank by two marks. His father, who understood the gravity of the situation, didn't say much and only asked him to focus on getting into the coveted Indian Institute of Technology as soon as he completed his senior secondary exams. It seemed his father was hungrier for the IIT admission than Nirmaan was.

Afsana scored better than her preceding years in the final exams. But she wasn't happy. Whenever she overheard Tarun and her father talk, she had a feeling that they were inclined to getting her married off the moment she turned eighteen instead of waiting until her graduation. The stronger her conviction grew that her marriage to Tarun was inevitable, the more she ignored his overtures to date her. The worst part of this was that she couldn't share her apprehensions with Nirmaan fearing his reaction. Although Raisa was always there, confiding in her would only relieve her momentarily. She wanted a solution that only Nirmaan could give her and yet she knew that they had gone past that stage now. She had become too close to him to reveal anything disturbing about herself. This was a strange lesson in relationships to her—the existence of a seed of distance within the womb of intimacy. That cherished closeness becomes the reason to protect the loved one from learning some hard truths.

Meanwhile, Tarun's desire for Afsana grew stronger with time although her repudiation of his advances only increased the depth of his humiliation. During a booze session with friends who constantly mocked him because he was the only virgin in the group, he finally zeroed in on a plan to get Afsana's attention.

The following week Tarun lay in wait outside Afsana's school. His plan was simple. He would tell Afsana that his father wanted to meet her and induce her to get into his car. He would then drive to a secluded place and ask for a kiss. If she refused to comply . . . Tarun was confident of his plan.

He wiped the sweat off his brow as the last bell for the day reverberated in the school. Soon students poured out in hordes. He was extra alert on the lookout for Afsana. Minutes later he noticed her walking out with two other girls. They parted ways at the gate and Afsana strolled over to the banyan tree where he had parked his car. She sat on the low brick wall around the tree. When Tarun reached her side, she frowned in surprise and irritation.

'What are you doing here?' Afsana stood up.

'Dad wants to meet you so I came to pick you up.'

'I don't want to meet him now.'

'This is important,' Tarun insisted.

'Okay, you go on ahead. I'll come along shortly.'

'I have my car here,' Tarun said.

'I don't want to go with you.'

'Why do you always make me feel like a stalker?' Tarun snapped as Afsana rose to move away from him.

'What is it with you?' he grabbed her arm. She tried to jerk herself free, but couldn't.

'Let go of me,' she said furiously. 'Let go, now!' she screamed.

'I won't. You have to come with me, now!' Tarun managed to drag the resisting girl away from the tree and almost to his car when someone called out.

'Hey, what are you doing?' It was Nirmaan. He parked his bicycle and came up to Tarun. Although the latter towered over him, Nirmaan held his ground with confidence.

'Get lost! This is none of your business,' Tarun snarled and continued to drag Afsana.

Nirmaan didn't know whether it was Tarun's supercilious contempt of him or the fact that he was manhandling Afsana that made him kick Tarun in the stomach. The latter released Afsana and knelt clutching his stomach in agony. Afsana ran to Nirmaan.

'She's my fiancée,' mumbled Tarun trying to stand up. Nirmaan kicked him again, this time on his knee joint, which made him sit down on the road.

'If you don't leave now, I'll call the school authorities,' Nirmaan said.

Eventually, Tarun managed to heave himself up. He wanted to beat up Nirmaan, but Afsana threatened to scream the place down. Tarun drove off in a dudgeon.

'Thank you, Nirmaan,' Afsana was clutching his arm with both hands. She was shaking.

'Isn't he the same guy with the rose?'

Afsana was silent.

'Was he speaking the truth?' Nirmaan had never looked so tough before.

'Let's sit down,' Afsana pulled him towards the banyan tree. Nirmaan broke free of her clasp and stalked off to sit on the bricks.

'Now tell me,' he said.

Afsana dithered for almost fifteen minutes before she relayed the whole sorry tale to Nirmaan, that she was indeed informally betrothed to Tarun. She explained that she had run away from home in protest and swore upon their relationship that come hell or high water she would never marry him. Nirmaan heard her out patiently and then simply said, 'If you truly love me, Afsana, you'll tell your father right away that you're not into this boy. You'll do this today.'

It's the existence of options, however unpleasant they may be, that cause dilemma. Without options, there can be no dilemma. With a simple conditional clause, 'if you love me, Afsana . . . ' Nirmaan had invalidated all her options. The smog of confusion lifted and filled her with the determination to prove to both Nirmaan and herself that what they shared wasn't an illusion.

That night, Afsana told her father about the incident outside her school and explained why she never wanted to see Tarun again. Although her father blamed her obstinance for Tarun's misbehaviour, her mother surprisingly rose to her defence and made it clear to her husband that business deals were all right but they shouldn't coerce their only child into an alliance with a loutish lunatic. Her father wasn't convinced until Tarun's father called that night and demanded an apology from Afsana for injuring his son. Following a long and harsh verbal duel on the telephone, it was decided that Afsana and Tarun would no longer be forced to marry. That night Afsana, for the first time in ages, hugged her parents. She wanted to tell them about Nirmaan, but decided that the opportune moment to introduce him to her parents would be when he cracked his IIT admission exams.

VOICE NOTE 31

Barely two months were left for the senior secondary board exams. Nirmaan remained immersed in the laws of physics, chemistry formulas and mathematical theorems all through the day. Talking to Afsana on the telephone before going to bed rejuvenated him for the next day. He would listen to the high-on-hormone love stories of his batch mates and noted the way they swore fealty forever to their beloved only for it to blow over the very next day. Nirmaan thanked the gods that the connection between him and Afsana ran so much deeper than mere hormones.

One Saturday, Nirmaan's parents had to attend a relative's wedding in north Bengal. Nirmaan would have accompanied them if he didn't have to prepare for his pre-board exams that were due to begin in a few weeks. Although his mother was worried, he allayed her anxiety and convinced her that he would manage just fine. They left on Friday night.

Eight hours later, in the wee hours of the night, Nirmaan cycled over to Afsana's place and smuggled her into his flat. Her parents believed that she had gone off on a school outing.

They watched television late into the morning and then cooked up a scrumptious brunch together. They sat down to study together, snacking in between. Neither of them knew when they fell asleep. Afsana was the first to wake up with a start when she heard the doorbell ring. She was disoriented for a while until she caught sight of Nirmaan asleep beside her. She shook him vigorously.

'There's someone at the door,' she whispered.

'What?' he leapt up. 'Let me check. Just stay here and don't make a sound.'

Nirmaan opened the front door.

'Were you sleeping, dumbo?' Raisa was holding a covered steel bowl. 'My hands are aching,' she said, marching into the kitchen. 'I made some chicken for you,' she said.

'You did?'

'Yes, I like to cook.'

'But how did you know I was alone?' Nirmaan asked standing by the kitchen door.

Raisa turned around, her arms akimbo, 'My mother is part Sherlock Holmes.'

'But I told my mom not to tell anyone,' Nirmaan protested.

'That's okay,' she sauntered into the drawing room, Nirmaan at her heels. 'Now eat it on time and let me know how it is. Why are the curtains still drawn?' Raisa grumbled and threw open the shades to let the morning sunlight flood the room.

'Actually I slept late so . . .' Nirmaan said weakly, finding it difficult to lie to Raisa with a straight face.

The telephone in his bedroom shrilled at that moment. Nirmaan stayed rooted to the spot. Raisa shrugged impatiently and quickly went into his bedroom and picked up the receiver.

'Hello, Aunty, it's Raisa. I brought lunch for Nirmaan. No, don't thank me. He was sleeping. Yes, he's here,' she extended the receiver to Nirmaan.

'Hello, Ma. Yes, yes, I'm fine. I was studying in the morning. Okay. Bye.'

As he hung up, he heard Raisa say, 'Who was here?' She was staring at his table that had two plates with the remains of food. Nirmaan looked abashed and started mumbling something, when the door to the en-suite bathroom opened.

'Hey, Rice!' Afsana emerged.

'Affu?' Raisa looked at Nirmaan, her mouth agape. 'Why did you lie to me, Nirmaan?'

Afsana and Nirmaan exchanged glances. For a moment they thought Raisa would throw a hissy fit, but she smiled, surprising them.

'It's okay, guys. I too have a boyfriend now and I do understand you need time together. Now enjoy, okay? I'm gone. See you later, Affu. Bye, Nirmaan.' She left. It was only when Nirmaan heard the main door lock itself with a thud that he flung himself on the bed. Afsana sat by the study table and stretched her legs on to the bed.

'Do you think she felt bad?' Nirmaan asked sitting up.

'What did you tell her?'

'I didn't tell her you were here.'

'Why? You could have.'

'I know. I don't know why I didn't. I've never hidden anything from her. Should I apologize?'

'Well, she said she too has a boyfriend. She should understand. Moreover we're no longer kids, if you know what I mean.'

Nirmaan lay back on the bed again. He sat up again within seconds.

'Don't you think she has changed a bit?' he asked.

'Maybe,' Afsana said, thoughtfully, 'honestly we aren't that close any more.' She looked up at the ceiling and continued, 'There was a time when we shared every little detail of our lives.'

'Same here. But the last time I saw her was like a couple of months ago and the worst part is that I'm realizing this only today,' he looked conscience-stricken.

'Same here,' said Afsana.

'Does it happen with every relationship?' Nirmaan wondered.

'My friendship with Rice is far from dead.'

'Of course! But . . . you know what I mean. I've seen how close you two used to be and now you're also seeing her after a long time.'

'Perhaps our priorities change as we grow and we no longer remain the persons we were,' Afsana said philosophically as she gathered up the two plates and carried them into the kitchen.

'I think,' Nirmaan was right behind her, 'As we grow, we consciously get away from our basic selves and get more and more conditioned by our surroundings.'

They entered the kitchen. 'I never thought there would be another girl in my life who could be closer to me than Raisa, but now I have you.'

'And I never knew I could ever love anyone so much,' Afsana kept the plates by the kitchen sink. She noticed a covered bowl beside the gas stove. She raised the lid and inhaled the aroma of the chicken gravy.

'Wow!' She dipped her finger in the gravy and licked it clean.

'Mmm! Rice's mother is an excellent cook,' Afsana said, deeply appreciative.

'Raisa cooked it.'

'What? She's a natural then. It's yummy,' Afsana dipped her finger again and gestured Nirmaan to taste it. He leaned forward and sucked the gravy off her finger.

A moment later he said, 'Now I'm confused. I think your finger is tastier.'

'Oh yeah, Mr Romantic? Let's get back to the books now. Exams are round the corner.'

VOICE NOTE 32

A month and a half had gone by since their senior secondary board exams. Returning from one of his tuitions one day, Nirmaan halted his bicycle by the Ultadanga footbridge. It had been almost twenty days since Nirmaan had met Afsana or even heard her voice. She had been bulldozed into accompanying her family on a Europe tour after their last board exam got over.

They had met in the evening at this very footbridge before she had left. When they had hugged, Nirmaan realized the significance of what had happened between the two of them in the last two years. They had become deeply attached. Although he was aware that she was only going away for a vacation, he felt as empty as one would feel staring into an oblivion.

'What if some day we don't remain together?' Nirmaan asked as he embraced her.

'Shut up,' Afsana whispered in his ear and tightened her hug.

'The more I'm drawn to you,' Nirmaan continued, 'the more vulnerable I feel because while a part of me believes that our connection is more permanent than anything else, the cynical side of me says it could be just as transient as everything else.'

'Honestly, I too feel the fear uncoiling within me. Our board results will be out in a few months. I'll have to introduce you to my parents otherwise they'll set me up with another boy. And—'

He broke the hug and completed her sentence, '—and I'm a Bengali and you are a Marwari.'

'I honestly don't know how my parents will react to that.'

They strolled hand in hand and sat on the steps of the footbridge. She took out a cigarette. She understood Nirmaan noticed the box a little too intently.

'You don't like that I smoke, isn't it?' she asked.

Nirmaan was quiet.

'You can tell me. I won't smoke,' she said, toying with the cigarette between her fingers.

Nirmaan though for a while and said, 'Affu, I don't want either of us to dictate ever what the other person should or should not do. If you want to smoke, you should; if you don't want to, don't.'

Afsana smiled at him and put the cigarette back in the box and stuffed it in her bag.

'What happened?' he asked.

'Don't feel like smoking now. And you are right. Just because people are in love doesn't mean that they have to control each other,' she said and leaned her head on his shoulder, still holding his hand, as he slipped his arm around her waist. They sat quietly with their emotions oscillating between calm and chaos for two hours before it was time for her to go home. Nirmaan dropped her home. The moment

Afsana reached her room, the first thing she did was pen the thought that had struck her in the last hour.

Duniya uss rishtey ko kamiyaab samjhti hai,
Jo ek kitchen, ek bistar aur,
Roz ki daud mein qaid ho.
Humare rishtey mein koi ghar nahi hai,
Na electric bill, na doctor ki fees aur na hi koi EMI.
Ek khula aasmaan hai bas,
Aur kabhi na khatam hone wali udaan.

दुनिया उस रिश्ते को कामयाब समझती है,
जो एक किचन, एक बिस्तर और,
रोज़ की दौड़ में कैद हो।
हमारे रिश्ते में कोई घर नहीं है,
न इलेक्ट्रिक बिल, न डॉक्टर की फीस और न ही कोई ईएमआई।
एक खुला आसमान है बस,
और कभी न खत्म होने वाली उड़ान।

Nirmaan cycled on hoping the remaining days would fly past and Afsana would be back from her holiday soon. As he cycled into his lane, he saw Raisa by the pharmacy. He got off his bike and joined her.

'Ma has a fever,' she said. They entered the RBI quarters together, chatting and catching up on their studies and this and that.

'Let me meet Aunty once,' he said. They went to her flat. It was her father who opened the door and flung some papers on her face.

'What the hell are you up to, you little bitch?' he yelled at Raisa.

VOICE NOTE 33

'Nirmaan, go home,' Raisa said quietly. Although he wanted to stay, seeing her father in such a rage, Nirmaan realized it had to be something acutely personal. So he left baffled.

Almost the entire RBI colony was set by the ears hearing abuses being hurled at Raisa by her own father. Nobody knew why. It was only when some of the concerned neighbours went to check on the family did they realize that Raisa was getting beaten. When his office colleagues sternly commanded Mr Barua to behave himself, he stopped beating his daughter and ordered her to get out of his sight.

Mrs Bose asked what had happened, but Nirmaan had no answer. He wanted to telephone Raisa, but realized this wasn't a good time. After dinner, Nirmaan, glancing out through his window, noticed Raisa sitting alone on a stone bench in the colony's courtyard. He didn't waste a single second to reach her.

'What happened, Raisa?' he asked, sitting beside her. She was sobbing and couldn't speak for a long time.

Nirmaan was at a loss and he placed an arm around her, gently patting her shoulder.

Suddenly the words came tumbling out, 'Two months ago Mihir and I made out. It was his birthday and he wanted my virginity as his gift. I loved him so . . . we did it without any protection. A month later I started having strange symptoms that scared me. I secretly visited a doctor and discovered that I was pregnant.'

Nirmaan felt like he was in a trance as he listened to her. He didn't want to believe a word of what she was saying, but he knew he had to because her eyes were swimming with tears and her woebegone demeanour told him it was the naked truth.

'I told Mihir and he broke up with me because his parents would kill him if they got to know of this. When I threatened to go public with the news, he mocked me saying I wouldn't be able to tell anyone that I'm pregnant. He was right. I couldn't even tell you,' she hung her head as the tears cascaded down her cheeks unchecked.

'Are you really pregnant?' Nirmaan asked.

'I was. Mohini, my friend from school, has a friend who took me to this clinic where I underwent an abortion in secret.'

'You aborted the child?' Nirmaan felt he was sitting beside a total stranger and not the girl he had known since he was eight.

'You actually underwent an illegal abortion?' Nirmaan rephrased to himself, still shell-shocked.

Raisa nodded and said, 'I was almost out of it unnoticed but—'

'But?'

'The doctor gave me ten days to pay his fee, failing which he said he would inform my parents.'

'How much money?'

'Fifty thousand rupees. My dad recently booked an apartment in New Alipore and he was going to make part of the payment in cash. I planned to steal the money as soon as I had a chance.'

'And you didn't get a chance?' To Nirmaan this all seemed surreal and more like a bad dream.

'I waited, but Deuta didn't bring home any money. The doctor grew impatient and this evening he visited my dad with the paperwork and told him everything. He went away giving him a two-day deadline to cough up the money,' Raisa wept.

When Raisa returned to her apartment, she received an international call from Afsana. Raisa faithfully promised to relay her message to Nirmaan, but didn't mention a word to her soul-sister about the upheavals in her own life.

VOICE NOTE 34

Two more weeks flew past and before Nirmaan could wrap his head around it, it was the day before the IIT entrance exam. It wasn't merely an exam for him, it was the door to a future involving both Afsana and him. He was dying to talk to her but there was no way he could. On an impulse, he called her house but nobody answered. *They're still in Europe*, he concluded with a heavy heart. The following day, he left home in good time to make it to the exam centre that had been allocated to him. But he never made it to the examination hall.

Midway to the exam centre, a car drew up alongside his bicycle. Two burly men got out, grabbed Nirmaan and bundled him into the car where he was immediately blindfolded. Although Nirmaan hollered, they quickly gagged him as well. The car drove around in circles and Nirmaan was held captive for the duration of the exam time. When the car eventually stopped, he was thrown out in the same place where he had been picked up. Nirmaan yelled and chased after the car, but it wasn't of much use.

Feeling wholly defeated, he reached home. Seeing Nirmaan's bedraggled state, although Mrs Bose understood something terrible had happened, she didn't badger him with questions. When Mr Bose called later that afternoon to find out how the exam had went, Mrs Bose said Nirmaan was asleep. It was only when he came home in the evening, all excited about his son's entrance test, that he learnt what had happened. Nirmaan hadn't been able to appear for this coveted exam for which he had been preparing for years. Mr Bose was thunderstruck.

'Who were they? Where did they take you? And why?' he asked. Nirmaan had no answers.

'Did you do this because you never wanted to be an engineer?' Mr Bose's final question struck Nirmaan dumb.

This was only the beginning of a father–son verbal duel at the end of which Mr Bose lost his rag. He accused Nirmaan and all his generation of having grown up with all the amenities of life without having had to work hard for anything. Mr Bose was obdurate in his conviction that Nirmaan had intentionally skipped the exam because, contrary to his father's engineering aspirations for his son, Nirmaan was determined to become a businessman. Both Nirmaan and Mrs Bose did their best to reason with him, but he was intransigent.

'He can always try again next year, can't he?' Mrs Bose had tears in her eyes by now.

'Of course, he will,' Mr Bose said sternly, 'but on his own.' He walked out of the apartment.

'If that's the way he wants it, that's the way it will happen,' Nirmaan said to his distraught mother, stormed off into his bedroom, locking himself in and skipped dinner.

The next evening, Raisa called him. They decided to meet on the footbridge.

Raisa's jaw dropped at Nirmaan's misadventures of the previous day.

'But who were those men who kidnapped you?' she asked.

'I don't know.'

'Did you fight with someone recently?' Raisa asked.

'Tarun,' he said almost to himself.

'Tarun, who?'

'Afsana was supposed to marry him. He came to meet her outside the school some time ago and was manhandling her. I had kicked him hard. The alliance was eventually called off. It has to be him.'

'Where will I find this guy? I'll kill him,' Raisa hissed. Nirmaan fell silent, ruminating. After a while, she ventured, 'So, what's the plan now?'

'There's no plan. I'm waiting for Afsana. Then I leave my home for good.'

'Leave? And go where?'

'I don't know. I'll decide only after Afsana returns,' Nirmaan said and abruptly stood up to leave. Raisa stopped him as he started ascending the stairs on the bridge.

'Nirmaan, listen. There's something I didn't tell you,' Raisa said, her throat going dry.

'What?'

She held his hands tightly and said, 'Affu is never coming back to India.'

Nirmaan failed to find any humour in Raisa's expression although his mind screamed that this had to be a bad joke. A really bad joke.

'What do you mean?' he snapped, snatching his hands free of her grasp.

'She called me. I wanted to tell you, but I was waiting for your entrance exam to get over. And now—'

'What happened to Affu? Why won't she come back?' he interrupted her. She could tell that they were teetering on the brink of an emotional landslide.

'I'll tell you, but you must promise that you won't cry or do anything crazy,' she said.

'Just give it to me straight, Raisa,' he gritted through clenched teeth.

'She called me last week, the night my dad crucified me in public. She called to say she had tried your number several times, but couldn't get through. Her parents had conned her into believing it was a Europe tour, but she soon realized that she was to be admitted into a grad school where one of her cousins is a student.'

'How could she—' Nirmaan trailed off.

'It's not her. It's her parents. They tricked her. She specifically asked me to tell you not to wait for her because it's possible she'll never return to India again. Not for several years at least,' Raisa spoke haltingly, but enunciated each word clearly.

'Did she leave any contact number or anything where I can reach her?'

Raisa shook her head sadly, 'No.'

Nirmaan looked at the busy city roads below the bridge. Everybody seemed to know exactly where they were heading, unlike him.

After a few minutes of silence, Raisa clasped his hands tight, 'I'm already fucked. Now you as well. What do we do now, Nirmaan?'

He gazed into her eyes. Life was going to change here on.

VOICE NOTE 35

Hi Shanay!

Last year, during a festival, I looked at an idol and pondered: man creates an idol, people carry it home, worship it, then immerse it in a sea or a river and pray that it returns to them, when it's actually they themselves who will recreate it when the time comes.

It's so much like the ordeal of love. We create this emotional deity within ourselves that we know we can't hold on to forever and yet we believe we can. We follow all the rituals only to watch ourselves immerse it in the river of our emotions eventually.

Realization awakens within the soul like a deep spring to quench the anguish of the loss of love. These realizations sometimes surprise us to the extent that we start hating ourselves because we know they aren't something we had sought while we were in love.

But then again, those realizations make us feel powerful and glad that we followed the rituals.

My next series of voice notes will have the second most important part of the story, so please listen with care, maturity and a free mind.

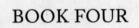
BOOK FOUR

BOOKFOUR

VOICE NOTE 36

Raisa and Nirmaan,
Bhubaneswar, 2012–17.

'Babloo bhaina, may I borrow your bike?' a twenty-four-year-old Nirmaan asked as he emerged from Shri Jagannath Sarees, a legendary shop in Shashtri Nagar, which was the biggest retailer of the famous Sambalpuri sarees and Baluchari sarees in Bhubaneswar.

'Leaving early today?' Babloo asked, tossing the motorbike's keys to Nirmaan.

Nirmaan nodded, unlocking the bike. He seemed unusually hopeful that day because something for which he had diligently worked for years was going to come to fruition at long last.

As the bike sped through a lonely road, the wind rushed through the raised helmet's visor on to his face fiercely, taking him back, for some reason, to the day he rode his bicycle for the first time with Raisa's encouragement. Although nothing as fierce as now, the thrill of the wind on his face was as it was then. The memory evoked others and slowly the past started playing in his mind with vivid clarity.

Seven years ago, when Nirmaan boarded the Dhauli Express from Howrah station at six o'clock in the morning, two nights after he'd sat with Raisa at the Ultadanga footbridge, he knew that leaving home was his way of accepting his father's unspoken challenge. Mr Bose had opted to disown his son, obstinately refusing to accept the explanation of Nirmaan's abduction on the way to the examination hall. Nirmaan took it upon himself to prove his mettle to a father who considered Nirmaan a typical product of his generation, spoilt silly and an ingrate. According to Mr Bose, Nirmaan was a rebel without a cause and had deliberately sabotaged his father's dreams of a wonderful engineering career for his son.

With little possibility of Afsana returning to India any time soon, there was no reason for Nirmaan to stay on in Kolkata. His only ally was Raisa who also had been ostracized from her family. It was at Raisa's behest that he had left a note for his parents vowing to kill himself if he ever got wind of them looking for him.

That morning, Raisa and Nirmaan had walked hand in hand into Howrah station without a destination in mind. The only thing that they were sure of was that they had to go away, far away. And 'going away' was as vaguely adventurous a feeling when they entered the chaotic station as the idea's allure had been to them the night before. Raisa learnt at the enquiry counter that the next train to leave the station was Dhauli Express. With no time or cash to buy any tickets, they boarded the train just as it started to chug along the track. When the ticket-checker came along, they had nothing to show him. He was on the verge of kicking them out at the next station when Jaya, a eunuch touting the train for *baksheesh* from passengers, noticed them. She pleaded in vain with the ticket-checker to spare the kids. She resorted to raising her voice and, in a flash, five more eunuchs materialized in the vestibule to which the ticker-checker had directed the runaway teenagers. The eunuchs surrounded him, clapping and raining racy comments on the hapless railway official until the man let go of Nirmaan and Raisa to avoid further embarrassment.

The eunuchs soon realized that the youngsters were from a well-to-do background because of their well-kempt appearance, deportment and manner of speech. Raisa thanked them in English and cooked up an explanation that they were siblings who had been evicted by a mercenary uncle upon the demise of their parents. Nirmaan remained silent, awed at Raisa's fertile imagination.

As soon as they reached Bhubaneswar, the kind-hearted eunuchs took them to their home, a ramshackle building that was a few miles from the station. That night, after a simple dinner of pokhaal, Raisa and Nirmaan were allocated a corner in the house where a tattered sleeping mat lay on the floor. As they lay down, Raisa fished out two small glittering objects from the pocket of her skirt and slipped them into Nirmaan's hand.

'Earrings!' he whispered.

'They're pure gold and belong to Ma. I stole them because I knew we couldn't carry cash.'

Nirmaan returned the earrings to her wordlessly. Silence reigned for a while and then she whispered, 'Are you missing Affu?' She waited but no answer came. Nirmaan was fast asleep. She closed her eyes as well, clutching the earrings in her fist.

Early the next morning, the head eunuch decided that they should take the youngsters to Manoj Ranjan Panigrahi, the school principal of the only public school in the area. Panigrahi was a benevolent philanthropist who had received an award from the state government for his selfless work to educate underprivileged children.

A large speed breaker jerked Nirmaan back to the present. He parked Babloo's bike in the shade of a tree, outside a freshly painted bungalow in Jayadev Vihar. He opened the main gate gingerly because that had also been given a new lick of paint. He made his way past the main house and into a small courtyard that had a picturesque well as its central feature, beyond which was the small house that Nirmaan had rented. The door stood ajar.

'Raisa! I've got good news. In fact two of them.'

Standing in the shower, Raisa could hear him. She had a fairly good idea what the bits of good news were.

VOICE NOTE 37

The first piece of good news was that Nirmaan's graduation certificate had arrived earlier that day. Raisa was delighted to see a certificate that read:

Nirmaan Bose
Bachelor of Commerce from Utkal University

'What's up?' Nirmaan asked expecting a spontaneous hug. She took the certificate and reverently placed it on the feet of a small idol of Lord Shiva that had been installed on a wooden platform over the kitchen counter. She shut her eyes and murmured a fervent and grateful prayer.

Nirmaan sighed at Raisa's piety. All along he had thought she was an atheist because she had found every ritual silly and every religion pseudo. However, their adventures and experiences over the last few years had wrought a lot of changes in her, her newfound religious bent one of them. There was no change in their relationship though and he was thankful for that.

His mind once again went back to the time when they had just arrived in Bhubaneswar, thanks to the kind and helpful eunuch, Jaya.

* * *

After the head eunuch had left the two runaways with Manoj Ranjan Panigrahi, both Raisa and Nirmaan were given a room to stay within the premises of Sarvodaya Shiksha Niketan. Although Raisa had fabricated a more viable reason for their flight from their parental homes, there was no need to use this revised version because their benefactor didn't subject them to an inquisition. For the next few days all Raisa and Nirmaan did was eat and sleep. The food, packed in a stainless steel lunchbox, would arrive like clockwork from the principal's home. A week later, Manoj Ranjan invited the teenagers to dine at his house.

'Would you like to study?' Manoj Ranjan asked.

'We do,' Nirmaan replied without hesitation.

'He does,' Raisa corrected. Although Nirmaan gave her a surprised look, she didn't return it.

'You two don't want to go back to—'

'Not any more,' Raisa cut in.

'Hmm. You said you had passed your senior secondary. If you can give me your mark sheet, I can get you admission into Utkal University, but only if your marks are good. Merit is everything.'

'He is our school topper,' said Raisa proudly.

'Good. Get me the mark sheet as soon as you can. Also, I'm afraid both of you will have to start working.'

Nirmaan and Raisa exchanged anxious glances.

'Look, children, only when you start working will you realize and appreciate the worth of everything. The one who understands the worth of sweat, understands a lot. And mind you, any activity that makes you perspire without harming anyone is productive labour.'

There was silence until Manoj Ranjan finished his dinner. 'What do you want to study?'

'Commerce,' Nirmaan replied immediately and caught Raisa's eye. Only she could decipher that look. She was happy for him.

The next day, Nirmaan telephoned his school in Kolkata and requested them to post his senior secondary mark sheet to the school in Bhubaneswar. The request was granted. He enlisted in Sarvodaya Shiksha Niketan School as a peon, running errands for the staff. A month later, he joined Utkal University to attend classes designed for working people—the classes were held in the evenings.

Raisa was also granted an opportunity to pursue her senior secondary in the same school, but she deferred.

'But, why?' Nirmaan asked.

'I have other important things to do.'

'What "important things"?' Raisa didn't reply.

Her actions in the days to follow were answer enough. She would rise at the crack of dawn to fix breakfast and lunch for Nirmaan and herself, spend the day working as an assistant to the school principal and return to make dinner and wait for Nirmaan to come home. Nirmaan was amazed at this transformation. He had never imagined that she could be so consistent and committed to anything in life. As time passed, he deeply appreciated the mantle of domesticity that she had donned, although he pretended not to notice her great attention to every detail. She maintained a list of their expenses, checked the grocery inventory and ensured that he always wore clean, freshly laundered clothes. As they hadn't brought any of their clothes with them, the first thing Raisa had done when they moved into the spare room in the school, was sell one of her earrings and buy two sets of new clothes for each of them, wisely setting aside the rest of the money for a rainy day. When she cooked, she ensured that she never repeated a dish twice in the same week. Nirmaan was astonished at her magical culinary expertise, which could have given any top chef a run for his or her money.

'When and where did you learn to cook?' he asked one day, sitting cross-legged on the floor of their room, having dinner.

'Cooking is mostly instinct and a little bit of experience, and good cooking is one of those things that just happens to you. No one can explain it much,' she remarked with a wry smile.

When observed closely, Nirmaan thought, Raisa was actually reverse-flowering. Every day since they arrived in Bhubaneswar, he could feel her curl back into a shell, whorl by whorl, in order to become the bud that she had never been. Ironically enough, from being his best friend, Raisa had suddenly taken on the role of a mother, a role in which no responsibility seemed too much to handle—only a woman was capable of transforming into so magnificent an avatar, he felt. The gentler sex, he concluded, was therefore far more adaptable than men could ever be. Although Nirmaan was still her friend, she was so much more. In the eyes of the rest of the world, they were siblings, but only he knew that there wasn't a single cubbyhole into which he could slot his relationship with Raisa.

Nirmaan worked in the school for two years along with Raisa before quitting to take up the job of a cashier in Shree Jagannath Sarees. When he told Manoj Ranjan about it, the kind gentleman readily understood Nirmaan's quandary with his yearning for greater responsibility with larger goals and let the lad go with his blessings.

Raisa, who also aspired to do something more challenging, decided to launch a cost-effective canteen in the school for the children, whose lower-income group parents were hard-pressed with overwork as well as financial constraints to provide nutritious food for their offspring. She charged a nominal amount from the school's management. Nirmaan wasn't very happy about this because he felt she was burning the candle at both ends: it was a lot of work for paltry returns. However, Raisa was adamant and Nirmaan couldn't argue because Manoj Ranjan instantly green-lighted her plan, appreciating the underlying altruism. It was months later that he heard Babloo, in the saree shop, praise the school canteen's special dahi vada with alu dum.

'How do you know about that? Isn't it exclusively for the school students?' Nirmaan was perplexed.

'The school watchman is my friend. When he told me about the dahi vadas, I asked him to bring me some. Oh man, I've never had such tasty vadas before.'

Nirmaan swelled with pride. However, at that juncture, he didn't know the effect that this one simple incident was going to have on their lives many years down the line.

* * *

After brushing the mark sheet on the idol's feet, Raisa said, 'I'll get it laminated tomorrow.'

'There's more good news,' he said, snapping out of his reverie.

Raisa stopped in the doorway of the bedroom. She had briefly forgotten that there were two pieces of good news.

'The loan has been approved. Your dahi vada–alu dum is going public soon,' Nirmaan's smile bore the essence of her joy.

VOICE NOTE 38

A dog barked on a deserted street in the distance and a small table clock ticked loudly, punctuating the night's silence. Raisa and Nirmaan were fast asleep on their separate beds in the shared bedroom.

Raisa sat up sleepily and gulped some water from the half-full water bottle beside her bed. As she replaced the bottle on the floor, she glanced at Nirmaan who was snoring softly. Raisa noticed and realized something to which she had been wholly oblivious before. The space between their respective beds—a few inches at most. Neither of them had ever traversed those inches in the darkness of the night or in the darkness of their desires. That gap, Raisa realized, was mute testimony to the platonic nature of their relationship and their implicit trust in each other.

On an impulse she was about to caress his forehead when she noticed his face contort and his lips move.

'Affu . . .' he muttered in his sleep.

Raisa withdrew her hand and sprang back into her bed in a flash.

She wept that night, with the sudden realization that deep in her heart, the relationship was perhaps not quite so platonic and that her heart had unexpectedly been torn apart at that moment more than any other; she hoped that her tears would mend her half-torn heart, even though she was also aware that half-torn hearts tended to bleed as long as one drew breath.

The initial business plan devised by Nirmaan, with the promised loan amount from the owner of Shri Jagannath Sarees, was to set up a stall outside the saree shop.

'Are you sure the location will attract people?' Raisa asked. She was fixing lunch in the kitchen while Nirmaan quickly and efficiently did the dishes in the adjoining space that had a tap.

'Whatever the location, your dahi vada, alu dum will bring in the crowds, so don't worry about it,' he said with supreme confidence.

'And how are we going to repay the loan?' Raisa was concerned because most of what they earned together, both from the school and the shop, went towards paying their rent. They had been able to move out of the school dorm and into the single-room house in Shahid Nagar using the funds that Raisa had raised by selling off the remaining gold earring. The cash surplus after this sale had been deposited into the joint bank account that they had set up shortly afterwards.

'A percentage of our earnings will go to Shree Jagannath Sarees on a monthly basis until the loan is paid off,' Nirmaan explained, turning off the faucet. He went into the bedroom to change into his work clothes.

'Any interest we need to pay?' Raisa raised her voice a bit.

'If we don't repay the loan in six months' time, we will have to pay interest on the remaining loan amount.'

'What's the interest rate?'

'Fifteen per cent.'

'That's far too much.'

'I know. But if I had protested, they would have assumed that I wasn't confident about my plan. This loan has been given without insisting on any surety. We won't get such a deal from anywhere else.'

'Hmm. Have you thought of a name for the stall?'

'How about *Dhai Kiri Kiri Vada Corner*?'

'What does that even mean?'

Nirmaan came to the kitchen door.

'Dhai Kiri Kiri,' he explained smiling, 'in colloquial Oriya means hurry up, or something along those lines. So in our vada corner, service will be quick, efficient and very fresh.'

'Not bad. It could work.'

Nirmaan set up *Dhai Kiri Kiri Vada Corner* beside the entrance to the saree shop. He employed an assistant for Raisa, a youth recommended by one of his colleagues at the shop. The lad was from the colleague's hometown, a small village in the area. He helped Raisa prepare the food and doubled as the waiter. Operating only in the evenings for a few weeks, it soon became obvious that Raisa would have to leave her school job to pay full attention to the fledgling business if they were to have any chance at repaying the loan before the moratorium on interest ended. Nirmaan continued to work in the saree shop to ensure at least one steady income.

Nirmaan had ordered special uniforms for both Raisa and her waiter. Hygiene-conscious, they used plastic gloves and hair caps and adhered to standards that no other food stall in the vicinity did. Price-wise, they were only slightly higher than the rest. Nirmaan's argument was that every business needed a unique selling point: he was confident that people would notice their ultra-hygienic food and service, which would attract families. Raisa was happy to let him have his way.

It didn't go very well, as was hoped. Six months into the business, they had not even made a quarter of the money needed to repay the loan.

VOICE NOTE 39

Nirmaan started smoking as a stress-buster when the sales from Raisa's stall took a sharp downward curve. As it sometimes happens with small businesses, the novelty wore off and the rush for Raisa's meticulously produced wares dwindled to a trickle. The income was inversely proportional to the build-up of pressure for the loan repayment.

Although Raisa knew that he had started smoking, she didn't say anything until one Sunday when she noticed him chain-smoke his way through an entire packet within a few hours. And she noticed the brand he was smoking. She understood what Nirmaan could never confess.

'That's it. No smoking from tomorrow,' she said decisively. Her voice startled him.

'What's your problem?' Raisa was truculent. She knew that the last three or four months hadn't quite panned out the way they had expected or hoped but she wanted him to talk to her about it and not subject her to this silent treatment. There was no response from Nirmaan.

'Isn't this the same brand Affu used to smoke?' she asked.

Nirmaan glanced at her furtively. After a pregnant pause he said, 'Please don't ask me to stop smoking. There are times when I crave to touch Affu and convince myself she wasn't a dream. This is the only way I can tell myself that.'

Grounding out the glowing stub with his foot, Nirmaan quietly went past Raisa and vanished into the house. He didn't notice her eyes were moist.

They had a quiet dinner. Although his hopes for the food-stall business project had waned into nothingness by this time, he felt that articulating this would only puncture Raisa's faith in him. Raisa had let go of her school job, which she loved immensely, without demur only because of her implicit faith in him. A woman's faith, he'd come to understand, was one of the most powerful things he had known.

'Are you running away from the truth?' Raisa said that night as they lay on their respective beds. She was frowning at the ceiling when he had stood up to switch off the fan.

'Leave it on,' she snapped and added, 'This can't go on,'

'I know. But I don't know what to do,' Nirmaan retorted, realizing that she was referring to their business.

'Do you think it would help if we expanded our menu? Perhaps that would attract more people.'

'I did think about that as well, but diversification will involve a further cost and we aren't ready for that. Moreover, we will also need to employ more people in order to expand. How will we pay them when we haven't paid our one employee for the last two months?'

'Why aren't we selling more? Aren't my dahi vadas good enough?'

'No! Your dahi vadas are perfect.'

'Then what is it? There has to be something. Did you ask around?'

Nirmaan nodded. 'Most of them said that they were intimidated by the uniforms, our sophistication and the standards of hygiene at our stall.'

'Intimidated?'

'I was surprised as well. I later learnt that the locals feel that our stall is considered an eatery for the hep and the affluent, therefore our target group, the lower-income group, stay away from the stall. The same items, although not quite as tasty but cheaper, are available in other places as well. Also, this city doesn't inherently have an eating-out culture. Not yet anyway.'

'But aren't they concerned about their health? We take so much care that our food is germ-free.'

'People don't give a damn for hygiene! They are used to a certain way of life and that is the only thing that might work.'

'Then should we follow the others?'

'Considering our investment, if we lower our rates, we won't be able to break even.'

Raisa pondered over the matter. Nirmaan was right. Cash flow was short, but they simply had to try something new, anything, otherwise the business would perish.

'Should we just pull out and revert to what we used to do?' Nirmaan asked. 'We can pay off our loan from our salaries then.' There was no conviction in his voice and Raisa hated his loser's tone and attitude.

He couldn't lose, she thought, *not while she was by his side*. 'No, we're not pulling out. There has to be a way. We have to think smart,' Raisa paced the room.

'What if nothing positive happens and we get stuck here for the rest of our lives?' Nirmaan sat on the bed with his knees drawn up and burrowed into his arms. It reminded her of a younger Nirmaan weeping in the stairwell because he couldn't cycle without the supporters. She remembered hauling him out of that crisis.

'I'm losing faith, Raisa,' his voice was choked.

'In just six months?'

Nirmaan slowly raised his head and eyed Raisa. He hadn't expected her to look quite so tough.

'It's not just about these six months. It's—' he buried his face in his knees again.

Raisa knew exactly what he meant and tried a different tack, 'I know it's been tough, but that's business. It was you who always wanted to become an entrepreneur. What's the fun when everything is served on a platter to us? Where's the challenge in that? Crisis management is the foundation and not the end. And what's passion if it doesn't overcome repeated failure? Moreover, someone who rebelled against his father can't possibly feel defeated within six months of doing what he always wanted to.'

Nirmaan took a deep breath and said, 'I need to sleep.'

'Okay,' she said. She also wanted to ask him not to smoke, but she didn't.

Raisa switched off the light and fell asleep. An hour before dawn she sat up with sparkling eyes. She shook Nirmaan out of his sleep.

'How about trying the empty lot outside a hospital? People who come to visit patients generally skip their meals. A hygienic vada corner outside a hospital's premises would be ideal. We'll only need to shift our stall there and that won't cost us anything.'

Raisa's enthusiasm made Nirmaan wide awake.

VOICE NOTE 40

For the next couple of weeks, Nirmaan used his lunch breaks to make a survey of all the hospitals and nursing homes in the city. However, he couldn't find that sweet spot that would be the ideal new location for their stall. Most places, he noticed, already had a lot of food stalls. One site, outside a government hospital, did seem like an opportunity, but Nirmaan was quick to understand that shifting their stall there would mean returning to ground zero because as a government facility, most of the patients belonged to the lower-income group who preferred eating at ultra-low prices and he wasn't ready to price himself down to those levels. Moreover, another discovery that he had made during this survey was that people visiting hospitals usually needed a proper lunch or dinner, rather than snack food.

He discussed his findings with Raisa over the weekend.

'What about the ones that don't have any food stalls nearby?'

'If we are the only stall in the area, we'll have to bribe the police and other authorities on a weekly basis. The only good thing when there are other stalls in the area is that this bribe payment is shared.'

'Damn!'

Both of them sat in silence. They had realized that they needed a place where they could cater to loyal customers on a daily basis otherwise the business would be tough to sustain.

'How about shifting into the forecourt of a bank?' Nirmaan asked.

'I already thought of that. The customers will be limited even if we get loyal ones because both employees and their clients in banks generally prefer homemade food, barring a few,' Raisa objected.

'You know what, I think we'll just have to stop being different and conform to the more traditional dahi vada stall. Maybe that's how we too can rake in our share of the profits. Perhaps people here aren't ready for anything that's more . . . Western in its approach,' Nirmaan said resignedly.

Raisa didn't reply. She was reluctant about giving up on their unique selling idea. Nirmaan went off to watch TV in the living room and Raisa drifted into the kitchen to fix dinner. When she heard her favourite Sonu Nigam song being played on TV, she wandered back into the living room. It was then that her eyes fell on something. Nirmaan was engrossed in a newspaper, holding it up with both his hands. On the last page of the newspaper was an advertisement of an engineering college.

'Nirmaan!' Raisa shrieked out.

Nirmaan looked at her and then followed her gaze to the back of the newspaper in his hands. He looked up at

Raisa and realized that he understood what had caught her attention.

They could open an exclusive dahi vada stall in a college. How could they have missed that? Like some of the south Indian cities, the city of Bhubaneswar was also steadily turning into a Mecca for college education in India. Private universities, engineering and management colleges had mushroomed everywhere, offering quality education to students across India. As Nirmaan didn't have a formal qualification in business administration, he began frequenting a cyber cafe nearby and together with Raisa, spent hours surfing the net for clues to make the perfect business plan. They made notes, went home, worked at night on the pointers and within a month, had the first rough draft of the proposal. While Nirmaan spent time to increase the number of unique selling points in their enterprise, Raisa experimented with recipes to diversify their range. According to the Internet, foreign junk food brands were a rage with the youngsters in India. They had two crucial things going for them: a key product and their brand promotion. So if they wished to make dahi vada popular among the college kids, instead of expanding their menu, they would need to diversify their key product. It only meant that they would have to build their menu with variations of dahi vadas that, as a business venture, would be the first of its kind. Raisa had already discovered seven varieties of the vadas, working with permutations and combinations of the ingredients. She christened her productions as: *First Love Dahi Vada, Heartbreak Dahi Vada, Virgin Dahi Vada with Kashmiri Alu Dum, Hi-five*

Dahi Vada, Friends Special Dahi Vada, Cupid Dahi Vada and Raisa's Special Dahi Vada.

The names impressed Nirmaan. He felt they were very identifiable with college students, and as youngsters are invariably curious about novelties, that was what their stall would provide. Although neither of them had any formal training in management, Nirmaan's instinct and tips from the Internet were their guiding stars. Their outlet beside the Shree Jagannath Sarees barely did any business but Nirmaan kept his counsel and didn't tell anyone about his plans. Nor did he mention it in his business proposal. He wanted to sell a vision to the authorities as a fresh entrepreneur rather than peddle a repackaged once-ran business.

For the next couple of months, both Raisa and Nirmaan scouted the various colleges listed in their plans and approached the students with pamphlets that explained their idea of hygienic food rather than the unhealthy items that were abundantly available in the campuses. It seemed to have struck the right chord with the students. Raisa was a crowd-puller with her chic appearance, especially the young male section. The two were brain dead by the end-of-play every evening, but were up bright and early the next morning, their passion unimpeded.

At long last they were ready with their business model. Their target market was a shortlist of engineering and management colleges from the ones they had surveyed. Nirmaan was deeply reluctant to approach the proprietors of the saree shop for a second loan towards capital for his project, but it seemed to be the only option. This time,

however, his employers insisted on a signed legal document
stating that if the profits mentioned on the contract weren't
forthcoming he would be liable for legal action. He knew
it was a huge risk, but then no dream was worth a chase
without risk.

Three months later, the authorities of a famous
engineering college, Samrat Group of Colleges, agreed
to meet with them to discuss their offer. Nirmaan and
Raisa were understandably nervous because this was their
first business presentation. According to their researches
on the net, image was everything. Nirmaan and Raisa
dressed up formally, transformed their plan on paper into
a PowerPoint presentation and left no stone unturned to
convince the organization about their earnestness to make
a success of their enterprise.

The presentation went well. However, during the
post-presentation question–answer session with the panel
representing the college, Nirmaan noticed the dean of the
college eyeing Raisa lecherously. The sixty-year-old pervert
touched his groin every time Raisa spoke to him directly
and Nirmaan gradually lost his focus on the negotiation.

When the dean said he'd like to talk to each of them
individually, he was on tenterhooks as he waited outside
in the corridor. Raisa emerged half an hour later looking
elated.

'They've agreed,' Raisa hugged Nirmaan excitedly. She
broke off the hug sensing his coolness and looked at him
enquiringly.

'We aren't going ahead with this one, Raisa,' Nirmaan
said abruptly and walked away.

VOICE NOTE 41

They waited for over a fortnight to get an appointment with their next client. In the meantime, Raisa and Nirmaan got into heated arguments about the offer that Nirmaan had turned down. When their second fight snowballed into an impasse, Nirmaan blurted out his objection to the old dean's salacity towards her.

'How was he eyeing me?' Raisa asked.

'Oh, you don't want me to say it.'

'Tell me, Nirmaan, how was the dean eyeing me?'

'It was like you were a toy that he wanted to play with. I loathed that look.'

'So?'

'What "so"?'

'That's your interpretation of his look. Why are you so judgemental?'

'I'm judgemental? Why do you assume that I don't know how a man's eyes rove over a woman when he thinks of her as a sex object? Give me a break.'

'Even if you're right, he didn't actually do anything! He didn't say anything suggestive or leap out of his seat to "*play*" with me.'

'He will! If we accept his offer, he most definitely will someday. I won't let that happen.'

'*You* won't let that happen?'

'Yes, I won't let that happen because . . .'

'Keep it down!' bellowed their landlord. Nirmaan lowered his voice.

'Because . . . ?' Raisa urged him to complete his sentence.

Nirmaan sighed and said, 'We're not going to Samrat Engineering College again. That's that.' He walked out of the house.

Later, Raisa perched on the low brick wall outside the house that evening pondering over Nirmaan's incomplete statement. She knew that the rest of that sentence would have swept the cobwebs of pretension off what they had become with time. The past seemed so simple in hindsight, and so much more attractive, almost surreal. She missed Affu ever since she came to Bhubaneswar. She had tried looking for her on Orkut and Facebook but she seemed to have disappeared without a trace. Old friends, old ties, old times, old self . . . when did they all become *old*? she wondered, her eyes welling up with tears.

Sensing what could have followed Nirmaan's '*because*', Raisa was now thankful that the landlord had interrupted their altercation. There were times when she gazed at Nirmaan when he was too busy to notice her glances. Those were the moments when she wanted to kiss him— as a friend, not a lover. Not to possess him, but to free

herself; to time-travel and become the person she had been
in Guwahati so that she could grow up the way she wanted
to and not the way she had to.

Their next presentation was at a management institute
in a sprawling campus. Raisa made Nirmaan swear that he
would focus on the presentation and not try to read the
minds of the men in the room.

In the sophisticated boardroom of the institute, the
panel consisted of two men and five women. This time
Raisa felt a knot in her stomach every time the women
smiled at Nirmaan.

VOICE NOTE 42

It took them four months to set themselves up in the management institute after their presentation. In another three months, they not only impressed the authorities but also found admirers amongst the students. With a letter of recommendation from the student council as well its dean, they managed to convince another engineering college of their worth. The following year, Nirmaan and Raisa were running two outlets and had employed five people. Raisa converted the drawing room of their rented house into a makeshift kitchen and produced the variety of vadas herself. Her assistants and errand boys delivered these, fresh off the oven, to their outlets every morning.

To be honest, there were six employees. I was the sixth. I helped Raisa in the kitchen. It was during our work together every morning that we bonded as only two women can. She haltingly opened her heart to me and I've pieced together their epic that I'm now narrating to you, Shanay, one voice note at a time.

The annual gross turnover for the first year from the two dahi vada joints was Rs 25,00,000. Nirmaan had already set up goals for the following year. He wanted to escalate their dahi vada brand to a Rs 50,00,000 business within the next couple of years. But before implementing his expansion goals, he repaid their loans along with interest as promised to the saree shop proprietors.

With time, Raisa noticed a growing enthusiasm in Nirmaan, the kind that had been in him before they left Kolkata. She understood that he was finally getting a grip on life. In the last few years, Raisa had surrendered her centre of happiness to Nirmaan without him realizing it. Each night, she only had to see the passion in his eyes as he recounted their customer feedback from that day; his aggressive expansion plans kept Raisa in full bloom. Nirmaan had finally come into his own.

The relentless kitchen-work however took its toll on Raisa's health, giving her dark circles and making her lose weight. The more outlets they opened, the greater was the pressure on Raisa. But as long as Nirmaan seemed happy, she never complained.

Time passed by until one day Nirmaan abruptly stopped talking to her about the business or, for that matter, any other matter. Raisa did ask Nirmaan whether something was amiss, but all he said was that things were better than they had anticipated. And yet he seemed to deliberately avoid making eye contact with her.

Finally, one night, he broached a topic that made Raisa's heart skip a beat.

'Do you miss Affu?' he asked. This was the first time in many years that he had consciously uttered the name.

Did she? Could she miss Affu? Raisa asked herself. Could years of once-upon-a-time closeness dissolve into nothingness? Nirmaan took her silence as an affirmation and said, 'I too miss her.'

'Why do you ask this all of a sudden?' Raisa asked.

'Do you think Affu and I could have had a life together if all those shitty things hadn't happened? What if Affu had never been hijacked to Europe by her parents? What if I had reached the examination centre on time?'

'Maybe,' Raisa whispered, her throat inexplicably dry. Lying on her bed, with her eyes closed, she could distinctly see the world she had lived in years ago and Afsana's face hove into view. She opened her eyes with a jolt.

'Are you regretting moving out of Kolkata?' Raisa asked. Not once had he ever mentioned his parents after leaving them.

'I regret nothing. Perhaps this is how it was always meant to be. But yes, sometimes I wonder,' Nirmaan paused before continuing, 'is it possible to have multiple realities? There is only one me, I know, but can't I have a lot of realities? And perhaps in one of those realities, Affu and I are married. Isn't that possible, Raisa?'

'Just like in this reality you and I are together?' she asked.

'Yes.'

'Do you want it to be possible?' she asked.

'We always have a thing for the incomplete, don't we? What-we-want-but-can't-happen is always an emotional turn on.'

Especially when we know what should have happened but didn't, Raisa thought to herself.

'I think this multiple reality thing is possible although it's a far stretch. Each time we make a choice, we create two realities. One we exist in and the other is a fantasy in our hearts,' Raisa said and thought, *but that fantasy is our ultimate desire.*

There was silence.

'You didn't answer my question, Nirmaan. Do you want it to be possible?' Raisa asked.

'I want to confess something,' he said.

'What?'

'I looked for Affu a few years ago on Orkut. I couldn't find her there. Nor on Facebook.'

Raisa didn't respond. She was guilty of doing the same thing.

'And then, a few weeks ago I looked for her on Facebook using a friend's profile. I found her.'

Raisa fell silent.

'I almost added her to my list of contacts, but then I saw her picture with a guy. Some Shanay Bansal. I read some of the comments on the picture and realized that they are engaged to be married soon.'

After a prolonged silence, Nirmaan said, 'This wasn't what I wanted to confess though.'

'What then?' Raisa asked softly.

'The day you and I left Kolkata, I promised myself that I would work hard and make something of myself. And then I would reconnect with Affu so that we could . . .' Nirmaan's voice choked at that point. He excused himself and went out. Raisa bit into her pillow to mute her sobs. Sobs that had a haunting story to tell but no listener.

VOICE NOTE 43

Hi Shanay,

There are many who keep ranting 'I love you' all the time, some who will even shower numerous gifts on you and pamper you silly and perhaps take you on exotic holidays but there's only one person who will actually go ahead and sacrifice everything he or she has to be a part of 'your' dream and to make it happen. The latter is Raisa's kind of love for Nirmaan. The kind of love where someone with wings decides to stay with you.

It was during this emotionally tumultuous time that Raisa opened up to me. She had no friends, then. I was a stranger and perhaps that was why she felt she could confide in me. I always looked up to her as an elder sister. I wept at her pain and that is probably why I became a part of the story—her pain absorbed me into her world.

One night, a month or so after Nirmaan confessed to her about his yearning to reunite with Afsana, Raisa packed her bags and left. Nirmaan was asleep when she applied deep red lipstick and kissed him on his chest. Her only kiss to him in all those years.

I'm not sure if Nirmaan looked for Raisa, although I'm sure he realized what that kiss on his chest meant. I stayed on to work there. Raisa had made sure to teach the vada preparations to a bunch of girls (including me).

There was no news of Raisa until, a couple of months later, I received a call from an NGO. They informed me that Raisa had acquired a rare skin disorder and was admitted to a hospital in Cuttack. I went to her, and pleaded with her to reconnect with Nirmaan, but she didn't. She made me swear I wouldn't tell him either. She died forty-eight hours after she was admitted to the hospital.

One month after her death, I dared to send you a voice note for the first time. As they cremated her body, I resolved to give her soul some peace. I tracked down Afsana in Kolkata to reach her and in the process, learnt about you.

You must be wondering about the choice that I had mentioned in my first voice note—the choice that you need to make now. I'll tell you everything, but for that I'll have to meet you in person, Shanay. Now that you know the story of Raisa, Nirmaan and Afsana, we must meet to bring about the most important part of their story: the end.

If you've heard the voice notes till now then I hope you won't say no to meeting me, Shanay.

BOOK FIVE

CHAPTER 1

Afsana and Nirmaan,
Bengaluru/Kolkata/New Delhi, 2018.

The first things that Shanay noticed when he opened his eyes were a butterfly hair clip and a packet of Classic Ice Burst cigarettes on the bedside table. A blue lighter lay on top of the packet. None of these belonged to him.

The next moment, Afsana stepped out of the washroom, the edges of her towel tucked in around her bosom, her wet hair still dripping. She threw him a cursory glance as she dragged the only chair in the room towards the window. The chair, Shanay noticed, had a notebook on it. He turned on his bed to get a better view of her, watching as she lit a cigarette and blew a cloud of smoke through the open window and ensconced in the chair, picked the notebook up. A moment later, Afsana started scribbling something in it.

Ek waqt hota hai,
Ghonsla banane ka.

Ek waqt hota hai,
Ghonsle ke bahar ghoomke aane ka.
Unke beech ka waqt hota hai,
Ishq ki gehrai ko samjhne ka.

Ek waqt hota hai,
Nasamjhiyon ka.
Ek waqt hota hai,
Manmarziyon ka.
Unke beech ka waqt hota hai,
Khichaav ki chingari ko lagao ke aag mein badalne ka.

Ek waqt hota hai,
Aahankaar ko adhikaar samjhke jatane ka.
Ek waqt hota hai,
Khamoshi ko khamoshi se samjhne ka.
Unke beech ka waqt hota hai,
Rishtey ki umra bhadhane ka.

Ek waqt hota hai,
Apne saanson se uske jism ke panno ko palatne ka.
Ek waqt hota hai,
Akele mein usse mehsoos karke tadapne ka.
Unke beech ka waqt hota hai,
Apne aasmaan ko, uske zameen se milane ka.

Ek waqt hota hai,
Ehsaanson ko ubaalne ka.
Ek waqt hota hai,
Jazzbaaton ko halke aanch mein pakane ka.

Unke beech ka waqt hota hai,
Juda na hone ke iradon mein, niyat ka namak swad anusar milane ka.

एक वक़्त होता है,
घोंसला बनाने का।
एक वक़्त होता है,
घोंसले के बाहर घूम के आने का।
उनके बीच का वक़्त होता है,
इश्क की गहराई को समझने का।

एक वक़्त होता है,
नासमझियों का।
एक वक़्त होता है,
मनमर्जियों का।
उनके बीच का वक़्त होता है,
खिंचाव की चिंगारी को आग में बदलने का।

एक वक़्त होता है,
अहंकार को अधिकार समझ के जताने का।
एक वक़्त होता है,
खामोशी को खामोशी से समझने का।
उनके बीच का वक़्त होता है,
रिश्तों की उम्र बढ़ाने का।

एक वक़्त होता है,
अपनी साँसों से उसके जिस्म के पन्नों को पलटने का।
एक वक़्त होता है,
अकेले में उसे महसूस कर के तड़पने का।
उनके बीच का वक़्त होता है,
अपने आसमान से, उसकी ज़मीन को मिलाने का।

एक वक़्त होता है,
एहसासों को उबालने का।
एक वक़्त होता है,

जज़्बातों को हलकी आंच में पकाने का।
उनके बीच का वक़्त होता है,
जुदा न होने के इरादों में, नीयत का नमक स्वाद अनुसार मिलाने का।

She undersigned it *Tushara* before closing the notebook.

Shanay had been waiting for this day for some time now. Everything had gone exactly according to plan. Afsana had flown out of Kolkata on Friday night, telling her folks she had to shop for a few things from Delhi for her upcoming boutique. And that she would put up with a friend there. Shanay had picked her up from Kempegowda International Airport.

She hadn't changed at all since the last time he had met her, and yet he couldn't shake the feeling that it was a new Afsana he was meeting. Now that he had been fed a lot of information about her, the voice notes had stripped bare her past for him, even though she was unaware that he knew. Shanay had once asked her if she had ever had a boyfriend. Afsana had promptly denied it. But now the voice notes were with him. Shanay didn't want to believe the anonymous voice-notes girl, but the narrative had sounded too real to be made-up so a 'what if' lurked strongly in his mind. *What if the story were true?*

They had had a cosy dinner at Liquid in Hyatt, where they drove straight from the airport. Between the two, Shanay was more of a chatterbox, however, he had been at a loss for topics to discuss last night. He remembered Afsana picking up on this and his mind went back to the events of the previous night.

* * *

'You seem a little off tonight? Is everything all right?' Afsana asked, finishing her dinner.

'Just a little tired . . . too much work,' he prevaricated.

'I can understand. I'm going nuts setting up this small boutique, while you have an entire business to take care of,' she said.

After dinner, they drove to his spacious, fully furnished, rented apartment in DLF Westend Heights at Akshaya Nagar. She remembered that Shanay had told her many times that he detested living in pokey, claustrophobic cubbyholes. After they changed into their nightclothes, they chit-chatted for a bit and then it was time for them to go to bed. He half-expected Afsana to be somewhat hesitant about sharing his bed but she got into bed first and left space for him on it, clearly indicating that she expected him there. He switched off the lights and lay down beside her.

Shanay kissed her, tentatively at first. And the next thing they knew, they were naked, passionately kissing each other all over. Shanay felt as if he had a point to prove to her even though she had never asked him to. The fact that there had been a person in her life whom she hadn't mentioned to him could mean one of two things: one, that person no longer mattered or, two, her mind-space was way too intimate to be shared with another person. Feeling her nakedness between the sheets, his sexual instincts took over. Shanay sought not only his own pleasure, but also to erase whatever emotions and memories she had of her past. His soft kisses soon turned into feral passion. His mild touches became hard squeezes. All the sexual positions they tried were with him dominating her. Afsana didn't complain even once. She didn't even wince in pain when he entered her, or so Shanay thought. When they were done, they slept without cuddling. It was 3.45 a.m. when Shanay opened his eyes and it was then that he saw her step out of the attached bathroom.

'May I ask you something?' Shanay propped his head up with his elbow, watching Afsana blow a smoke ring into the air. She had stretched out her legs on to the windowsill.

'Sure,' she replied.

'Were you a virgin before tonight?' It came out easier than he thought it would.

Afsana smirked, 'Yes. Why do you ask?'

'Just like that,' he said.

'Is it because I didn't cry out?'

Shanay hung his head in an I'm-so-busted manner.

'It's not a necessity,' she said.

Shanay knew it wasn't. Nevertheless, he wanted to hear it from her. Their eyes met.

'Is there anything else you want to ask me?' Afsana asked.

'Do you want to tell me anything that I don't know about you?'

Afsana took her time before she asked, 'Can I ask you something, Shanay?'

'Sure. Anything.'

'Is it important for me to tell you everything about myself? If so, why?'

'We'll soon be life partners. I think it will help solidify our relationship if we know as much as we can about each other.'

'This "as much as we can" is actually "as much as we say", isn't it?'

'It is. And that's why I'm asking,' he sat up in bed.

'Do you think one can really tell another person everything about oneself overnight? Or even over several nights?'

'What other options do we have?'

'To discover as we go along. Let me be to you how you interpret me and not what I say about myself to you.' She stubbed out the cigarette butt on an ashtray and rose. Shanay watched her drop her towel to the floor wholly impervious to her nudity in his presence. She slipped on her panties, extracted a tee from her bag and put it on and joined him in bed.

'We should sleep now,' she said and turned to face the other way.

'Good night, Affu,' Shanay whispered. A second later she turned around.

'What did you call me?'

Shanay, completely immersed in his thoughts, hadn't realized the slip—he had never ever called her that. Raisa and Nirmaan had.

'Affu. Why?' Shanay asked cautiously.

'Nothing. Don't call me by that name. Please.' She turned away and slept. In the in-between silence, he felt unsure whether she hated the ones who called her that . . . *or loved them too much*. He wanted to shake her and wake her up, to ask if there had indeed been a Nirmaan and a Raisa in her life. But he was scared. What if there had been? What if there still were . . . ?

After a couple of hours, a sleepless Shanay sat up on the bed. He went over to her phone and drew the password pattern that he had inadvertently watched her draw when he had driven her from the airport. He quickly pulled up her contact list. There was no Nirmaan there. He checked her phone further: the photo gallery, her social media messages, emails. Nothing. Shanay sighed with relief. He looked at a sleeping Afsana. He wondered why the mere mention of 'Affu' had made her turn around.

CHAPTER 2

The month following Raisa's sudden disappearance, Nirmaan contacted every possible person he thought might know about her whereabouts, but all his efforts were in vain. He hadn't gone to the police because he knew that she wasn't missing or been abducted, she had just upped and left. She had deliberately left the lipstick mark on his chest indicating her absence to be one of choice rather than coercion. Why did she leave so suddenly? And why now— just when the sun was about to shine on them after all the shitty miles of life they had travelled together.

The lipstick mark of her lips . . . was it a clue, a confession or just a plain goodbye? It was during the third week that a new thought struck him: what if Raisa had gotten in touch with Afsana in Kolkata? A week later, Nirmaan received an email from Raisa. It had only three lines:

Reach out to Affu. Tell her I'm sorry. Don't try to find me.

Nirmaan immediately e-mailed back:

Where the hell are you? Get back ASAP. I'm waiting.

No response. Nirmaan tried to track the email's IP address. It said Kolkata. He immediately packed his bag and took the next flight to Kolkata, intending to visit the place from where they had both run away thirteen years ago.

He checked into The Park on Park Street and took a cab to the RBI Ultadanga quarters. The place, although it was actually the same when he left it, seemed to Nirmaan to have shrunk in size. Everything seemed to close in on him. Or was it the memories that came flooding back into his mind? He went to Raisa's flat, hoping against hope to find her parents there and a possible clue as to where she might be. He found neither her parents nor any clues. On the verge of taking the elevator down, he took it to the topmost floor instead. He ascended the stairs to the mezzanine floor below the terrace. It was here that Afsana had been provided sanctuary by Raisa. Life had been so simple then. He remembered the night he had smuggled her dinner. She had apologized to him for something but he couldn't quite remember what that something was. That was the first time he had noticed her in the only way that a young heart could notice another. With the tumult of past scenes hurtling through his mind, Nirmaan quickly walked out of the housing colony.

On a hunch he called the landline of his ancestral home from his mother's side in Chandannagar, about thirty-five kilometres from Kolkata. When he asked for his mother, he found that she was there. In the next four hours, he reached the place.

Mrs Bose couldn't believe her eyes. She embraced Nirmaan and nearly collapsed with sheer joy. Her son had

come back to her! Nirmaan learnt then that his father was
no more.

'After you left, he fell ill and never quite recovered. He
had a stroke. I begged him to find you, but he didn't. You
know how egoistic and rigid he was. Three years later, he
had a second stroke that he didn't survive,' Mrs Bose was
in tears.

She made all his favourite dishes for dinner, during
which he brought her up to speed with his journey through
life from the time he had left Kolkata.

'How is Raisa?' she asked.

'She is good. We work together,' he said, deliberately
not mentioning that she had left.

'I knew you two would get married. I always liked her,'
she said.

'Ma, Raisa and I aren't married,' he said. The look he
gave her discouraged her from probing further.

'Do you know where her parents are?' Nirmaan asked.

'The last I heard, and that was almost a decade ago,
they had shifted base to their hometown in Assam. I don't
know where to, exactly.'

'Hmm. I'm going to be in Kolkata for some time.
I'll be back. You'll stay with me from now onwards,' he
said. He hugged her, touched her feet for her blessings
and left.

Despite the lateness of the hour, his car had to nose
through traffic as it made its way towards his hotel. At a
traffic light in the outskirts of Kolkata he noticed a huge
billboard for a new boutique that was due to open the
following evening. Above the address there was a name:

Designer Afsana Agarwal's boutique, *Tushara*, opens
tomorrow at 5 p.m.

Tushara . . . the name nearly choked him.

That entire night and the following day he kept asking
himself whether he should visit her or not. Then Raisa's
email ricocheted in his mind. *Reach out to Affu.* He decided
to attend the boutique's inauguration.

There was not much hullaballoo outside the boutique
except for the entrance that was festooned with flowers
and had a red carpet reaching halfway across the street. He
stepped inside. There was a crowd inside—photographers,
family members and many guests. There was also the
man—her fiancé—whose photograph he had seen on
Facebook once. In the middle of them all he saw her.
Afsana Agarwal. He wished she had become only a name
to him. She wasn't. It was a name that harked him back to
a story that reminded him of what he could have had but
never did. What he once coveted but never got. What he
once was but now wasn't. He felt like he was walking into
a lucid dream where everything was real and at the same
time, unreal.

A warm smile touched his face. He had always longed
for this moment but never for the life of him thought that
he would actually see her again. Not even from a distance.
He wanted to shout out her name like a victorious war cry.
He wanted to run to her and hug her tight. He wanted to
convince her that the last thirteen years never happened.
But all he did was wipe the warm tears that misted his
vision. Seconds later, he walked towards her.

CHAPTER 3

Afsana had developed a passion for dress-designing during her graduation years in Europe. For the first six months, she had stubbornly refused to study when she realized she had been tricked. She had hoped that poor academic performance would lead her to be rusticated from the grad school, out of Europe, back to India, back to Kolkata, back to Nirmaan.

When she got an opportunity to call him up, she tried his number but couldn't get through. She called Raisa instead, and explained her predicament. Six months later, when she again got a chance to call Nirmaan, his mother told her that he had left home with Raisa. *Left home with Raisa . . .* how was she supposed to interpret that? Unhappy thoughts assailed her all the time. Was Nirmaan's love for her entirely fake? Afsana sank into clinical depression for a long time without talking about it to anyone. It was during this time that she started sketching dresses, in an effort to cheer herself up as well as a vent to her pent-up frustrations. Very soon designing clothes became a passion for her. She enrolled herself into a fashion design academy in Milan immediately after graduation. When she completed that, she joined a top designer in Paris as an intern first and then an assistant. Somehow or the other, she kept eluding her parents' desire to get her married for the longest time. It was only when her parents flew down to Milan and under an emotional breakdown insisted that it was now time for her to settle down that Afsana returned to Kolkata with a dream of opening her own boutique chain. No matter how successful she had or would become, she could never find the answer to that one question: why did Nirmaan leave her? Why didn't he wait for her?

The questions, repeatedly intruding her thoughts, seared her soul just a little bit more each time they made an appearance. Alongside the hurt and the betrayal she deeply felt, she ached for what might have been—a world in which she and Nirmaan were together. When she decided to name her boutique 'Tushara' she surprised herself more than anyone else. She realized, with a shock, that Nirmaan had become her soul's fragrance and that nobody else could impact her, ever, to the point of erasing or replacing this fragrance. She was quite certain that she would never meet him, much less have him for herself, but it appeared that everything she did would, consciously or subconsciously, reflect his essence residing within her, just as the name of her boutique had done.

Afsana agreed to marry Shanay for a very simple reason: he had asked the fewest questions. He seemed more interested in her present while the others had all seemed to want to view her through the prism of her past.

They weren't present from the beginning of her story, so how would they understand even if she narrated it to them? she often wondered. Would they be able to understand her better if she gave them a quick synopsis of her past? The explanation and the interpretation: did they go hand in hand in a relationship? If they did, the world would have had many more happy couples. The thing was, she knew, people always explained what they wanted to and people always interpreted or misinterpreted these explanations as they wished. What suffered was the truth of that relationship.

Afsana's and Shanay's families attended the inauguration, which turned out to be a fair success. Earlier that morning, T2 of the *Telegraph* had carried a one-page interview of hers and this brought a good number of women in to take advantage of opening-day discounts and goodies on offer along with a few people from the local press. The photographers made her pose with Shanay for some pictures, hopefully to be featured in the papers the following day. After the event was over, both their families waved their goodbyes and left. The press and the other guests also vanished.

Shanay was waiting for her in his car outside the boutique. He wanted to escort her to a new restaurant for dinner. The fact that he hadn't seen Nirmaan's name in her telephone's contact list gave him hope and enough reason to ignore the girl of the anonymous voice-notes, who had injected him with a curiosity for things that he was better off not knowing. Shanay honked a couple of times indicating his impatience.

'Ma'am, please go. I'll do the needful, tidy up and lock up before leaving,' assured one of Afsana's store assistants.

'All right. See you girls tomorrow,' Afsana said and was about to leave when she noticed another of her assistants giggling at the messages in their guest book.

'What's it?' she asked.

'In all we have 102 comments in the guest book. Only one is by a man. I don't know what he needed in a woman's boutique,' the girl laughed.

'Perhaps something for his wife, girlfriend, mother or sister,' Afsana said with an amused smile and turned to leave.

'His comment says "please call". Why would we call him?' the girl asked.

'That's fine. I'll call him tomorrow. What's his name?' she heard the other assistant ask.

'Umm, Nirmaan . . . Bose.'

Afsana stopped dead in her tracks at the boutique's threshold. She could see Shanay in his car outside. But she turned and asked, 'What did you say the name was?'

CHAPTER 4

At the airport, on his way back to Bengaluru, Shanay's hug felt longer than usual, like he was unwilling to let her go. Afsana had had a similar feeling when he had hugged her on her way back from Bengaluru earlier. Ever since her visit to Bengaluru, each of his embraces had been getting tighter and a few seconds longer than the previous one. Something told her it wasn't out of true love; as far as she could make out, he had fallen head over heels for her the moment they'd met but she put that down to an infatuation, a physical attraction. If only love happened that spontaneously!

'I'll call as soon as I reach home,' Shanay promised.

'Sure,' she replied and he gave her a quick peck on her cheek before striding off into the airport. As soon as Shanay disappeared from sight, Afsana got back into her car and drove a short distance out of the airport premises and parked on the side of the road. She wasn't able to forget the voice. Although she couldn't identify Nirmaan's voice after thirteen years, she was sure it was him. She took out a diary and opened it to the last page

where she had scribbled something last night after she'd
called the number.

Dard ke bichone mein,
Kal raat hum saath soye the.
Ajeeb pagalpan tha humari saanso mein,
Ek dusre se lipatkar roye the.

Apne rooh ki chadar se humne,
Janmo ke daag, bari-bari, dhoye the.
Tez bukhar tha humari aankhon mein,
Kal raat hum behosh se khoye the.

Waqt ki ganga mein jo na baha sake, uss raakh ko,
Humne kal chand phoonkon se udaye the.
Ek unkahi kahaani thi humari hassi mein,
Har shikve ko humne gehri saanso ke kafan chadaye the.

Barson se bilakhte ghavon ko,
Humne siskiyon ki lori se sulaye the.
Ek darwani awaaz thi humare sparsh mein,
Andar ke khwayishon ko pehredaar banake jagaye the.

Shikayetein bohot se thi, lekin,
Kal raat jism ke har kone mein,
Humne hothon se sulah ki mashallein jalayin thi.
Hume yaadon ke mandap mein saath dekh,
Dono ke maazi baraat mein aaye the.

Dard ke bichone mein,

Hum subah tak jage the.
Pehli baar khud se nahi,
Hum duniya se dur bhaage the.

दर्द के बिछोने में,
हम कल रात सोए थे।
अजीब पागलपन था हमारी साँसों में,
एक-दूसरे से लिपट कर सोए थे।

अपनी रूह की चादर से हमने,
जन्मों के दाग़ बारी-बारी धोए थे,
तेज़ बुखार था हमारी आंखों में,
कल रात हम बेहोश-से खोए थे।

वक़्त की गंगा में जो न बहा सके, उस राख को,
हमने कल चाँद फूंकों से उड़ाए थे,
एक अनकही कहानी थी हमारी हँसी में,
हर शिकवे को हमने गहरी साँसों के कफन चढ़ाये थे।

बरसों से बिलखते घावों को,
हमने सिसकियों की लोरी से सुलाया था,
एक डरावनी आवाज़ थी हमारे स्पर्श में,
अंदर की ख़्वाहिशों को पहरेदार बना के जगाया था।

शिकायतें बहुत-सी थीं लेकिन,
कल रात जिस्म के हर कोने में,
हमने होठों से सुलह की मशालें जलाई थीं,
हमें यादों के मंडप में साथ देख,
दोनों के माज़ी बारात में आए थे।

दर्द के बिछोने में,
हम सुबह तक जागे थे।
पहली बार खुद से नहीं,
हम दुनिया से दूर भागे थे।

As soon as her assistant told her the name of their sole male guest in the boutique, Afsana felt a thrill of anticipation run through her. Did Nirmaan attend the launch? Why hadn't she seen him? Had he changed so much that she couldn't recognize him? She borrowed the assistant's telephone and dialled the number.

She heard a man say 'hello' a few times. Then a silence before he said softly, 'Affu?'

She immediately hung up. Only she knew the effort it had taken to control her tears. Afsana had blocked and erased the number in the assistant's phone before leaving the store but not before memorizing it.

Now, sitting in her car a little outside the airport, Afsana took a deep breath and called the number again. It rang. With every ring she could feel her heart thump harder. Suddenly a voice said, 'Hello?' No response from Afsana. In that moment her mind flashed back to the time when she had prank-called his landline all those years ago. That was different. This was—

'Hello?' he repeated.

'Hi,' she said softly, doing her utmost to sound normal.

'Affu?'

'Afsana speaking.'

There was a pause.

'Hi, Afsana.'

It seemed to her that Nirmaan suddenly had nothing to say.

'What is it?' she asked.

'I need to meet you. Once,' he replied. The last word came out after a lot of hesitation.

'But I don't,' she said and hung up. She knew he wouldn't call back. He didn't.

It was only in the evening that she understood it wasn't she, but her ego talking. She had asked him to wait. *To wait, damn it!* She would have returned from Europe for her first summer vacation anyway. And she could have sworn on her life that she would have never gone back, even if it had meant that she would have had to elope with him. The way Nirmaan did with Raisa. All through that day she did her best to focus on her work, but every alternate minute an incident from the past came alive in her mind. In these thirteen intermediate years, she had convinced herself that she had moved on, but all it took was one telephone call to disillusion her. She was still stuck in her past. The moving-on part was an illusion. Unable to bear any more, Afsana called him that night. This time he answered the call, but waited for her to speak.

'Where do you want to meet me?' she asked.

'I'm staying at The Park.'

'I can't meet you in a hotel,' she was curt.

'Then wherever you say,' he said.

'I am in South City. Downstairs, in an hour,' she said and hung up. The next second she called him again.

'One second extra and I'm not waiting for you,' Afsana snapped spitefully and cut the call again before he could reply.

She could see the South City entrance from her flat's window. Minutes later, she saw a cab drop a man by the gate. He simply stood there looking around. A moment later, she received a message: *I'm here*. She saw the message but didn't respond. She was about to walk down, when she stopped and checked herself in the mirror. She hurried out with a quick step.

Afsana saw him smoking, standing by the entrance. His back was to her. She went and stood beside him. Quietly. Nirmaan exhaled and casually turned around. As the smoke dispersed, he saw her. He immediately dropped the cigarette, grinding the stub with the heel of his shoe. She was looking at him in a way that made him acutely uncomfortable.

'Hi,' he said. She hadn't changed much. The same rebellious instinct in her eyes. The same don't-fuck-with-me attitude on her face. The same . . . she was wearing a nose pin. He wanted to compliment her for that but he didn't.

As a response to his 'hi', her look turned more intense. Nirmaan understood she wasn't there to converse. He didn't know where to begin. Should he start explaining why Raisa and he ran away together? How much he had wanted to wait but things had gone awry in his life as well?

'Did Raisa, by any chance, contact you recently?' Nirmaan asked.

'No. She didn't try to contact me. Not in the last thirteen years. Nor did anyone else,' if the first part of her speech was laced with spite, the last part had pure venom.

'I—' he began but was cut short.

'Anything else?' she asked. Nirmaan's eyes remained on hers for seconds. Then he shook his head, 'no.'

'I'm about to get married. It's better that we don't meet or contact each other again,' she said and stalked off. As the lift soundlessly rose towards her floor, Afsana pressed the stop button between floors. She slowly sank into the middle of the elevator and wept. She could have been rude to the entire world, but never with Nirmaan. But life had made her do that.

That night, when Shanay was returning home in Bengaluru, he received a picture on his WhatsApp. It was from Lavisha, the girl who had sent him all the voice notes. She had been desperately trying to reach him ever since he returned to Bengaluru but he hadn't responded. The picture was of Afsana and Nirmaan by her apartment. The caption beneath the picture read: *I think you won't ignore me now.*

CHAPTER 5

Shanay stared at the picture. It was Afsana and Nirmaan standing face to face. He couldn't be sure how recent the image was, or where they were exactly. It looked like a dark place, on a sidewalk or beside a road. He zoomed in to try and see the detail, in a vain attempt to read all the hidden truths behind their expressions and body language. He ignored Afsana's call that night. He drank more than usual and then called Lavisha on the number she had used to send the photograph. Unlike the number from which the voice notes came, this matured into a call instantly.

'Thanks for calling, Shanay,' Lavisha said.

'Who clicked that picture? Where was it and when was it?' he immediately asked.

'I clicked it. I'm in Kolkata right now. It's right outside Afsana's housing society. They met earlier tonight.'

'Why did you send it to me?' he asked, trying not to slur.

'I'm sorry. I know it wasn't the right thing to do, but I'm helpless.'

'Why are *you* helpless? If anyone should be helpless, it should be me. I love Afsana.'

She could feel the emotional embers in his voice.

'I'm helpless because I don't have options. You do, Shanay,' she said.

'Oh really? What are my options?'

'Leave Afsana. She isn't for you. I know you're supposed to marry her, but trust me whatever she or even Nirmaan says now, they will never love anyone else, ever. Even if they end up living with someone else, they won't belong to them. Staying together doesn't always mean that the other person is into you, does it? Right now they may not realize this themselves, but soon they'll know that they are shards of flint that will always yield a spark when in proximity. And this isn't a spark of lust or physical communion. This spark will lead to a raging conflagration that could incinerate the world, but their love will be forged into something stronger, for it is genuine. It is natural. And when something is natural, one doesn't feel guilty about it. One doesn't think in terms of wrong and right. When there's no wrong and right about something, then there's no decision to be made. It's just there—a kind of love that you and I won't be able to fathom easily because we'll never experience it. That's why, like everyone else, we will only judge it, without understanding even a fraction of what's between Afsana and Nirmaan. There will always be a difference between you and Nirmaan from her perspective. Nirmaan will always love her without demanding or expecting anything. But you'll love Afsana until she provides you with whatever you are seeking. If it doesn't make sense now, one day it will. You also have the option to make sure it isn't too late by then.'

Lavisha realized she had been talking for some time and added, 'Do you understand what I'm saying? Are you there, Shanay?'

There was a stark silence for almost a minute, then Shanay snarled, 'Go to hell!' and hung up. Next, he called his mother.

'Hello, beta, what's up? Why are you calling so late?' his mother sounded worried. It was rare for Shanay to call after eleven o'clock at night.

'Mumma, let's get done with this marriage this very weekend,' he said. He had never sounded so desperate about anything.

CHAPTER 6

The last time the Agarwals and the Bansals had met for a family dinner was when Afsana and Shanay's marriage had been fixed. It was in one of the restaurants in JW Marriot. When Mrs Bansal invited Mrs Agarwal, along with her family for dinner, the latter was a little suspicious of the motive. The Agarwal family was further surprised, as was Afsana, to see Shanay at home.

'You never told me,' she whispered to him as she hugged him. Shanay flashed a tight smile and thought, *like you tell me everything*.

'It's good to surprise people sometimes,' he shrugged. Afsana's alarm bells tolled.

After some pleasantries, the Agarwals were ushered into the dining room. It looked like the proverbial big, fat family dinner. Right in the middle of tucking in, Mr Bansal said, 'There is something we want to share with you.'

Everyone felt the joyous energy give way to a nervous one.

'There's nothing to worry about,' Mr Bansal assured everybody and smilingly continued, 'Shanay wants the

wedding date to be brought forward so the youngsters can
marry a little earlier.'

There was a sigh of relief.

'That's not a problem at all,' Mr Agarwal said.

'When do you want to get married, beta?' Mrs Agarwal
asked.

'He wants it to happen this weekend,' Mrs Bansal
replied on her son's behalf. Shanay glanced at Afsana and
noticed her keying something into her phone. *Was she
relaying the info to Nirmaan*, Shanay wondered.

'Let me consult our panditji and get back to you first
thing tomorrow morning,' Mr Agarwal responded.

'Sure. I hope you don't have any problem, Afsana beta?'
Mr Bansal said, looking at her.

'Certainly not,' she smiled.

Everyone seemed happy except Shanay. He was sure
that she would have had a problem with this sudden
urgency. He had hastened their wedding date thinking it
would be the right way to strike back after she squashed his
ego by meeting Nirmaan on the sly. His phone buzzed with a
message. It was from Afsana. It read: *let's go for coffee after this*.

Sure, he responded via message. In his mind, Shanay
was smiling. After all, the news did affect her.

The two went to a café close to Afsana's place. She
had been living alone in this apartment for the last two
years. It had started off as her work studio, but eventually
became her abode as well. With work as her cushion,
loneliness seemed cosy. Monday to Friday she was at her
three-bedroom apartment in South City but she spent her
weekends in her house at Salt Lake.

'I love the coffee here,' Shanay said.

'Why didn't you tell me?' she asked, direct as ever.

'Tell you what?'

Afsana studied his face for a few seconds and then asked, 'Are you marrying yourself?' She knew she was being unpardonably rude, but she didn't want to go about it in any other way.

'What?'

'If you were marrying yourself then you have the right to take a decision alone. Since you and I both are getting married, don't you think that before anything goes to our parents, you should bounce it off me once?'

The waiter came to them and Shanay ordered.

'I'll have an Irish coffee. And you?'

'Black coffee without sugar.'

Shanay glanced at the waiter. He noted their order and left. There was only one other couple in the café. An English song was playing softly in the background.

'Do you think you've told me everything?' Shanay said, looking piercingly at her. He wanted her to interpret the look as an accusation.

'I've told you whatever you should know about me,' Afsana said without giving out an inkling of the whirlpool beneath the placid surface.

'And who decides what this "whatever" is? You?' Shanay leaned back a little.

'Can you please tell me straight up what's on your mind? This is the first time I'm seeing you beating around the bush,' Afsana said leaning forward truculently.

Shanay leaned forward as well and asked, 'All right, let's get to the point. Who is Nirmaan Bose?'

Afsana wasn't ready for this. She changed her posture, wondering, *I wish I could tell you who he is and what he means to me.* His steady gaze never left her face. She knew that the more the time she took to respond, the wider the window of opportunity she was giving him to jump to whatever conclusion he wished to.

'You seem to be lost,' Shanay accused, with a condescending smirk. He brought out his phone and tapped on a picture in his photo gallery. He turned his phone to her and said, 'The name didn't ring a bell, it seems. Hopefully this will.' Her picture with Nirmaan was in front of her. She took his phone in her hand with a look of disbelief.

'How did you get this?' she asked, still staring at the picture.

'That's not the point.'

'How did you get this Shanay?' she sounded more insistent this time.

'Are you having an affair?' Shanay asked, his teeth clenched on the last word.

'Are you following me?' she charged.

'Now who is beating around the bush?'

The coffee arrived. Shanay took a sip. Afsana didn't care to even touch the black coffee.

'I can tell you the truth but I don't think you will accept it as the truth,' she riposted.

Shanay chortled derogatorily.

'Nirmaan approached me,' she began, 'after more than a decade. He wanted to know if a common friend of ours had contacted me. He thought I would know something about her. That's why we met. For less than two minutes.'

Shanay looked at her for some time and said, 'You're right. I don't think that's the truth.'

'First answer me, how did you get this picture?'

'Your friend Raisa Barua is dead,' Shanay said bluntly, sipping more of his Irish coffee.

Afsana frowned looking at him. Something about his body language told her he wasn't bluffing.

'Are you going to tell me how you know all this?'

'A friend of Raisa—Lavisha—told me,' Shanay took a moment to tell her whatever the voice notes told him about Raisa's death.

'I need to leave,' Afsana said.

'Are you going to meet Nirmaan now?' he asked reaching for her hand.

She turned to glare at his grasp and said, 'Let go of my hand, Shanay.' He did. Afsana left the café. She went straight home, but couldn't sleep the whole night. Raisa's face kept haunting her. In the wee hours, she couldn't hold back her tears any more. She repeatedly told herself that Raisa couldn't be dead. There had to be some confusion. At around eight o'clock, the next morning, she called Nirmaan. He answered almost instantly.

'I want to meet you,' she said.

There was silence. Then he said, 'Where do you want me to come?'

'Ultadanga footbridge.' *Like old times*, she wanted to add.

Silence.

'Okay.' *Like old times?* he couldn't ask.

CHAPTER 7

Afsana was driving to the same Ultadanga footbridge where an important part of her past had once played out. It was also the place where many a time she had parked her car after she returned to Kolkata from Milan to simply stare at the bridge. Every time she could see two teenagers sitting by the stairs, wholly in love with the other. And then . . .

This was the place she'd met Nirmaan for the last time before she left for Europe years ago. She didn't know why she decided to meet at the footbridge. Perhaps in a corner of her heart she was dying to relive her past and this was the only way she could. As she parked her car by the stairs, she could see Nirmaan standing atop the bridge. He was pacing up and down. Afsana left her parking lights on, got out of her car and took the stairs. She was by his side in a matter of minutes. She had tried to rehearse her speech to break the news to him as gently as possible, but a great big lump formed in her throat when she stood before him.

'Do you know any Lavisha?' she asked abruptly.

Nirmaan repeated the name under his breath, as if lost in his thoughts, and then replied, 'I know a Lavisha who used to work with us. An employee really.'

'Us?'

'Raisa and me. We have a start-up running,' he explained.

Raisa and Nirmaan have created something together, Afsana swallowed the lump.

'How do you know Lavisha?' he asked.

'It doesn't matter,' it was clear to her that Nirmaan wasn't aware of Raisa's death. *If at all that were true*, Afsana thought. *And if Lavisha knew Nirmaan, why didn't she call him instead of reaching out to Shanay?*

Afsana was about to say something when she heard a traffic policeman yell, '*Kaar gadi eita?*' He was standing beside her car.

'Is that—' Nirmaan began and stopped seeing her nod.

'Mind if we drive around and talk? I'll drop you off at The Park,' she offered.

'Sure.'

She made her way to the stairs and began descending to the sidewalk. By then she had decided not to tell Nirmaan anything without crosschecking the truth herself.

She messaged Shanay: *give me Lavisha's number*.

As Nirmaan sat beside her in the car, Shanay's response came: *forget it*.

Afsana felt frustrated. She asked Nirmaan, 'Do you have Lavisha's number?'

'I should, but what of it? How come you even know her?' he asked.

'I think you should talk to her as soon as possible,' Afsana replied. Nirmaan gave her an intent look, looked for Lavisha's number on his telephone contact list and called it. He put the call on speaker. They both listened as the ring went through, but nobody answered.

'She left the job almost a year ago. Or maybe more. I don't know,' he shrugged.

'Please, just talk to her about Raisa once,' Afsana said. They drove quietly. By a traffic signal Nirmaan saw another hoarding for Tushara Boutique.

'I'm glad you named it Tushara,' he said with a tight smile. As a response she extracted a packet of Ice Bursts from her bag and lit one cigarette. She took a long drag and exhaled outside the window. Nirmaan didn't react. This wasn't the first time that he had seen her smoke, the last time was when she and Raisa had been blowing a cloud together.

Afsana chain-smoked three cigarettes and they sat pretending to be oblivious of the other's presence. And then suddenly Afsana asked, 'Are you and Raisa married?' She had intended to ask something else altogether and couldn't really believe the question that she had blurted.

'No. We aren't,' he replied after a thoughtful pause.

'Why? You guys eloped, right?'

'We did run away, but not to get married. I never loved Raisa that way.'

'Which way?'

'The way I love . . .' Nirmaan sighed and lamely finished, 'someone.'

'What happened between you and that someone?' she asked inexorably. Nirmaan was silent. She kept driving.

He told her that he was staying at The Park but he had a business meeting at Novotel.

As they approached the hotel's entrance, Nirmaan replied, 'Life. Life happened between me and that someone.' He noticed Afsana turn away. A valet came and opened the passenger side door.

'Are you all right?' Nirmaan asked sensing her body was shaking. She turned to look at him.

'Don't I look absolutely all right?' she asked, hot tears coursing down her face. Nirmaan got out. She drove off before he could say anything more.

Nirmaan was about to summon an Uber after his business meeting when he saw Afsana's car drive up into the portico.

'Get in,' she commanded, he obeyed. She drove off. She was about to light a cigarette when she saw Nirmaan lighting another. It was her old brand. She kept her cigarette back and said, 'May I?'

'Sure?' He offered her one from the cigarette box in his hand. She took and lit it.

'When did you start smoking?' she asked.

'Some time back,' Nirmaan said and thought, *just don't ask me why it did it.*

'Why did you guys run away?' she asked.

'How much do you know?' he asked.

'I know nothing,' she replied. Nirmaan couldn't guess her emotions.

'I couldn't sit for my IIT entrance exam. I was kidnapped and held prisoner for the duration of the examination. I still don't know who did it, but my hunch says it was Tarun.'

Afsana slowed down and parked the car.

'Tarun? You mean that Tarun?'

Nirmaan nodded, 'The one and only.' Afsana felt that she was to blame for that terrible experience that Nirmaan must have had. Tarun, after all, was connected to her, not him.

'And then?' she asked.

Nirmaan took a while to give her a synopsis of the last thirteen years. From Raisa's illegal abortion to their staying together, her amazing cooking skills and their business model . . . everything. He sighed in the end, adding, 'I looked for you on Orkut and Facebook all the time.'

That was when I was deeply depressed and had cut myself off from everything, Afsana thought. But what she couldn't understand was: *Raisa and Nirmaan lived together for so many years but neither proposed to the other? I can understand Nirmaan might have been in love with me, but what about Raisa?* she thought.

'Didn't Raisa have a boyfriend or—'

'Not that I know of.'

That's weird. Afsana dropped Nirmaan at The Park. He didn't ask if they were meeting again and neither did she.

'Talk to Lavisha and let me know,' she said before leaving him at the entrance of the hotel.

Afsana didn't go to work that day. She remained in her flat trying to sort through her utterly confused mind. How could Raisa not have fallen in love with Nirmaan in all these years? Something did not add up.

It was also the day when her bestie from her graduation days, Dipannita, was supposed to come to Kolkata from Singapore with her husband for a week. They decided to meet up at 10 Downing Street later that night for a drink.

After congratulating Afsana on her business venture and raising a toast to it, Dipannita realized that her bestie didn't look her usual self.

'What's up, hun? Is it just a case of bridal nerves? I felt exactly the same, d'you remember?' Dipannita said chuckling. Afsana sat still, like she hadn't heard her. She started murmuring some lines in Hindi.

Mera dil ek chota sa gaanv hai.
Log kam hain yahan.
Roshni bhi nahi, na hi bijli.
Lekin jab tum milne aaye,
Barson ki raat mein bhi,
Sab kuch subah sa saaf dikhne laga.

मेरा दिल एक छोटा सा गाँव हैं।
लोग कम हैं यहाँ।
रौशनी भी नहीं, न ही बिजली।
लेकिन जब तुम मिलने आए,
बरसों की रात में भी,
सब कुछ सुबह सा साफ़ दिखने लगा।

Dipannita looked at her bestie with wide eyes for a moment. 'Hey, what's up, darling?' she asked, gripping her friend's cold hands.

'I met Nirmaan,' Afsana replied.

Dipannita's eyes grew even wider, 'You mean Nirmaan Bose?'

Afsana nodded, gulping down her Jack Daniel's. Dipannita knew who and what Nirmaan Bose meant to her. There were times when she badly wanted to meet him after hearing so much about him. She knew that Afsana wasn't an easy girl to impress, and if she thought highly of someone—especially a man—then he had to be really special. Exceptional. And rare.

'Where did you meet him? On Facebook or for real?' Dipannita's excitement was palpable.

Afsana paused for a bit before she started talking. 'Even now I feel like I hallucinated both our meetings.'

'You met him twice already? And you're telling me this now? I want the details. Come on now,' Dipannita pushed her glass aside and looked at her friend expectantly.

Afsana absentmindedly moved her whiskey glass around in circles, gazing unseeingly at it as she said, 'He said he doesn't love Raisa the way he loves someone else.'

'Is this someone . . . you?'

Afsana looked up. Tears welled up in her eyes as she answered, 'All these years' she said, 'I thought things were dead between us. I really believed time would bury us both and whatever we once shared. But after meeting him again, I realized that what two persons create for each other in the privacy of their hearts can never die. We may become egoistic or stubborn or even indifferent and look the other way but that creation is a permanent edifice. With time it becomes such an intrinsic part of our existence that to demolish it we'll have to destroy ourselves too. To be honest, there have been times when I envied Raisa. I always asked myself why I couldn't have been the one with whom he eloped. You know, I just got to know that he and Raisa have a start-up together. And I wondered why couldn't I be the one with whom he created something so strong that nothing could challenge it? Why couldn't I have been the one with whom he could be both domestic and wild?'

The pub reverberated with loud music, but there was silence between the two women.

'Does he know you're getting married soon?' Dipannita asked.

'He does. I broke the news to him baldly the first time I met him. But then I wondered who it was that I was kidding. Can I really be taken by anyone other than Nirmaan? What does "being taken" or "become someone else's" mean anyway? Can any ritual, oath or social ceremony rinse a heart of memories? For nearly fifteen years I've both loved and hated Nirmaan. I loved him for what he is and what he made me experience and hated him for not waiting for me. It was difficult to accept, but with time I did accept it. And one of my ways of acceptance was to surrender to the choices of my parents in life-defining matters. Just consider this, Dippi: a man staying with a woman for thirteen years, sharing a room, sharing all the small incidents of life and all his experiences with her, still doesn't give her the space that he reserved for me. For me!'

Dipannita swallowed a lump. Although it sounded too perfect to be true, she knew that if Afsana didn't believe in it, she wouldn't have shared it with her.

'Today, after Nirmaan implied that he is still in love with me, I'm yearning for him more than ever. He was committed to "us" even when we weren't in a relationship for more than a decade. Even when there wasn't a remote possibility of that "us".'

Dipannita sipped her drink and noticed Afsana had an amused smile on her face. 'It's a funny thing really, but Nirmaan effectively destroyed my capability to love someone. The man I'm about to wed, I don't love him. Marriage is just a social and legal contract. And the love that stems out of such an arrangement is more often than not a convenience of and for the contract.'

'What are you saying?' Dipannita sounded scandalized.

'Rare men give the rarest kind of pain and the rarest kind of pleasure. When you love a rare man like that you are proud to be a woman in a way that is also rare. My impulse, right now, is to be with Nirmaan but my social impulse tells me never to meet him again,' Afsana said.

'I think you shouldn't. There's too much risk involved. Your parents, Shanay, his parents. And Shanay is a good man as well. He'll keep you happy.'

'I don't want to be happy. I want to be at peace every day for the rest of my life. And I never said Shanay is a bad guy.'

Neither said anything. They finished their drinks and went out for a smoke. Just then Shanay telephoned and she answered after two rings.

'Your dad just called,' he said without preamble. 'Your family's panditji has said that the best date that he could zero in for our marriage is a month from now. I'm okay with that.'

'Okay.' Although her head was reeling with the alcohol, she did her best to focus.

'However, you'll have to stay with me in Bengaluru until we get married,' Shanay said.

Afsana was silent and he added, 'I've had a talk with our parents. They are okay with it. So pack up. We will fly tomorrow evening together.'

He hung up. Afsana stared blankly at the phone screen and then chuckled.

'What's up now?' Dipannita asked.

'You know, Shanay always said that he never could understand me.'

'So?'

'I have a feeling he soon will.'

Afsana took a long drag from her cigarette.

CHAPTER 8

'I'm parked outside your house. Come out,' Afsana said on the telephone and hung up before he could respond. Shanay drew back the curtain of his room and peered out but couldn't see any car. He walked into the street in his pyjamas and noticed her car at the far end of the lane.

'What's happened?' he asked as he climbed in, then quickly added, 'Are you drunk?'

'Not so much that I can't talk,' she replied.

'We can talk tomorrow. I'll drive you home,' he said. Shanay was about to get out when she reached for his hand.

'I've connected the dots,' she said, smiling sarcastically.

'What do you mean?'

'The prolonged hugs of late, that urgent fuck when I was in Bangalore, the wish to get married immediately and now to cohabit until we are married so I don't stay in Kolkata. All this because you're a *fattu* and your ego has been squashed. You're like any other man; scared of competition, childishly insecure and suspicious of everybody to the point of being paranoid.'

Shanay felt deeply embarrassed because Afsana had read him like a book. He gave her a steely look and said nastily, 'Yeah, sure. So when your partner has a secret rendezvous with her ex- mere months before your wedding, you're expected to celebrate with a cocktail party, right?'

Afsana returned the steely look as she replied, 'If you don't know it yet, his name is Nirmaan Bose. Who told you that he's my ex-? True, he was there in my life before. But I met him again after more than a decade. I met him this morning again and realized that he is my present as well. Moreover, the fact that you thought keeping me away from Nirmaan until our wedding day will sunder us forever tells me that your definition of marriage is moral captivity. It's like, let her become my wife, I'll fuck her as many times as I want to and then, even if she has an affair, I won't care. Or is it like, marriage will make her too guilt-ridden to ever cross the "line"? If it's the latter, then you don't know even one per cent of Afsana Agarwal yet.'

Shanay's awkwardness gave way to anger. He took his time to speak.

'Look, Afsana, let's act like adults here and be done with it. Our marriage is fixed. I have the right to know whatever it is that's brewing between you and this guy.'

Afsana chuckled softly, 'Oh okay. So, you have the right! But do you have the sensibility to understand what it is that has been forever there and will always be between me and "this guy"?'

'Stop it. Just tell me whatever it is that I should know. This is your last chance. I'll forgive you.'

'Forgive me?' she swivelled around to face him now. 'For what?' This was the loudest he had ever heard her speak.

'For keeping me in the dark, damn it!' he hissed.

'I didn't keep you in any darkness.'

'Really? I'm your husband-to-be, for god's sake. You kept your past, the past that you're now flagrantly flaunting as your present, a secret from me.'

A smirk appeared on Afsana's face as she said, 'My dear husband-to-be, my past is none of your business.'

This new, audacious side of Afsana needled the chauvinist inside him.

'So, you're saying that if you were to realize that I've been having an extra-marital affair behind your back, it wouldn't have bothered you?'

'I'm saying I'm not having an affair. Not yet.'

'You have nothing to prove that. But I've got a picture that shows you meeting him outside your building at night. Who knows where you two were before that picture was taken? Perhaps you guys had just emerged from your cosy apartment.'

Afsana was ominously quiet. A part of her was glad that they were having this conversation now. It wasn't just a conversation, it was turning into an eye-opener. By the end of it, she knew that both would know each other's cores.

'All I know is that you're my fiancée and he is the other man who is out to destroy my life by trying to steal you from me emotionally,' Shanay darted a fierce look at her and added, 'and who knows, perhaps physically as well.'

'Shut up, Shanay!' Afsana snapped as she opened the car's door and stepped out. It was getting suffocating inside.

'Really?' He got out as well. Looking at her over the hood of the car, he said, 'Guess what, I won't shut up because I'm not the sort to hand over his fiancée on a platter to her lover.'

'I don't want to discuss Nirmaan and me any more.'

'Now that you've brought this conversation to this point, tell me one more thing.'

'What?'

'Tell me, has Nirmaan ever fucked you?'

Afsana fumed at the man she was supposed to marry. At that moment he looked no different from any random stranger on the street.

'Your silence tells me—' Shanay began, but was interrupted by Afsana.

'Yes. Nirmaan has fucked me,' she retorted and watched Shanay's face drain of all colour.

'You're right. That night we didn't just meet outside my building. He visited my flat.' She knew the lies would only pile up once they started, but she also knew that the truth had been discarded as a lie as well.

'Not once,' she was on a roll now, 'not twice, but he fucked me so many times that every inch of my skin has been branded with the scent of his touch. And it doesn't matter how much you, my husband-to-be, possess me, I'll never smell of you. And no amount of your sanctimony will rinse me of Nirmaan.'

'You're saying this to humiliate me, right? Answer me!' Shanay walked across and shook her roughly by the shoulder. She stood unresisting.

'Tell me,' he repeated, 'that you're kidding.'

Afsana laughed mirthlessly, 'I told you exactly what you wanted to hear, and now you want me to take back my words. Tsk, tsk, tsk.'

She shook herself free from his hold and retorted, 'Nobody can fuck me better than Nirmaan. And do you know why? That's because I *love* him. I always have and always will. It's the kind of love that I'm sure you've never felt or come across, and seriously doubt that you ever will with such shitty thoughts.'

Shanay let go of her like he had been scalded.

'You are such a—'

'Bitch? Slut? Whore? Go on, say it. Say it, Shanay Bansal, that your fiancée, the woman you're going to marry, is a slut. Just say it! That's the most that your sort of men can stretch their bloated brains to when it comes to their women. But do you know why women like me are sluts? It's because there's a dearth of stalwarts like Nirmaan who can stand beside a woman and never use any flimsy excuse to ask for her body in return. Would you consider renouncing everything you always craved and become something else for me or for anybody? Like fuck you can. You can't even suspend your insecurity and trust me. You can't see the woman beyond my body.'

In the silence of the night, Shanay could hear his heartbeat clearly. Afsana got back into her car and started the ignition. Popping her head out of the window she hollered, 'You said Nirmaan is the other man. You're wrong. The other man is you. I was married to Nirmaan long before my relationship with him even began. Our marriage wasn't forged in fire, didn't need the chanting of mantras or witnesses; it had two simple things: a yes from me and a yes from him. And we stuck together forever. That's a marriage, Shanay. What you and I are supposed to have would only be a social licence to cohabit. A farcical attempt by the nomads to tame their savagery. So yeah, so-called husband-to-be of mine, you are the fuckin' other man in my life. And it always will be so even if I apply vermilion on my forehead in your name for the rest of my life.' Afsana drove off.

Shanay stood still for a while and then turned away and gingerly made his way to the street lamp. He sat there weeping.

The next day Afsana went to her boutique. She felt the urge to message Nirmaan, but didn't. Her mother told her that Shanay had extended his stay in Kolkata until the wedding. That night Afsana was emotionally blackmailed by her mother to join her along with the women of the Bansal house for a dinner where they wanted to discuss certain marriage details. As the families met to dine at Marco Polo, in Park Street, Afsana received a message on her phone from Nirmaan:

Can we please talk?

She responded: *sab baithe hain* [everyone's sitting around].

Nirmaan read the message and replied: *sorry. I'll wait.*

You sure?

Yes.

As Nirmaan wrote the 'yes' and sent it, a teardrop fell on his phone. He stood up and went to the washroom in his hotel room. He looked at the reflection in the mirror and said intently, 'Don't you get it, Nirmaan? You are an illegitimate part of her life. And illegitimate people can never be anyone's priority. Just understand this, Nirmaan, doesn't matter how genuinely you love Afsana, you are an illegitimate part.' He kept repeating the last part to his reflection with bloodshot eyes and then suddenly punched the mirror. An image popped up on his phone at that time. As asked by him, one of the nursing home personnel had sent him an image of a death certificate in the name of Raisa Barua.

CHAPTER 9

Post the dinner, instead of going to her flat, Afsana drove as fast as she could to The Park. Nirmaan wasn't taking her calls and she sensed something bad had happened. She asked the girl at the reception to call him. After three attempts, and Afsana also rang his mobile phone, he responded to the room telephone. Afsana rode the elevator up to his room.

As she stepped out of the lift, she spotted his door immediately. It was ajar. Afsana pushed it open and entered a darkened room. As she switched on the light, the first thing she noticed were cigarette butts littering the floor. A laptop was on the bed. The shades were drawn across the window framing a faint view of the Kolkata city line outside. A dishevelled Nirmaan was sitting on the floor by the bed. He held a lighter that he clicked on and off absently. His right hand was blood smeared. He looked up at Afsana.

'Please shut the door,' he said softly. Afsana complied, saying, 'What happened to your hand?'

She came close and knelt before him and their eyes met. She touched his injured hand, frowning. Their first

contact after more than a decade. Nirmaan almost leapt to
her. He buried his face in her bosom and wept.

'Raisa is dead, Affu. Our Rice is no more!' his voice was
muffled in her chest.

Afsana couldn't keep her balance and they toppled on the
floor with him on top of her. He held her, tight, close and
intimate, his arms like bands around her, his rapid breaths
warm against her exposed cleavage. It was an emotional
arousal of the highest order. Her eyes were so drenched that
she couldn't see his pain or loneliness, but could feel his body
shudder in her embrace. She wanted this moment to end
immediately, because he was crying, and also stretch forever
because he had chosen her for his catharsis. Both sobbing,
their within welded together by the common pain.

They didn't realize how long they stayed like that. And
just as suddenly as he had embraced, Nirmaan released her.
Rubbing his eyes he said, 'I'm sorry, Afsana.'

She sat up, 'I've got a request. Call me Affu.'

Both smiled weakly through their tears. She called for
first aid immediately. After his nursing was done by her,
Nirmaan perched on the bed. Afsana parked herself in the
armchair by the window. Her hands were still shaking.
Raisa, her soul-sister, was no more. They both sat in silence
for the longest time. The night had turned into morning
without them realizing it.

'How did all this happen?' she asked.

'I'm not sure,' he said. 'I had a chat with Lavisha who
told me about it and I crosschecked with the nursing
home. They said she had succumbed to a rare skin

disease.' He looked up at the ceiling, still trying to get to grips with it.

'I don't know why she didn't tell me about her illness,' he added.

'Perhaps she knew that it would hurt you badly to learn of her terminal condition,' Afsana said.

'You know, the day she left me, I found a lipstick mark on my chest as if she had kissed me when I was asleep.'

'She loved you, Nirmaan,' said Afsana softly.

'She never gave me those vibes.'

'She didn't want you to know. If a woman decides not to show her feelings, she won't.'

'After living together for so many years, what was her reason for not expressing her feelings?'

'Only she can answer that. But would you have accepted her if she had told you about it?'

'I don't know.'

'Perhaps that's why.'

They sat in quietude for some more time. Afsana's phone rang. It was her mother. She answered it.

'Ji, Mumma.'

'Shanay has been nominated for some big business award. That ceremony is two days before your wedding. I'm so proud. When are you coming home? Your dad is looking at some wedding card options. We need to shop for a lot of things as well.'

'Mumma, stop stressing. I'm coming home right now. We'll talk then.' She hung up and noticed Nirmaan watching her. She shrugged.

'I'm sorry, Affu, to have interrupted you. This isn't right. You should leave. You're supposed to get married and—' He stopped.

'And?'

'You shouldn't meet illegitimate people in a hotel room like this,' he said realizing something inside him had burnt while he said it.

Afsana gave him a studying look and then said, 'If you are an illegitimate part of my life, then let me tell you everything legitimate in my life is an illusion.'

'Just leave now, Affu.'

'I'll leave. But not alone. You're coming with me.'

'Me? Where?'

'To my apartment. I live there alone. I can't leave you here alone, like this. Not after knowing what we know. And what you are up to,' she said looking at his wound.

Despite Nirmaan's half-hearted protests, Afsana packed his bags and they were ready to check out in a matter of minutes.

Afsana made him comfortable in her flat and made him a cup of coffee with a couple of mild sleeping pills in it. She knew he needed to sleep but was too keyed up for it.

'Sleep tight. I'll be back as soon as possible,' she said from the door. 'I'll lock it from outside.'

'Thanks, Affu,' he said softly.

She grinned, 'Thanks from you sounds like profanity so, please.' Then she left.

The news of Shanay's marriage being brought forward spread like wildfire among his close circle of friends. They insisted on a bachelor bash and he booked Club Boudoir for the party. That was also the first time that he showed Afsana's picture to his friends. They ribbed him good-humouredly.

'You're a lucky dog to find such a hot girl.'

'So when are we going to meet *bhabhi*?'

'Soon, soon,' Shanay assured them.

After several toasts, one of them noticed a girl eyeing them from the bar. They nudged one another.

'Stop it, guys, behave!' Shanay said.

'We haven't started anything yet,' they protested with raucous laughter. They quietened down as the girl came over to them.

'Hi, Shanay,' she said.

'Go for it, boy. One last fling before the wedding bells toll,' his friend whispered to him.

'Do we know each other?' Shanay asked, standing up.

'I'm Lavisha. May I have a word with you alone, please?'

CHAPTER 10

Given half a choice, Shanay would have cheerfully ignored the girl but in front of his friends he couldn't risk it, because then he would have to answer a million of their stupid questions.

'Sure,' he led the way to the smoking area.

'The last thing I need to hear is that Afsana or Nirmaan sent you here,' Shanay snarled as they stood facing each other in a corner. They were the only two there who weren't smoking.

'No. I don't think they know what I'm seeking and why,' Lavisha replied.

'Why and what are you seeking anyway?' he asked.

'For Raisa.'

'She is no more.'

'All the more reason to find the answers. That's not why I came here, though. The reason I've contacted you and not Afsana or Nirmaan is because only you can decide how their story should end.'

Shanay smirked, 'To hell with you and whatever you are seeking. Do you even know what Afsana told me? She said I'm the other man. I, her husband-to-be, am the other man in her life. Can you beat that?'

'I'm not surprised at all. From whatever Raisa told me about her, she was never the doormat kind. You needled her and got what you deserved.'

'Deserved? Really? Who decides what I deserve? You? Or your dead friend, Raisa?' Shanay was clearly on edge. It was also evident that his last meeting with Afsana had left a scar that he was still nursing.

'I've already told you this and I'm telling you again, please forget Afsana. She'll never belong with you. And it's not about you per se. She'll never belong with anyone for that matter, except—'

Shanay cut her short, 'She will belong to me. She concealed the fact that she had such a deep relationship with Nirmaan. She could have told me so the very first day and I wouldn't have pursued her thus far. But she didn't. In fact, if you hadn't sent me those voice notes, I would have never known about it. Ever.'

'Exactly. She didn't conceal it intentionally. She didn't know she would meet him again. In her mind it was over. She was carrying it in her heart, that's all. Not all men are allowed into a woman's heart. It doesn't matter if that man is her husband-to-be or someone else,' said Lavisha, her poise unfaltering.

Shanay narrowed his eyes, 'I suspect that it is you who brainwashed her, but let me tell you here and now, I mean to marry her and I'll show her who the "other man" is. One day she'll apologize and belong only to me.'

She studied his face in silence and said, 'So you're marrying her to avenge the insult that you brought upon yourself. Brilliant! When I started narrating the story of Raisa, Nirmaan and Afsana to you, I didn't realize that you were a petty person. Had I known, believe me, I wouldn't have even tried. You say Afsana didn't choose to tell you about Nirmaan. She was right. That's her choice, not your prerogative. I'm sorry to have wasted your time, Mr Bansal. I guess some things should be left to destiny. You won't hear from me again. Enjoy your bachelor party.'

Shanay watched Lavisha walk out of the smoking zone. He took a deep breath, quickly thinking up a plausible explanation to satisfy his friends and then returned to them. On some level he was glad that this stupid and sad joke that this mystery girl had been trying to pull off was finally over and done with.

It was close to eleven o'clock at night when Afsana unlocked the door of her flat. Her parents had taken her on a shopping spree after which they forced her to have dinner with them. They wanted her to stay the night with them, but she claimed that she had a project to complete and returned to her apartment. For the first time she was returning home to someone; someone she never imagined even in her wildest dreams would come and reclaim, in a subtle, indirect and compassionate way, his place within her.

Afsana went into the bedroom. The room was cold. The temperature of the air-conditioner was exactly the same as she had set it before leaving. Nirmaan was lying on his side, facing away from her. She went around the

bed and noticed a moonbeam directly on his face. He was
sleeping like a baby. She dragged a bean bag to the bed
and sat on it. Afsana noticed that his lips were parted. She
leaned forward until she could feel his breath on her face.
For a moment she simply inhaled the air that he exhaled.
She turned her face so his breath could touch every inch
of her face. She felt an irresistible urge to touch him, but
was irrationally afraid that he would disappear if she did.
What if all this were a dream? A fantasy that would never
materialize into reality. She feathered a kiss on the tip of
his nose and then grew still.

Raisa left a lipstick mark on my chest. Afsana
straightened, feeling a knot in her gut. Raisa was
obviously deeply in love with him, with the kind of love
that bordered on devotion. That which is beyond touch
and lovemaking. She rose and took out her diary from
the drawer in her study table. She sat with it, looking at
Nirmaan and scribbled a poem.

Zamane se chupke,
Ek band kamre mein,
Parde kheech ke,
Bistar pe beeche chadar ko kuchalke,
Ishq nahi hota.

ज़माने से छुप के,
एक बंद कमरे में,
परदे खींच के,
बिस्तर पर बिछे चादर को कुचल के,
इश्क़ नहीं होता।

Once done, she didn't realize when she had dozed off.

Afsana awoke with a start. Nirmaan wasn't on the bed. A shadow moved on the floor and she turned to see him standing by the window with an amused expression.

'I didn't know you snored,' he said with a naughty smile.

'Shut up!' Afsana stood up and stretched.

'Whoa, that's sexy.'

'Shut up! Did you sleep well?'

'Haven't slept this well for a long time now,' he replied.

'Good. Just give me a minute,' she went into the en-suite bathroom.

Afsana took an impromptu day off from work and coaxed Nirmaan into postponing his business meeting. They spent the entire day, evening and night talking about the past. About Raisa. About Nirmaan's memories of her in Guwahati. About Afsana's memories of her in Kolkata. About how Raisa had supported him through his every-day struggles in Bhubaneswar. It was then that Afsana realized how easy it was to become a man's fantasy queen. But to soldier on beside someone for over a decade . . . it sounded amazing to her.

After a late dinner, when Nirmaan had retired to bed, Afsana telephoned Dipannita from her room.

'You better be free now. I need to talk,' she said.

'I was anyway getting bored with my aunts badgering me about starting a family, so I'm all yours, darling. Tell me, what's up?'

'Nirmaan is in the other room,' Afsana said with childlike fervour.

'OMG! Do you mean Nirmaan is in your flat?'

'Yes.'

'You guys—'

'Lived together today,' Afsana could feel a sense of peace pervade her being.

'Don't tell me you guys did it?'

'No, we didn't.'

'*Achcha?* You two in the same flat all day long, and you guys didn't do it? Please!'

'We did not do it.'

'Not even a kiss?'

'No.'

'Okay and I'm Mother Teresa,' Dipannita scoffed.

'Shut up and listen. I've other important things to tell you.'

'Shoot, I'm listening.'

'I cooked for him, did his laundry and also helped him shave.'

'Shave what?'

'His beard, stupid. Now just listen, don't interrupt. I feel like I've achieved nirvana at long last. I'm not the subservient sort, but I chose to be one today. I mothered him although we are the same age. When he was taking a bath, I wanted to barge in and soap and shampoo him. I didn't, but I wanted to. I've collected the cigarette butts of all the cigarettes we smoked as we reminisced. I'll string them together and use them as a bookmark for my personal diary. While I was in the kitchen, he stood by the door simply watching me. His eyes on me . . . I can't explain how sexy it felt. The talks satisfied my soul, but the silences in between were simply orgasmic. His sheer presence, however quiet, was making me wet. Only I know how I controlled myself.

'I noticed a mole on his shoulder. I wanted to scribble a few words before to make the mole a natural full stop. There was an instance late in the evening when we were standing in the balcony. We just stood there looking at each other. I don't know about him, but I wouldn't have minded if he had ripped off my clothes and taken me like an animal. If he had done so, he wouldn't have just stripped me of my clothes, he would have stripped my body as well to free my soul. Just before dinner, he read all my poems out loud. As he read, I kept staring at him. The words were the same but the meanings seemed different. The life was the same, the living seemed different. I think when he finished reading, he wanted to kiss me. I don't know why he didn't.

'While we laughed about the stupid things we did in our past, I wanted to hold him and cry. Just cry. No reason why. I wanted my tears to dry on his skin and become a part of him. Like he is a part of me.' Afsana let go of a relaxing sigh.

'Can I say something now?' Dipannita cut in sounding a little tense.

'Yes, now you can.'

'What are you doing really? On the one hand you're shopping for your trousseau and on the other you are getting excited like a teen because Nirmaan is in your flat? Aren't you seeing the obvious or are you deliberately ignoring it?'

There was silence.

'You there?' Dipannita asked.

'Yes,' it was a soft confirmation.

'Do consider what I'm saying right now, hun. Love and all are fine but you're getting married real soon. Have you thought about what's next? Are you going to invite Nirmaan to your wedding? Or get into an extra-marital relationship with him? If you're thinking along those lines then, as your best friend, I would suggest you to back off. And back off right now. We're adults. We're more about the society than about our own desires. Tell me, have you had a talk with Shanay? What does he think about you and Nirmaan? And what's your plan exactly?'

Afsana was quiet. A moment later she said, 'Let's talk later.' She hung up and switched off her phone. Dipannita was spot on, she realized. The terrible thing was Afsana had no answers to her questions. Her folks were unaware that Nirmaan was in her apartment. Of course, things couldn't go on like this forever, however much she may desire it. Perhaps she knew this as well, deep inside, and was therefore trying to live a lifetime in this one day.

Afsana went into the bedroom where Nirmaan was sleeping. She interlaced her fingers with his and rubbed his hand on her face gently. She was so busy revelling about getting Nirmaan back into her life that she forgot that she needed to find ways to make sure he remained in it. And not as an extra-marital affair, but as the one single, genuine and only relationship she could ever have with a man. For that she would have to talk to Shanay. And real soon.

CHAPTER 11

Shanay, along with his mother, Afsana and her mother were in PC Chandra Jewellers on Elgin Road to select the rings that the bride and groom would exchange before the wedding ceremony. With the short notice, a lot of the itinerary had telescoped for the families. Afsana had messaged Shanay to meet her privately but he had responded with a blunt no. She understood that he was prepared to talk to her only after they were safely shackled to each other. After selecting the rings, the ladies decided to have lunch. Shanay drove everyone to Zing restaurant in Spring Club. The two mothers asked their kids to order and vanished into the ladies' room. Shanay handed the menu to Afsana. She put it aside and said, 'I'm sorry for the other day.'

Shanay pretended to be busy on his phone and ignored her apology.

'We need to call off this marriage, Shanay,' she said. His eyes met hers. 'Trust me, this marriage will not make either of us happy, ever. I'm telling you this because nobody will listen to me if I tell them I want to back off. But if you tell them, perhaps they will question you for a while, but eventually they'll accept it. Shanay, I . . .' her throat went dry and she sipped some water, '. . . beg you.'

Shanay stared at her blankly and then chuckled.

'Good. I like it. Keep begging.'

Afsana could have dunked the water on his head but maintained her poise.

'Why aren't you getting it, Shanay? I don't love you. I love Nirmaan. All I'm asking you is to tell everyone you aren't interested. I'll handle the rest. It's not like you're emotionally invested in me. We've known each other for only six months. Also, you could get any girl to marry you.'

'Any girl? Why not the one with whom it's already fixed?'

'Why don't you understand a simple thing?'

'Perhaps you aren't begging enough,' Shanay said with a condescending smile.

Afsana wanted to retort but by then the ladies were back from the powder room.

'Did you guys order?' Mrs Bansal asked.

'Afsana is dithering, but I know exactly what I'll have,' he replied. Afsana was livid.

After lunch she was dropped off at Deshbandhu Park where she would meet Dipannita at Café by the Lane while Shanay drove their mothers home.

Dipannita joined her soon.

Their order came promptly—*Wanna Whole Lotta Love*—and was placed in the centre of the table. Dipannita helped herself to a scoop. 'Did you imagine that Shanay would tamely agree to your scheme?' she scoffed. 'No guy would.'

'I don't understand his fixation in getting hitched to me. He can't come to terms with my past with Nirmaan but he still wants to marry me. Why?'

'It's a conquest for him now. Had it been nothing, he would've backed off the moment he saw that picture of you and Nirmaan,' replied Dipannita.

Afsana toyed with the spoon but ate nothing of the dessert.

'Nothing can be done to back away from the wedding. Just accept it and instead of talking to Shanay, talk to Nirmaan. He seems more mature. He will understand and stay away from the two of you. Everyone and everything will be sorted satisfactorily that way,' Dipannita added. But her friend was gaping at the dessert totally lost.

'Just talk to Nirmaan today, all right?' Dipannita reiterated.

'You're right. He wants to marry me because he wants to win an imaginary battle against Nirmaan. That's more important for him right now. His male ego has been challenged after I blasted him the other night. So, he will be a stubborn ass now even if it means his decision may destroy three lives.'

'Blasted Shanay? Gosh, when did that happen? What did you tell him?'

'Chuck it. What he doesn't know is he has taken this ego-fight up with the wrong person. If it's really a conquest for Shanay, then I'll beat him at it once and for all,' Afsana said through clenched teeth.

'What do you have in mind?' Dipannita asked, her spoon halfway to her lips.

'Cheque, please,' said Afsana, snapping her fingers to the man at the till; to Dipannita she said, 'let's go.'

CHAPTER 12

Afsana dropped off Dipannita and drove to Salt Lake. She picked up Nirmaan from an engineering college, and drove back to her apartment. Nirmaan sounded excited about the prospects from his business meeting—he seemed to have found an opening to help him spread his start-up to Kolkata's academia.

'You've no idea how much I missed Raisa today,' he said.

'Did you guys go to business meetings together?' she asked as soon as they were ensconced in the balcony with steaming mugs of coffee.

'In the beginning, yes. Then she took over the kitchen section while I concentrated on the business,' Nirmaan replied. His phone buzzed and he talked for a minute before hanging up.

'My tickets are done.'

'Tickets?' Afsana sounded genuinely surprised.

'Back to Bhubaneswar for a few days and then I'll return to Kolkata. I'll shift the company here.'

'Are you running away from Raisa and her memories?' she asked.

Nirmaan nodded. 'I'm staying away from what her memories can do to me. Come what may I don't want the company to suffer. It was her dream as well. I feel more responsible now.'

She flashed a smile at him, appreciating his noble dedication.

'When are you going to Bengaluru?' he asked.

'Bengaluru?' She glanced at him and realized he couldn't ask the obvious: when was she getting married. She took her time to answer. But it was with a question.

'Tell me, Nirmaan, what after I get married?'

'As in? I didn't get you.'

'What about us after I get married?' she rephrased.

Their eyes met and she looked away first. The sky was overcast.

'I want to remain with you always, but the love I have for you tells me that since you're the one getting married, you get to decide this "what about us" thing.'

'What if I say I want to stay away from you?' she pursued, still unwilling to look at his face.

'I would say you won't be able to,' he replied glancing at her profile.

'What if I say I want to have an illicit, extra-marital liaison with you?' she asked.

Nirmaan sipped his coffee and moved to stand directly in front of her.

'We've taken years, but we've always maintained the sanctity of our relationship. It's unique. Two people who reunite after thirteen years and still haven't gotten over the other. I agree that some of it has been destiny, but I'm sure you'll agree that some of it has been our choice as well. We chose to belong to each other.'

'So, what's your answer?' Now she looked straight at him.

'D'you know why it's special? Because it's rare. Let's not make it just another sordid "relationship". I'm not judging anybody. It's just that I'm not comfortable meeting with you after you're married. I would always feel guilty if I became the reason for you to be shunned or scorned by the people you will live with. I can't allow that. I can't let either of us be the reason or excuse for society to sling mud on our relationship or on your character. I won't be able to take it.'

Afsana could have kissed him right then, but beamed at him instead. She got the answer that she had been fishing for.

After dinner, Nirmaan went to his room to work on a PPT while Afsana went to hers and sat still on a chair. She heard the sound of rain outside. The next moment she felt a hand on her back. She turned to see Nirmaan.

'Let's go to the terrace,' he said.

Nirmaan stopped at the terrace door, looking at the lock in disappointment. Afsana smirked, slid out a bobby pin from her hair and jimmied the lock in a matter of minutes.

'Locks were never an issue for me.'

As they pushed open the door, they realized it was bucketing down. They stepped on to the terrace, with no umbrella. Nirmaan sat on the low cement wall across the terrace. Afsana sat beside him uncaring that they were both completely drenched.

Nirmaan looked at the city's skyline and said, 'Years ago Raisa and I had sat on a terrace under an umbrella. Life was so simple then and . . .' He felt Afsana clasp his hand. He looked at her.

'Can you make such love to me, Nirmaan, that after we are done I feel stronger than I am right now?' she asked. The next second his lips were on hers. Their eyes were closed. The moment their lips parted, a hunger was unleashed. A hunger whose face was, perhaps, lust, but whose soul was a deep longing that had been pent up within them for a long time. He cupped her face as he kissed her. She held him. Caught up in the rapture of their kiss, neither realized that the torrential rain had diminished to a drizzle. He was about to say something when she put a finger on his lips and said, 'Don't say a word and make me feel it's all real. I want it to be a dream. Take me home. And . . . take me.'

Nirmaan grabbed her hand and pulled her along with him. She didn't know he had such strength when outwardly he looked so gentle. In no time, they were inside the apartment. As soon as the door clicked shut, they looked deeply into each other's eyes. Their breathing grew heavier with every passing second. He lowered his face and gently rubbed his lips against hers before flicking his tongue over its contours. He shifted her in his embrace to kiss her nape. Goosebumps rose all over her. Afsana guided his hand to her drenched shorts. Nirmaan slowly slipped his hand inside and caressed her clitoris through her panties. He could feel her stiffen as he rubbed her. His eyes were on her face but her eyes were shut as she revelled in his lovemaking.

When Afsana couldn't take it any more, she shoved him away. Nirmaan staggered. In one fluid motion she divested herself of both, her shorts and her panties. Nirmaan flipped her around, pinned her to the wall and pressed himself against her back. The bulge in his trousers was rubbing against her bare butt. He gently nibbled her shoulder, licking the raindrops off her skin as his hands helped get rid of her tee. In a flash he unhooked her bra. The next moment, Afsana stood naked before him. He cupped her breasts in his palms while his thumbs caressed the erect nipples gently. She squirmed a little to turn around in his arms and looked into his eyes that were ablaze with passion. She couldn't remember the last time she had felt so aroused that her knees gave way. She simply let herself go in Nirmaan's capable hands. The suddenness of it startled him and he stumbled. They both collapsed in a heap on the floor. Her long hair, still very wet, brushed his face. He could feel her breasts crushed against his chest. Afsana sat up, looking into his eyes, and coaxed his tee up. She caressed the hair on his chest lovingly and kissed his chest once. Then twice. And then multiple times until he caught her face and claimed her lips again. He helped Afsana undo his trousers and slipped out of his shorts.

'Affu—' he started, when Afsana stopped him.

'Sshh.'

Nirmaan sat up with Afsana straddling him. Holding her intimately, he gazed up at her. She gazed down into his eyes. Their breaths fused together as their lips met. Nirmaan slowly shifted and placed her beneath him. He stretched her arms wide and kissed each of her fingers, sucking them, then the palm, then he moved up her arm worshipping every inch of her skin. Every kiss seemed like a love letter that he held within him, but could never post to her earlier. Before she could read one, there was another. And another. And yet another. Nirmaan's lips traversed every possible inch of her. He wanted to kiss her more but she held him at bay with an unspoken command in her eyes. He obeyed. Nirmaan entered her. Afsana's lips parted with pain as her eyes rolled up in pleasure. After that all she remembered was the sound of his breathing in her ears as he held her tight and continued with his thrusts. When she caught his eye again, she was mesmerized and couldn't look away. It was like their eyes were holding a conversation of their own.

I don't believe this is happening, his eyes said.

Neither do I, her eyes responded.

How will I survive without you after coming this close?

Maybe we don't have to. Maybe we came close for a reason and perhaps we were supposed to be together from here on.

I hate maybe. Tell me we will.

We will.

Scream it out that we will.

WE WILL.

WE WILL.

He finally collapsed on her. His weight on her made her feel incredibly powerful.

Afsana's eyes fluttered open after a couple of hours. Their naked bodies were still intertwined on the floor. She could feel his breaths on her forehead. She freed herself, careful not to wake him up and walked naked into her room. She sat at her desk and opened her diary again. She sighed and completed the half-written verse.

Zamane se chupke,
Ek band kamre mein,
Parde kheech ke,
Bistar pe beeche chadar ko kuchalke,
Ishq nahi hota.

Ishq khule mein hota hai.
Logo ko lalkarke hota hai.
Mann ke talon ko todkad hota hai.
Takht-o-taj hilake hota hai.
Kisi purani soch ki tanashahi to girake hota hai.
Tez hawa ka rukh modhke hota hai.
Oonche-oonche lehron se sambhalke hota hai.
Sadak ke beech chilla ke hota hai.
Ishq sirf khule mein hota hai.

जमाने से छुप के,
एक बंद कमरे में,
परदे खींच के,
बिस्तर पर बिछे चादर को कुचल के,
इश्क नहीं होता।

इश्क खुले में होता हैं।
लोगों को ललकार के होता हैं।
मन के तालो को तोड़ कर होता हैं।
तखत-ओ-ताज हिला के होता हैं।
किसी पुरानी सोच की तानाशाही को गिरा के होता हैं।
तेज हवा का रुख मोड़ के होता हैं।

ऊंचे ऊंचे लहरों से संभल के होता हैं।
सड़क के बीच चिल्ला के होता हैं।
इश्क सिर्फ खुले में होता हैं।

As Afsana stared at the words, she knew it was time to enact her plan. A plan that would bring her and Nirmaan together but would destroy everything else that she was associated with. It was like burning up one world in order to keep another alive. Picking up her cell phone, Afsana went back to Nirmaan, and lay down beside him on the floor. She clicked pictures of their naked bodies taking care to ensure that his face was not very clear although hers was in each of them. She replaced her SIM card with a new one and switched on the phone. She tapped on the WhatsApp icon on the phone and registered the new number, made a new group that included Shanay, his parents and everyone in his family whose number she had. She loaded all the pictures she had just clicked, shut her eyes and muttered the lines of the poem that she had penned a moment ago. Afsana pressed the 'send' button. Then she extracted the SIM and splintered it. *Sometimes the present needs to be eradicated so that one can build the future afresh*, she thought as she put her arms around Nirmaan and buried her face in his neck. She had never felt stronger.

CHAPTER 13

Every picture sent to the group was seen by each member of the group. Instead of finding out who sent them, the photos were forwarded to their respective wives and other relatives, who further forwarded them to their extended families. In no time it was an established fact in the entire Bansal family, far and near, that Shanay's wife-to-be was having a torrid pre-marital affair.

The pictures were sent to Afsana's parents as well. An urgent meeting was arranged between the two families. Shanay wanted to intervene but Mr Bansal asked him to keep quiet.

'I know who sent these pictures,' Shanay was one hundred per cent certain that it had been masterminded by Nirmaan to sabotage his marriage.

'It doesn't matter who sent the pictures to us,' Mr Bansal said, 'what matters is whether what was sent is true or not.'

When Mr Bansal telephoned Mr Agarwal, he only wanted Afsana to confirm or deny the truth of those pictures. Afsana was asked to remain at her parents' home where both families were to meet at noon and discuss the implications of the scandalous photographs.

When Afsana came home, without telling Nirmaan anything about it, she knew she would have to face the music. Her disgusted father categorically told her that she was the biggest mistake of his life and had never given him a moment's peace from the time she had been conceived. Now she had maligned his name so badly that the entire Agarwal family was reduced to a laughing stock in their community and business circles.

Afsana was silent.

Only Shanay's parents arrived to represent the Bansal clan. Mr Bansal asked her a simple question, 'Beta, is there another man in your life?'

Afsana nodded.

'And you want to marry him and not Shanay?'

Afsana nodded again.

'Why didn't you tell us before?' asked Mrs Bansal.

Afsana remained silent.

Mr Bansal suggested to Mr Agarwal that he get his daughter married to the man of her choice. As for the marriage alliance between the Bansal and the Agarwal family, it stood cancelled.

'Whoever sent those pictures sent it to almost everyone in our family. However much both my wife and I love Afsana, it will be very difficult for us to accept her as our daughter-in-law now. I hope you understand, Mr Agarwal, and not make a fuss about it,' Mr Bansal said regretfully.

In the silence that fell, the Bansals walked away.

'I'll not spare the bastard who sent those damn pictures,' Mr Agarwal muttered furiously. He glared at Afsana, 'If I knew I had sired a slut, I would have killed myself a long time ago.' He shut himself up in his room.

Afsana knew it would be impossible to conclusively trace the origin and sender of those images. Her mother remained strangely quiet throughout this altercation.

An hour later, driving back to her apartment, Afsana checked her phone and found Shanay's message: *Are you ready to get married to a man who circulates your private pictures? Great! Both you and I know that Nirmaan has done this, and you know what? You actually don't deserve me. You deserve that dog. Goodbye.*

She promptly deleted the message.

Nirmaan, dressed in a formal suit, was waiting for her on the couch. He was due to fly to Bhubaneswar later that evening after a business meeting in Kolkata. When Afsana entered the flat, Nirmaan immediately sensed that something was terribly wrong. He rose to hold her hands and draw her down to sit beside him.

'What happened?'

She smiled at him wanly, 'I destroyed myself today for you. Now I want to begin again. With you . . . beside you. I want to resurrect myself holding your hand,' her eyes were moist, she raised his hand to her face.

'What happened, Affu?' Nirmaan repeated. She buried her face in his chest, 'I had to burn my world to start a universe with you.'

Nirmaan broke the hug and cupped her face.

'What did you do?' he asked. Afsana took a few minutes to summarize everything that had happened after their passionate encounter. The obvious consequence was that the marriage had been called off.

'Please tell me you didn't do that,' Nirmaan urged in disbelief.

Afsana gazed at him, smiling.

'I did,' she confirmed.

'You . . . actually sent those pictures . . . yourself?' Nirmaan was still having trouble coming to grips with reality.

'I tried explaining to Shanay that we weren't meant for each other. But he simply wouldn't listen. And I couldn't live with him. I want you, Nirmaan. I lost you once but then when you met me again . . .' Nirmaan hugged her tight.

'*Kehte hain peepal ke ped ko ghar pe nahi lagate. Lekin peepal ke ped mein hi ghar mil jaaye, toh?*' Afsaan whispered in his ears. Nirmaan whispered back, '*Kehte hain talaab ke paani ko, rasoi ke matke mein nahi rakhte. Lekin, zindagi ki pyaas talaab ke paani se hi mite, toh?*'

'*Kehte hain ishq mein qaid nahi, azaadi honi chahiye. Lekin, kisike qaid mein hi azaadi mile, toh?*' Her body shuddered as she whispered again. Nirmaan broke the hug, wiped her tears away and said, '*Kehte hain khuda mein koi aeb nahi hota. Lekin, kisike aeb mein hi khuda dikh jaaye, toh?*'

She sealed his lips with hers.

'I swear, Affu, if I'm a real man, I won't let you regret this decision of yours ever,' he promised fervently. 'Wait for me here. I'll be back soon. Get packed and be ready,' Nirmaan kissed her forehead and walked out.

CHAPTER 14

With Nirmaan gone, Afsana stayed where she was as the enormity of her actions sank in. She hadn't asked when he would be back. She simply sat on the couch staring out of the window and gradually dozed off. When she woke up in the wee hours, memories of the first cycle ride she had had with Nirmaan to the lovemaking that had happened the previous night returned to her vividly.

Nirmaan came home that evening.

'I'm sorry to have kept you waiting. I've already signed it and you can follow suit after reading it,' he said, handing her some official-looking documents and gathering her into his arms.

'What are these?' she asked, peering at the papers.

'When one has the right connections, anything is possible. I called up a few people and got hold of a marriage registrar who prepared these papers for us overnight,' he said beaming triumphantly.

Afsana felt as if she were dreaming. She hurriedly signed the papers before someone woke her up and told her that none of this was real. She noticed three witnesses had already signed it.

'They're my friends, don't worry,' Nirmaan assured her. She hugged him tight.

'Have you packed?' he asked. 'We'll leave right away. We'll stay at The Park for a few days and after that we'll shift to a three-bedroom rented apartment in Rajarhat. I've had a talk with a broker as well,' he murmured holding her close as she seemed reluctant to let him go.

'You wanted me to pack everything I need. I'm holding everything I need right now,' Afsana said. He kissed her forehead.

After a few minutes, she said, 'Tell me, Nirmaan, this isn't temporary. Tell me this is permanent . . . for always.'

Nirmaan cupped her face and gazed into her eyes, 'You and I are all about permanence, Affu. D'you think we met again just like that? I deliberately held back from confessing that I couldn't survive without you. I knew that if I said anything like that you would have no qualms about setting your world ablaze to return to me. But you . . .' he kissed her hard.

'I'm glad you realized it without my having to spell it out,' she kissed him harder.

Nirmaan finally excused himself, saying wryly that he needed to wash and shave and become human again. Afsana relaxed, feeling normal after ages. She was about to sort through her stuff to pack a bag, when the doorbell rang. Her father along with a contingent of her male cousins barged in as soon as she opened the door.

'Where is that scoundrel?' Mr Agarwal demanded furiously. Her cousins were already in the bedroom.

'What are you doing?' Afsana asked.

'I know that bastard is here. He's the one who circulated those pictures to the Bansals,' Mr Agarwal hollered.

Afsana was about to reply, when Nirmaan responded, 'Yes, I did.'

He stood in the doorway of the en-suite bathroom. The cousins converged on him looking like jackals to a kill.

'Papa—' Afsana began.

'Affu, don't worry and stay out of this,' Nirmaan picked up the marriage registration papers from the centre table as he approached her father.

He faced Mr Agarwal. 'I have loved your daughter for the last fifteen years. She loves me as well. Now, she is not only your daughter,' he waved the documents in his hand, 'but my legally wedded wife as well. If you want to fight me, you're welcome to try. Is there any law in this country that can separate two consensually married adults?'

'Is this the truth?' spluttered Afsana's father. She nodded.

'You—' Mr Agarwal's face was red with fury.

'I request you to lay off calling my wife names.'

One of her burly cousins stepped threateningly towards Nirmaan. Mr Agarwal and the other cousins deterred him from launching an onslaught. Mr Agarwal considered Nirmaan with fulminating eyes, took the registration papers with shaking hands and perused them.

'Don't show me your face ever. Let's go,' he said hurling the documents to the floor. All of them left.

'I'm sorry, Affu. You had to fight with your family for me.'

'Don't make us sound like hormonal teenagers, Nirmaan. We have chosen each other. I know my father. He's angry because he doesn't know you. With time, he'll get to know you. He isn't as evil as he sounded.'

Afsana grinned. 'But thank you. When the person you love turns out the way you always thought he would, life seems like a blessing.'

'"Thanks" coming from you sounds like a profanity, so, please,' he smiled and she joined in.

They stayed for a week at The Park. Afsana's mother phoned to convey her blessings. However, Afsana didn't disclose her whereabouts to her mother. A week later, they moved into a swanky rented apartment in Rajarhat.

'After we get back from New Delhi, I'll bring Ma here.'

'I'm dying to meet Aunty. It has been a long time since I last saw her.'

With a reminiscent smile, Nirman said, 'she once said she wanted a daughter-in-law like you.'

Afsana smiled and said, 'I remember, the Bangali-meye avatar.' And then added, 'But why New Delhi?'

'Our start-up has been nominated for an award by *Business Right Now*.'

Afsana was surprised to learn that Nirmaan would be competing for the same award as Shanay. It was during their flight to New Delhi that she told Nirmaan about it.

'If you aren't comfortable, we can fly back without attending the show. I don't have a problem,' he offered without a moment's hesitation.

'No. Let it be,' she shook her head. After a pause she added, 'I want to confess something.'

'Sure.'

She held his hand tightly and said, 'I've slept with Shanay. I lied to him about my virginity but I don't want to lie to you. I first had sex with a French painter whom I had met in Milan. We were not in love but whenever we made out, we always said we loved each other. Then I was briefly with a client of mine in Milan. I think he genuinely loved me. I may sound like a bitch but I wanted him to crave me. I don't know why. So, I would make out with him time and again. I even promised him that I'll return only for him. I wanted someone to wait for me . . . I'm not in touch with anyone any more.'

Nirmaan looked at her impassively.

'Say something,' she said.

'Affu, it does not matter who you were with earlier. It doesn't change anything. I respect your choices. During all those years when we were apart, I realized that the purest love is that which you set free, which you don't try to alter. You love the other person for who they are and not for what you want them to be. I would never want to change you, Affu. You're my inspiration. As long as your love for me stays uncompromised, I don't really care about your past boyfriends or flings.'

Afsana was touched. She leaned her head on his shoulder as their flight entered a crowd of clouds.

The award ceremony was a gala affair at the Leela. Business magnates from across the globe, political leaders and distinguished dignitaries from various walks of life

were present. Shanay snagged the award in the category
that Nirmaan was also competing. Although he noticed
Nirmaan and Afsana at the cocktail party that followed, he
steered clear of them.

The next morning, Nirmaan and Afsana were at
terminal 3 of the Delhi airport, waiting to catch a flight to
Guwahati.

'I want to visit the RBI quarters there. I want to see
if the mango tree is still there. That was how I first met
Raisa,' Nirmaan had explained as he booked their tickets.

'I'll go with you,' replied Afsana promptly.

As they waited for the boarding call, Afsana said,
'Dipannita was asking—'

'Dipannita . . . oh, yes, your friend who thought we were
going to have an extra-marital liaison,' Nirmaan grinned.

Afsana elbowed him and continued, 'She wanted to
know whether we would go off on a honeymoon now that
we're married.'

Nirmaan looked at her and asked, 'What did you tell
her?'

'That we are each other's honeymoon.'

Nirmaan gave her a you-are-incorrigible smile and
kissed her hand.

'Your hands are frozen. D'you want some coffee?'

'I wouldn't mind.'

'Wait,' Nirmaan wandered off to the hot beverages
stall.

Shanay was watching them from a distance. His flight
to Kolkata was around the same time as theirs. As Nirmaan
left, he approached Afsana.

'Hi,' he said, as she looked up at him in surprise.

'Don't worry I'm not here to fight or anything. I just wanted to clear a small doubt.'

'What is it?' she asked.

'Ever since our relationship started going downhill, I've hated you so much and bad-mouthed you. But perhaps that was just my way of dealing with the thought of losing you. I realized something only a few days ago when I ran into one of your cousins at a pub. He told me that you've married the man who had circulated those pictures. Something about that didn't sit right with me. I wondered how a feisty girl like you could tamely give in to a man who had so thoughtlessly put out naked pictures of the woman he allegedly loved. And then it struck me. It was you who did it, isn't it? You chose to crucify your own character to be with the man you truly love.' He paused for a beat before continuing, 'My blood ran cold even thinking about it. I don't think I could ever have done such a thing—destroy myself for someone else. It was then that I realized that I never deserved you. Strangely enough I feel a lot better now and happy for you too. You were right. We would have driven each other mad if we had gotten married,' he laughed mirthlessly.

Afsana didn't know what to say.

'I've a final request. Can I stay in touch with you until I find a life partner? I told my parents not to look for alliances for me. I'll tell them when I've found someone who is worthy of me and I'm worthy of her.'

Several seconds ticked by before Afsana said, 'Of course, we can remain in touch.'

'Thank you. Fly safe.' Shanay was gone. Half a minute later, Nirmaan joined her with two paper cups of coffee.

'Shanay was here,' she said.

'I saw. But I didn't want to interrupt you two.'

'He seemed apologetic. He wants to stay in touch with me until he gets someone in his life. I said yes, but—'

'But?'

'Will you be okay with it?'

'As I said, Affu, it's your choice. I trust you. And when you trust someone you don't ask questions. You just know the answers.'

She gave him a peck on the cheek as the boarding announcement was made.

As Nirmaan and Afsana disappeared into the aerobridge for their flight, another flight was ready to depart to Kullu. The first person to cross the boarding gate for the flight was Raisa Barua. She waited impatiently till her flight took off and steadied in the air; she unbuckled her belt and went to the washroom. She gagged her mouth with a handkerchief and cried so hard that the veins on her neck stood erect and her eyes got all bloodshot.

EPILOGUE

Two days later,
Spiti Valley, Himachal Pradesh,
11.11 a.m.

The temperature outside is two degree Celsius. Raisa is standing naked in the shower of the small room she has rented. She squeezes her eyes shut and turns on the shower. Icy cold water cascades down her skin, freezing her to the bone. She communes with her spirit, willing the physical body to overcome the extreme discomfort and analyses her thoughts during this process.

These days I feel at peace. I'm rather glad to be free of the turbulence that had plagued me when I was with Nirmaan in Bhubaneswar. The furore in my mind was actually the manifestation of a guilt that I couldn't share with anybody, so much so that at times I did my best to keep it away from myself as well.

Some damages can never be fixed. There are some mistakes from which even the wisest sage would be at a loss to find a life's lesson. And there are tumults to which one can never get inured.

These upheavals encapsulate the meaning of love. Nobody will ever know the truth about my fictitious illegal abortion or that Mihir was a mere figment of my imagination. I had asked the older brother of a classmate's boyfriend to reach out to my dad on that fateful evening thirteen years ago with some forged abortion papers, and demand money from him for an abortion that never happened. I knew that my infuriated father would severely chastise me and perhaps even ostracize me. Everything happened as I had expected.

However, that was but one part of the plan. The other part happened when I sought out Tarun, instigated him against Nirmaan and motivated him to keep him captive during his IIT entrance exam. I thought these two lies would suffice to launch Nirmaan and me on an adventure like no other, far from everyone else and together forever.

The third lie was necessitated by Nirmaan when he swore blind to wait for Affu. I didn't tell him all of what she had told me when she had called me. I didn't tell him that she would come back in a year and had asked me to tell him to wait. How could I have told him that? I was blinded by my love for him.

Although I didn't hate Affu, I realized that she had eclipsed me in Nirmaan's eyes. So what if I was his oldest friend? I was his oldest everything. It was only when I repeated a year without him that I understood how much Nirmaan had come to mean to me. No matter how shitty reality becomes, there's always that one person who makes you believe in fairy tales. Nirmaan was that person for me and I couldn't let the fairy tales slip away with him. Although I knew I wasn't ready to part with him, I wasn't sure if I loved him. I've not understood this 'love' thing even to this day. I only wanted to be with him.

That was all. When Affu said she was in love with him and Nirmaan reciprocated the sentiment with equal fervour, I was really happy for them. However, with time, I understood that the moral of their love story was that they would be together and the more they were together, the more I would have to stay away from Nirmaan. That's the norm, right? Three's a crowd . . . who made these diktats?

I did my utmost to stay away from both of them, but it didn't help. I knew that eventually I'd have to go away from him, but I wasn't ready for that. When I went over to his place one day with a chicken dish that I had made and found Affu there, I excused myself and left immediately, but I couldn't sleep for days. Their intimacy troubled me, inflamed my inner demons and took me to a place where prayers didn't work.

I swear that when I thought up the lies, I didn't know that they would lead to where they did. My then innocuous mind thought that my lies could make me stay close to Nirmaan. One of those lies made me revel in its possibilities to such an extent that I didn't bother to calculate its consequences. I was, in any case, the dumbest of the trio. I really thought he could and would forget Affu with time; that we would get married, have babies and start a family. But I was wrong. In the thirteen years that I lived with Nirmaan, I realized—spool by spool—that he was all about Affu. He was born for her. And she for him. I was merely their stepping stone to happiness. I hated myself. But by the time I realized my blunder, I was in an irreversible situation. I didn't have the guts to call off the bluff. Hence the disturbance; the guilt started chewing at my conscience from the time I heard Nirmaan utter Affu's name in his sleep. And then him taking up smoking the same cigarette brand as Affu only to feel her presence. It dawned on me only then that I was the ogre in their fairy tale. What was even worse, they had no inkling of this.

They'll never know of it. If I had confessed the truth to him, Nirmaan would have left me hurt. I can accept that he doesn't love me, but to have him hate me is nigh unthinkable.

The fact that we err doesn't make us human. I think the fact that we want to correct that error and redeem ourselves is what makes us human. Ever since I realized my grievous error, and even though I have cried a million tears of remorse every night, I couldn't assuage the guilt. Each time I looked at Nirmaan during our long Bhubaneswar stay, I was reminded that he and Affu could have easily been together and enjoyed a happy life, had it not been for my interference, my stupid lies and my stubbornness to gain his exclusive proximity. Whenever he was happy, I was in a dilemma: to be happy with him or to be sad because he didn't know at what cost his happiness had come. Only I did. Although I constantly reassured myself that I wasn't all bad, that one unacceptable action of mine—those lies—called my bluff every time.

I understood that although Nirmaan and I could be an ideal couple, we weren't made for each other. People never understand the difference. I could have left him years ago hoping he would reconnect with Affu, but at that time he had not made anything of himself. His dream of being an entrepreneur became my dream as well and I devoted myself to it because in that devotion I found redemption. I worked, overworked, and pushed myself beyond limits as never before, I became a different person and when Nirmaan's dream was fulfilled, I knew it was time. I couldn't have left him midway so I left him when he had

something solid to fall back on. His successful business and . . .
Affu.

Even though I was gone just like that, overnight, I did keep
track of Nirmaan through my confidante at work, Lavisha.
When I learnt that she too had left the job, I contacted her only
to learn that she had been diagnosed with an obscure and rare
skin disease. As she was an orphan, I took her to an NGO and
admitted her under my name. When she died a couple of days
later, it was 'Raisa Barua' who was dead. In the meantime, I
located Affu on Facebook and was upset to learn that she had got
engaged. I found Shanay's details from her profile and went to
Bengaluru to talk to him. I almost met him once but something
told me that if he didn't know the story of Affu, Nirmaan and
me, he would never be able to make an informed decision. That
very night I started sending him the voice notes with the alias
of the long dead Lavisha Mishra. And later met him as her. I
chatted with Nirmaan as Lavisha to provide him with proof of
my death. If he comes to know that I'm alive, he will look for
me. I know it. And if he comes for me, so will Affu and our cycle
will play itself again.

For this cycle to stop, this emotional suicide of mine was
necessary. I had to strike myself off from his life. Once and for all.

My first deception, a set of lies really, as an eighteen-year-
old was fabricated to remain close to Nirmaan so that I could
live; the second deception about my demise was invented as the
means to stay away from him so that he could live. After my talk
with Shanay at his bachelor bash, I felt that all my efforts had
been in vain. I was praying the two to stick it out somehow.
I'm delighted that everything has fallen into place: Affu and
Nirmaan are together at long last.

Life lulls a lot of things to sleep within us as memories fade. As long as Nirmaan and Affu keep me awake within them, I'll feel worthy. I'll feel alive even if I'm dead for them. I'll feel I have redeemed myself even if they never knew my sins. The ripe mango that I once gave Nirmaan will never lose its aroma.

Raisa steps out of the shower drying herself. Her eyes fall on an old photograph pinned on the wardrobe—a snapshot of a pair of eight-year-olds, Nirmaan and Raisa, dressed as Krishna and Radha. She kisses the picture and wonders, *Krishna may have married Rukmini, but he would always be idolized with Radha, isn't it? I think I can live with that.*

ACKNOWLEDGEMENTS

There are some books that aren't just books. They are part of an author's life. *Half-torn Hearts* is one such book for me. It made me depressed, tested my patience and at the same time, helped me introspect that which I'd consciously shied away from. The process and experience of penning this book will always remain special. In the end, I'm happy the way it shaped up. And I can't take the credit myself for sure.

Heartfelt thanks and immense gratitude to:

As always (in all ways), Milee Ashwarya, for having an unfaltering faith in my stories. Here's to creating bigger and better things together in the near and distant future.

The entire sales and marketing teams of Penguin Random House India, for lending their prompt support to my books whenever needed.

Indrani, for the awesome edits as usual.

My family, for being there like a prayer.

My friends, for not judging me when I tell them my favorite time pass is to dance on Govinda numbers.

My readers, for appreciating my work each time I present something to them.

Paullomy, Titiksha, Kratika, Ankita, Vaishali, for listening to me patiently when I am impatient. About what? You girls know better!

A: For destroying me so poetically. I only wish you knew the consequences of those three words you'd once told me. It altered my life.

Ra: Just be there, okay? Just. Be. There.

R: My everyday light, for you anytime. Anywhere. Anyhow.